SOMETHING IN THE BLOOD

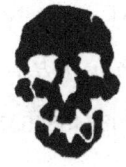

H. H. Mika

This book is entirely fictional.
All characters, places, and events are products of the author's imagination or used fictitiously.
Any resemblance to an actual person—living or dead—business establishment, happening, or locale, is purely coincidental and not in any way representational.

Copyright © 2024 by Stephen Lo Biondo

ALL RIGHTS RESERVED. NO PART OF THIS BOOK MAY BE REPRODUCED OR TRANSMITTED IN ANY FORM OR BY ANY MEANS, ELECTRONIC OR MECHANICAL, INCLUDING PHOTOCOPYING, RECORDING OR BY ANY INFORMATION STORAGE AND RETRIEVAL SYSTEMS, WITHOUT THE WRITTEN PERMISSION FROM THE PUBLISHER, EXCEPT BY A REVIEWER WHO MAY QUOTE BRIEF PASSAGES.

Second paperback edition, November 2024.

Illustrations by H. H. Mika

ISBN 9798345555378 (pb)

Published independently by H. H. Mika

For my father

and Sexy Betty.

Contents

PROLOGUE   13

ACT I: RED WINDOWS   15

CHAPTER I: The Volkers   17
CHAPTER II: Sick   21
CHAPTER III: Sullivan's Café   32
CHAPTER IV: Card House   39
CHAPTER V: Spartacus   44
CHAPTER VI: Lonely Boys   47
CHAPTER VII: "Fullsend Steve"   50
CHAPTER VIII: Autopsy   70
CHAPTER IX: Briefing   74
CHAPTER X: The Letter   77

ACT II: DISSOLUTION   81

CHAPTER I: Joycie   82
CHAPTER II: Amarok   86
CHAPTER III: The Unipqaaq of the Quiet People   90
CHAPTER IV: The Thompsons   91
CHAPTER V: Herod   96
CHAPTER VI: Kynikós   104
CHAPTER VII: Paige   107
CHAPTER VIII: The Tuquji Iceman   111
CHAPTER IX: The Architect   118
CHAPTER X: The Boy with No Shoes   126
CHAPTER XI: Black Glass   131
CHAPTER XII: Papa and the Wolf   136
CHAPTER XIII: The Unipqaaq of the Quiet People   142
CHAPTER XIV: Miss Meliss   144
CHAPTER XV: THE BLOODRUN BUTCHER   148
CHAPTER XVI: Lashes and Lips   155
CHAPTER XVII: Tashira   164
CHAPTER XVIII: The Unipqaaq of the Quiet People   168
CHAPTER XIX: Brass   169
CHAPTER XX: Redeloos—Radeloos—Reddeloos   173

ACT III: SOMETHING IN THE BLOOD — 187

CHAPTER I: Pins — 189
CHAPTER II: Last Call — 192
CHAPTER III: Johnny Cocheroo — 197
CHAPTER IV: Split a Piece of Rotting Wood — 202
CHAPTER V: INCLUSIVE CASE REPORT — 205
CHAPTER VI: 3 — 212
CHAPTER VII: Descenntial — 222
CHAPTER VIII: The Word Becomes Flesh — 225
CHAPTER IX: Dry — 229
CHAPTER X: Acts 20:29 — 232
CHAPTER XI: The Room at the End of the Hallway — 236
CHAPTER XII: Ruined — 238
CHAPTER XIII: |T|O|O| |C|O|L|D| |T|O| |C|H|A|N|G|E... — 253
CHAPTER XIV: Detective Koyukuk — 255
CHAPTER XV: Sublimation — 257
CHAPTER XVI: 98.6°F — 262
CHAPTER XVII: The Abyss — 264
CHAPTER XVIII: Red and Raw — 267
CHAPTER XIX: The Unipqaaq of the Quiet People — 269
CHAPTER XX: The Water — 272
CHAPTER XXI: 83.5°F — 275
CHAPTER XXII: Syrpynt — 278
CHAPTER XXIII: Scars — 283
CHAPTER XXIV: 75.6°F — 289
CHAPTER XXV: ASAP — 291
CHAPTER XXVI: Only Death and Death Alone — 294
CHAPTER XXVII: Rot — 298

EPILOGUE — 305

SOMETHING IN THE BLOOD

Ah, how sad it is that I still remain in this muddy swamp of death and rebirth even now, after countless ages without beginning or end."

- The Tibetan Book of the Dead

PROLOGUE

I T ' S C O L D E N O U G H this morning that the air itself is freezing. Pillars of light can be seen in the distance stretching up until they meet the black sky. Mostly streaks of whites and yellows—a few pale blues and oranges. They reflect off the otherwise imperceptible ice crystals which suspend in the atmosphere below the clouds.

Even more imperceptible than this ice fog—and the gentle tinkling of the air freezing—is a black timber wolf. He stands at the edge of the pines which encapsulate the source of the various lights—a town. Frost covered streetlamps; early opening storefronts; the tip of a water tower. He stands cloaked in the darkness and surveys the optical illusions glowing in the sky and all the strange things that the people build which rest motionless below.

He seems to be waiting for something—not making a sound—appearing to not even breathe, until a train's horn drones in the distance as it nears. Another beam of light casts up into the sky. Then another. Soon, he hears a car snaking down Hilldrum Road—its engine roars through the trees and echoes off the crisp snow.

The people are beginning to rise.

For a second, the wolf vanishes into the darkness as he blinks his sapphire eyes and then turns tail and disappears completely into the pines from which he came.

ACT I:
RED WINDOWS

CHAPTER I:
The Volkers

PIPES CREAK from behind a shower curtain as a man turns off the water. He drips onto the bare floor as he reaches for the rolled-up towel that he left on the sink. The bathroom has an unusual atmosphere to it for right after a shower—cool, dry and still. No lingering cloud of steam floats in the air. No aroma of soap. The only real sign that someone has been bathing comes from the sound of the dripping showerhead.

    The man wraps himself in the towel and steps out of the tub, closing the curtain behind him. In the fogless mirror, he observes his reflection. He's overdue for both a shave and a haircut, but he pays little attention to this. Instead, his eyes go to his chest—which has been beaten red from his deliberate use of cold water.

    There's a scratching sound coming from the other side of the bathroom door, but he ignores it. He can also hear his cell phone buzzing, but he ignores that too. In the mirror, the reflection of one of his pink hands rises towards his neck, stops before his collarbone, and presses lightly on his blood rushed skin. Pale fingerprints are left behind, but they quickly return to the color of raw meat as he lowers his hand away.

    A small hieroglyph-looking tattoo marks his forearm, which swings faintly for a moment as his hand steadies and then hangs. At a glance, it resembles the iconic "peace sign," with a few variations. Peace *is* the first of the three virtues that are used

17

as the motto for the police precinct where he works—the other two being *bravery* and *justice*—but his tattoo appears much different when examined closely. It's not often examined closely though, or at all, really. The strange marking is almost always hidden by his sleeves, but even when they're occasionally rolled up, there was only one person who ever recognized it.

He stands there for a few minutes—ignoring the sounds outside of the door—and stares at his skin in the mirror as the red flush slowly fades away. When all the sounds return to silence— the scratching, the buzzing, the creaks and drips from the shower—he notices that his skin has completely dried. His chest has also paled back over and it's once again ready to bear the badge of the Bloodrun Borough Police Department.

HE PLACES A BUNDLE OF BLANKETS down onto the steps outside of his front door to grab some letters from his mailbox, and then resumes down the shoveled path to his old but well-kept Bronco. With the blankets held in one arm, he checks the time on his cell phone with the other:

8:26am—two hours late.

As he reads the time, he also sees two voicemail notifications from his "partner" Eddie.

Most detectives in the Bloodrun precinct earn their rank through merit alone, but it's not unheard of for patrolmen like Eddie to shadow under a veteran detective for training— especially when they're as shorthanded as they are. Despite feeling that Eddie might have a screw or two loose, the detective took to him quickly and already thinks of him as a partner rather than a protégé.

"Sh, sh sh—it's okay," he says and places the bundle of blankets down in the back of the Bronco before getting behind the wheel.

ONE OF THE LETTERS in the small stack of mail catches the man's attention from the corner of his eye as he drives recklessly while swiping through his missed calls. He places his phone between his head and shoulder to get a better grip on the steering wheel as he listens to his voicemail, and then probes the envelopes blindly with his free hand.

"Terry," a voice on the first recording says with an unfamiliar tone—too serious for Eddie, who normally likes to fuck around. He stops fingering through the bills and flyers to listen more intently now, but he's already spotted the dreaded white envelope.

"There's a dead body at Point Woronzof," the voice continues. "You need to come quick." A short silence follows and the message ends. Terry exhales as he pulls the heavy letter from the rest of the pile and then plays the second message. This one is just a few seconds of static that ends with an inarticulate syllable.

Terry flicks on his roof lights and notes that he didn't hear Chief Eddowes in the background yelling about where he was. In fact, there wasn't any noise at all besides some breathing and the failed attempt to say something. Point Woronzof, like many of Bloodrun's scenic views and attractions, doesn't draw as much activity in the winter, but it still usually has plenty of dog walkers and children playing.

It's even possible to hear the train from it.

T E R R Y P A R K S on Brigantine Boulevard—or "the Brig," as it's referred to by the locals—behind three BBPD cruisers, but instead of opening the door and heading to the crime scene, he just stares down at the envelope. It's normally his custom to get right out; to lift up the yellow tape—to restore the peace of Bloodrun. But normally, there are only restaurant coupons and bank statements in his mailbox. Half of him knows that he should deal with this letter later, but the stronger half—or perhaps the weaker—cannot wait. It tears the envelope open without his consent and yanks out the contents.

The first line reads:

HANNAH VS. TERRANCE VOLKER—

and Terry's hands drop to his lap.

On any random day, without even seeing what awaits him beyond the circle of tape, Terry Volker could always call out if he needed to. He could tell them that he just can't do it today; that something came up—something awful. He always does his job and usually sees to it fairly well—enough to garner the position of a small-town detective, at least. Although he's recently developed a habit of coming in late, he can't remember a time when he's ever called out before. They'd understand. But this is not his nature.

He can't bring himself to pull out his phone and make the call, but he's also unable to get out and leave the divorce papers behind. Trapped inside his own vehicle, Terry looks across the street.

Ordinarily, the Brig is relatively full of life, but peaceful. Standard small-town shops dot the sidewalks—amiable places to buy saltwater taffies and coffee or hunting knives. All family owned. All handmade. Locals would carry their groceries, tourists would tote gift bags. But now, the Brig is nearly desolate. Ten yards or so away from where Terry parked, he sees Eddie and other Bloodrun PD illuminated by a spotlight in the dark Alaskan winter morning. Their figures shroud whatever the light is shining on, but he knows what it is.

There's no time for this, Terry thinks.

He watches a group of frightened pedestrians be ushered across the street and then sighs heavily as he leans his head back onto the headrest. Only a second of solace is given to him before a memory flashes in his mind: the time when he vainly uttered, "I can fix this—"

It makes him flinch, but act.

He takes one last look at the summons send to him from Hannah's lawyer and then shoves them into his glove compartment and slams it shut.

CHAPTER II:
Sick

A GOOD MAN has no desire to do evil, because a good man has no desire. A good man can sleep easy knowing that he may die at once—at any minute—because he never worries himself with things that are out of his control. A good man can pull back the scrim and not become fixated on what he sees.

A good man, Terry Volker is not, yet he's not all bad either.

A cold shower can help make some men good, at least, Terry believes—so he compulsively tries to wash away everything that's wrong with him down the drain in raw stinging water. A cold shower, despite the wonders that it can do for the body and soul, will not protect either from the eternal end. Terry knows this and he fears it with disgrace.

But it isn't so much the dying that bothers him; it's doing it alone.

"Jesus, Ter—sick fuck," Eddie embarks a few steps away from the perimeter. "I've never seen anything like this," he admits. Eddie hasn't seen a lot at all really, compared with Terry or some of the others on their meager force—but no one was ready for this. Behind him, Terry can see pale flesh belonging to a pair of legs lying on top of the snow.

A woman's legs.

"She's been..." Eddie tries again, but Terry strides around him and he can see the awful butchery; a naked body in two pieces. His eyes dart across her feet and up her thighs, but then stop abruptly at her waist. Where her abdomen is supposed to begin, emerges a scarlet void—a red stained window into something that never should've been opened. It's so jarring to lay eyes on that for a few moments, Terry can't even make sense of it.

None of them can make sense of it, yet there's no mistaking the sinister reality of what lies before them; that *someone* did this. What they're looking at didn't occur from the result of some horrific accident or cruelty of nature—no matter how much they'd like to convince themselves otherwise. There's no hope for them in believing that they're just spectators to some perverse prank, or heinous prop—or even an optical illusion in the snow.

"Aha!" one would say, sliding up a plane of glass, revealing the dead girl to be still alive and intact on the other side.

"Magic!" another would cheer with relief as he helped her to her feet.

They all know that there is no smoke or mirrors anywhere creating a twisted trick of the eye, but many of them still rather check before getting any closer to her—before they can't come back from seeing that it's real. They want to hold on to a feeling that they aren't really here, like they're just acting out a scene in some sick theatre that they've all been forced to appear in. But no amount of wishing that some incompetent magician just opened his box up to discover that a slight mishap occurred while sawing his pretty assistant in half will make it so.

Abracadabra, Alakaza—

The oldest of the officers recall the baffling cases of cattle mutilation that occurred across the Lower 48 during the 1970s—all of which were chalked up to things like alien abductions, government conspiracies, sacrificial cults and in the end, lightning strikes. Eddie Koyukuk, the youngest amongst them, comes to recall the story about a monster that his mother scared him with before bed as a child. None of these will do though—these are all nonsense.

Someone did this, and that disturbs them more than the body itself—that a person could be so depraved to commit such a heinous act of violence. Somewhere out there is a human being made of the same flesh and blood as theirs, but in a way they didn't care much to discover, far more monster than man. It shouldn't be real, but the fact that it is, disturbs them so profoundly that it distorts their perspective of the world around them.

Everything that normally appears mundane is now bizarre; the glints on the snow shudder with a mysterious light; the steam from their breaths escapes them like departing souls. There's even an unspoken feeling amongst them that something seems to exude from the frozen halves of the body itself and seeps into their pores. It hums in the air like a marvelous ball of electricity that encapsulates the corpse and dares them all to come a bit closer—just a step—and complete the circuit. Like that odd anticipation that comes sometimes right before falling asleep—a phantasmal jerk—as if something is hovering above you and about to bop you on the tip of your nose and jolt you awake. They feel it prowling—vibrating between every molecule in the air—and it consumes their thoughts. The very sound of someone's voice might even wrench them from this dream with a convulsive shock.

It'd relieve them from having to unearth any of the dreaded answers to this vicious crime, but still, none of them say a word. Something holds their heads behind the curtain, shoving their faces down into the magician's box and forces them to see how horribly his trick had gone wrong. Simply turning away from it—as if even an option—doesn't mean that it will turn away from them.

"Sick son of a bitch," someone eventually brings themselves to say, and then they all repeat it like some sort of compulsive rite. They can hardly tell if they're saying it themselves or only hearing someone else say it. Along with Terry and Eddie, more officers and other personnel show up one by one and join in the chant.

"Sick son of a bitch."

"Twisted fuck," some deviate.

Terry stands at her feet—looming over her body—and stares into the red frozen display of her abdominal cavity. For a moment far too brief, it appears less like a dead girl—

"Sick son of a bitch,"

—and more like a slide from some graphic medical journal; a sagittal slice from a donated cadaver which consented strictly for the purposes of anatomical study. He stares at the thick layers of muscles and finds that he can identify the psoas and the obliques from the days when he had time to lift weights. The rest of it remains viscera to him though, which reminds him that he isn't glancing at a medical journal or poking his head into the observation window of some grotesque surgery. He wishes that he could identify more because it made her easier to look at. Chief Eddowes had advised him to do similar things in the past, in other lurid cases—ones that involved children.

"A view from above", Eddowes called it.

But even those cases were nowhere near as disturbing as this.

"Twisted mother fu—" another tries to join in but stops to catch his stomach.

Terry looks over to Rudd Hasson—the retiring detective whose position Eddie hopes to fill—and sees that the older man also looks sick. Terry doesn't want to be the one to crouch down and examine this one, but he knows that he must—even if it wasn't for Rudd's bad hip. For whatever reason, Terry always has a strong stomach when it comes to the unpleasantries of the job.

It's the fact that this girl was someone's daughter that makes Terry need to look at her from some other point of view—but unfortunately, he's out of anatomical knowledge. All that he can observe now is how it all seems to be so neatly tucked into place; the large empty aorta and vena cava tubes; the pink labyrinth of small intestine on top of a sliver of her right kidney; and then at the bottom, the exposed bone where the spine curves, making it impossible for whatever cut her in half to pass cleanly in between her spinal column. He even notes the careful arrangement of her hair.

He didn't just dump her, Terry thinks.
He wanted her to be seen.

It all horrifies and confounds him as much as it angers and disgusts him. He wishes he could be back in his Bronco right now. He'd rather face the music notated on his divorce papers than look at this any longer.

WHILE TERRY STARES AT THE CORPSE, Eddie feels a shameful pride when one of the other officers gets sick—a steaming puddle of coffee and half-digested donuts on the other side of the yellow tape—and how he is able to hold it down like Terry.

"Sick bastard," another voice from the choir winces.

Terry may have a strong stomach, but he *is* sick. Frankly, Terry is lucky to have only been to a few crime scenes with dead bodies. Most of them were already dead before he arrived, but what's far worse—the ones who died after.

"She appears to have been drained and cleaned to some degree," a voice says as Eddie walks over to the other side of the girl's severed body. Terry tries to listen without breaking his gaze, even as someone hands him a pair of blue nitrile gloves which he puts on unconsciously.

"She must've been killed somewhere else," the voice continues, this time followed by the *click-click* of a camera. "Out in the open like this—someone would've seen it. Plus, the killer would've needed a place to clean her up."

Terry and Eddie look across at each other with apprehension—

"Sick son of a bitch."

—and then all they can do is look down and listen.

"THERE APPEARS to be no other signs of fatal injury, indicating that the laceration through the waist could be the cause of death—via an extremely large and rapid amount of blood loss," the woman's voice says bleakly. "That is, given the victim wasn't mercifully poisoned or fortunate enough to suffer from cardiogenic shock first."

"Wait, you think that she was alive when this happened?" Eddie asks.

"The ligature marks around her wrists and ankles indicate that she was held captive, so, it's possible that she could've been restrained during the…" the woman says, hesitating to use the word "operation." She spins a dial on her camera, adjusting the exposure and then photographs the bruises on the ankles above the dead girl's white feet. Terry looks to the pale face and becomes mesmerized by the endless gaze of her eyes which almost stare back at him through a thin casing of cloudy frost.

"Sheri," Terry addresses the woman taking pictures without looking away from the dead girl's eyes. Terry's good at remembering names, unlike his protégé—he even has a neat trick that helps him remember faces. "What do you think this was… a chainsaw?"

"I'm not sure," she says. "Helduser will be able to figure it out, but that's what I'm leaning towards." Eddie shakes his head as Terry scans the rest of the body.

"Did you get the head and shoulders yet?" he asks.

Sheri nods and raises the large camera, as if to say, "Right here." Terry presumes to delicately lift the corpse's head without disturbing the hair as much as possible—which all flows out to one side above her right shoulder. Eddie crouches down to examine the back of her head and immediately finds a small "C" shaped wound.

"Looks like she was hit with something round—maybe the edge of a pipe," Eddie says in Sheri's direction. Hearing this, "the woman with the camera"—which is how Eddie refers to her when she isn't around—comes over and crouches next to him to photograph the wound.

Sheri hates it when she gets pulled away from her initial sweep—especially by patrolmen—and on any other day may've politely told him to wait. Detectives are usually keener in understanding how easily oversights can occur from this, but she isn't about to make Terry touch this one a second time. After

Eddie makes sure that he didn't miss anything, Terry puts the head back in place and Sheri returns where she left off photographing the dead body and the area surrounding it.

As the late dawn finally approaches, the first indications of light from behind Mount Tuqujuq begin to illuminate Point Woronzof and the dead girl's body with an orange twilight. The winter solstice passed a few weeks ago and the days are officially opening back up again, but it's a slow process—agonizing for some. On a clear day, it's possible for Bloodrun, Alaska to get about five hours of daylight in the winter, but the sun doesn't fully rise—if that's how it can even be described—until about 10:00am at this time of year.

They keep the dead girl's body outside longer than usual so that Sheri can take an abundance of photographs—and then she takes more. The Southcentral Alaska chill—which bites their cheeks at 3 degrees this morning—has kept the body well preserved, according to Bloodrun's small forensic team. They estimate that she's been dead for about six hours. Had it been the summer, nature would've provided a host of other threats of contamination beyond a much faster decomposition; coyotes and ravens could very well have dragged her off and picked her apart before she was ever found.

"Who would do something like this?" Terry asks.

The skin of the corpse is so clean and pale that it almost blends right in with the snow. From a distance, the only things that stand out are the two scarlet ovals of the body's open waist. Her legs are positioned together but tilted to one side, which causes them to bend slightly at the knees with her feet pointing away. Her torso lies face up with her palms resting near the sides of her head and her frozen eyes fixed on the sky. Terry catches himself thinking there would be something seductive to the pose, if you found her like that in your bed—alive and in one piece. She's young and good-looking and has striking hair that floods the snow to the right side of her face.

"Do you think it could be related to another crime?" Eddie asks after a moment. "One from somewhere else, maybe... I mean, this sort of thing doesn't happen here."

Despite the macabre sounding name of the town, Eddie's assertion rings true—the area that the Bloodrun River flows through is largely a quiet place—like many of the small towns across the state. The borough does receive a reasonable amount of skiers in the winter, but its big stir usually doesn't come until the summer; when tourists hope to catch a glimpse of the natural phenomenon which once caused the great river to run red thousands of years ago—something that hasn't happened since, and is unlikely to ever happen again. To the relief of most of the town's residents, it's a steadily dying attraction with only one place in town profiteering from it.

"Didn't the Black Dahlia cut a girl in half somewhere in California?" Eddie ventures, unsure if the nickname belonged to the victim or her killer.

"Yeah," Terry replies. "But that was too long ago—the killer would be an old man by now, if he's even still alive."

"Don't rule out old men," Rudd Hasson says, but no one acknowledges him.

"Maybe a copycat?" Eddie suggests with a raised brow.

"It's possible," Terry says and snorts. He can feel his nose hairs prickling the insides of his nostrils as they freeze stiff from the moisture in his breath. "But something tells me this is different. That girl down south had extensive mutilation done to her in addition to being cut in half."

Terry pauses for a moment and tilts his head to one side like a confused dog and stares into the girl's eyes which appear to follow him as he stands.

"This girl is almost untouched," he says. "That wound you found on the back of her head was most likely just to put her off her feet."

Besides the positioning of the body, the killer left no sign that he was even here. No little game pieces that beckoned them to find him like on some silly television show—no little totem, calling card—or even a goddamn eyelash. He simply didn't want to be found and had no interest in playing any games of cat and mouse with them. Not even a single useable footprint can be pulled from the snow around the body. The dense white blanket, which hasn't received fresh powder in two weeks, has since crusted over and remains sharp and hard—more like a rough sheet of ice.

"No witnesses," Terry says, and Eddie shakes his head. "Who found her?"

"Marlene Foster," Eddie says. "She was out for a run this morning with a headlamp on when the light bounced on 'two red blobs.' She thought it was an animal at first—from road hunters or poachers again—so she went in for a closer look. She said she called us immediately after she saw the feet—waited over there until we showed up," Eddie says, pointing to one of the benches that face Brigantine Boulevard. "Dispatch told her to try and keep anyone else from coming over to it, but she said that she was too shaken to think straight—understandably so I guess, hence all of the bystanders we had to move across the street."

"Did any of them get pictures?" Terry asks.

"There weren't any reporters in the crowd when we got here if that's what you're aski—"

"That's not what I'm asking," Terry says sharply. The mentioning of *reporters* makes Terry cringe with bitter resentment. "There's going to be pandemonium once this gets out, Eddie."

"I mean, we couldn't confiscate anyone's cell pho—" Eddie tries to rationalize but gets cut short again.

"You didn't have to *frisk* anyone to get their cooperation in keeping this hush," Terry says. Eddie thinks about his next words more carefully before speaking this time.

"Well, I don't think Marlene is in any condition—or more to the point—the type of person to go gossiping all over town about this. As for the others, I don't think anyone wanted the sight that they came over here to see. They were probably all too dumbfounded to do anything but stand there, which is what they were doing when we arrived—zombies. Our own men barely knew what to do—*I* didn't know what to do, but I certainly didn't feel the urge to take a picture. I should hope that the people in this town are more human than that." Eddie pauses for a moment and Terry nods.

"I think any journalists we might have in town are probably over at the community center for the Native Women vs. White Men Tug-o-War, anyway," Eddie continues, "but I imagine there's at least one grilling those people across the Brig by now."

This time, Eddie's use of the word *journalist* inadvertently compels Terry to remember two headlines that were printed about him in *The Crest* after the tragic shooting at The Rod & Reel Tavern 15 years ago:

"TEEN SHOT IN THE BACK"
and
"UNARMED AND SLAIN
BY OFF DUTY PATROLMAN"

The families of the victims that the shooter massacred before being gunned down himself were appalled reading them. They consider Terry a hero for what he did—regardless of the circumstances in which the nineteen-year-old boy was subdued—but Terry never got over the smear.

"Missing Persons has been notified?" Terry asks, bringing his eyes back to Eddie's.

"Of course," Eddie says.

"Did you talk to anyone in the shops across the street yet?" Terry asks as they duck under the yellow tape. "It would've been dark out, but the candy shop and Sullivan's open early," Terry says and stares at the CLOSED sign hanging in the front door of the tattoo parlor on the corner.

"Old Sully," Eddie begins with sarcastic cheer as they approach the sidewalk, "stone walled me and called me a 'flatfooted lickspittle'—whatever that means."

"It means you're a kiss ass."

"I am not," Eddie says, stopping at the curb.

"Do you think she saw something?" Terry asks and turns around to read Eddie's face. After a moment of consideration, Eddie nods and Terry continues walking.

"She'll talk to me," he says over his shoulder.

"What—why?" Eddie asks following behind, trying to hide that he already knows all about the "Acid Cop" story which accounts for Terry and Tina Sullivan's relationship.

"For one, you're dressed like a cop—"

"I am a cop," Eddie says and looks down at his uniform. "Chief said no tie and jacket until I comple—"

"Tina *hates* cops," Terry says turning back around. "And two," he continues, "I guess you could say she kind of owes me."

"For what?"

"Well," Terry says, thinking of the simplest way to recount the debt. "I caught the kid that killed her husband."

"Really?" Eddie asks, still hoping to get Terry's version of what exactly happened—opposed to the gossip that he's heard around the station, and the old microfiche article he found—another blow courtesy of *The Crest*. "When?"

"A long time ago," Terry says as he steps up onto the curb on the other side of the street. "While you were still at the academy licking spit."

"Ter," Eddie changes to a more concerned tone.

"What?"

"You were pretty late getting here this morning... You and Hannah still working it out?" Eddie asks and fruitlessly searches Terry's blank face. "Has she responded to any of your calls?"

"Yeah," Terry says and opens the door to the local coffee shop.

CHAPTER III:
Sullivan's Café

TINA SULLIVAN is an old, stout, little woman whose attitude only gets worse with her age, and perhaps—at least, a bit—rightfully so. The image of a witch ladling from a cauldron appears in the minds of many of her customers while they wait in line watching her make their morning coffees. Terry always finds her endearing for some reason though, even before he closed her husband's murder case and she took to a more motherly affection with him…

* * *

BILL SULLIVAN STOOD OUTSIDE the café opening up a birthday present which he waited thirty years to gift himself. It was a pack of cigarettes. There was no wrapping paper to peel away that concealed its contents—only thin clear cellophane. Tina was inside counting the drawer and intermittently gave him the evil eye. She hated that at his age he would have the audacity to start the habit back up after going so long without it. She remembered how she used to plead with him to quit until finally—thirty years ago to the day—he complied. Some old men weren't necessarily old-fashioned, but Bill was, so when he made a promise, he kept it—something that he believed was going out of style.

The promise did come with a clause though; if he lived to see 60 without a single cigarette, he could fill the rest of his days blowing smoke signals to India when he had nothing left to lose. Tina only agreed because she believed that it'd be ludicrous for him to actually do—which it was. Aside from the brief period of cold turkey withdrawal and the nicotine satiation that smokers often crave after a belly full of food, Bill wasn't plagued all that much by the temptation through the years. Still, he never forgot how much he thoroughly enjoyed it—especially when lying in bed with Tina after a round or two of lovemaking.

Bill and Tina had no idea what a "web presence" entailed and it never occurred to them to do any traditional promotion for that matter. They had no need to draw in customers by punching coffee cards or having free Wi-Fi. Sullivan's Café was a thriving business and a staple of Bloodrun Borough all on its own; partly because Bill imported fresh beans directly from a small ranch in Colombia, but more so, because Tina truly was witch-like in her ability to brew the strong delicious tonics.

Of course, there also wasn't a Starbucks in town, which surely would've bled them dry by selling their coffee flavored piss water in cutely signed cups. Fortunately for the Sullivan's, someone in the borough had the foresight back in the 1950's to establish an ordinance that prohibited franchise operations on the grounds that they destroyed small towns.

Along with there being no Dunkin Donuts or Horton's, tourists often remarked that Bloodrun seemed to be without any fast-food restaurants as well, but it wasn't. There was Charlie's Hamburger, Los Machetes, and even an Indian takeout place called The Green Vajrā. The borough was too small for the likes of a Little Italy or China Town, but it did have two corner pizza parlors and Yuki Hana; a small Asian buffet which served the closest resemblance to the Szechuan style Chinese food that Terry craved. For some reason that he could never get to the bottom of, it was impossible to find what he referred to as "authentic" Chinese food anywhere in Alaska. The things they passed off as wonton soup were absurd to him. But all this aside—quick, greasy, comforting, Americanized food, Bloodrun surely had—it just didn't have any fast-food *chains*. Most of the businesses in town were original shops and restaurants that have been around for decades—just as Bill and Tina's café.

ONCE BILL GOT THE CELLOPHANE stuffed into his pocket, he pulled one of the cigarettes across his nostrils and breathed in deeply.

He always wished that they had the same smell when they burned. The smell of the leaf itself was a lost scent to him, or at least, a dying one. There was nowhere in town left to smoke and the smokers that were pushed out to the street weren't even "smokers" by definition; they blew steam clouds that smelled like strawberry iced cream—

Pansies, Bill reckoned.

He closed his eyes and breathed in again, giving the cigarette another good sniff before lighting it. His lungs, which had returned to a healthy shade of pink years ago, seemed to squirm imperceptibly below his ribs. He pressed the filter to his lips and prepared to shield it with one hand and light it with the other when he heard commotion to his right. On the same side of the pavement that Bill stood, only a few storefronts down, two girls on vacation were walking out of Donahue's candy shop. Bill could hear them laughing as they pointed and made disapproving noises at something a little further down the sidewalk.

A STARK NAKED YOUNG MAN was walking down the Brig and heading right for them. The girls' innocent and amused reaction quickly turned to terror when they saw that he held a knife. Bill, who was unafraid of confrontation ever since he was a young man—and as a result, had his nose broken so many times that Tina became an expert at resetting it—immediately rushed over to the sound of their cries. He didn't see the knife, however, until it was too late, and the unlit cigarette dangling from his lower lip fell to the ground amidst the turmoil.

The naked young man held one of the girls by her hair while the other girl desperately clenched the arm with a long kitchen knife grasped at the end of it. Her nervous system dumped adrenaline into her veins, and she discovered a strength that she never knew existed in the human body's seldom tapped will to survive. The wild instincts of all her ancestors who fought to live at one time or another raged within her and she refused to die with ardent defiance. Still, this new fervor could only delay the young man's strength, and his knife soon began to cut across her cheek as she screamed. Blood flowed down her face as her heart made determined vows with every one of its frantic beats:

More travel.
More sunsets.
More laughs.

More candy.
More—

Bill seized the young man's wrist and pulled the knife out of the girl's face before it could reveal the back rows of her teeth and end her heart's desperate plea.

"Get out of here!" Bill shouted at her as he grappled with the boy's strong arm like a thrashing python. She hesitated for a moment but released her grip to try prying open the white knuckled fist which remained closed around a knot of her friend's hair. A fierce bite on his wrist opened his clasp at last and the two girls ran into the café screaming and bleeding.

Alone now, with the boy's other hand free to push down on the knife, Bill Sullivan learned that at 60 years old, he was no longer the man who toughed getting hit with cue sticks in bar fights at the top of the world while defending the honor of his young acid tongued bride.

B I L L G R U N T E D as he stared into his nude assailant's eyes. The boy's irises appeared black because his pupils were dilated so widely that the thin ring of color around them could hardly be seen. Bill recalled this as the tip of the knife punctured him right below his sternum. It only pierced him shallowly at first, but soon began sliding in unobstructed. Bill kept grunting and fighting until the front of his jeans were soaked in blood. His grip didn't weaken until the knife sank all the way inside of him to the hilt. It was then that Bill's heart began to beat its own vows:

More Tina.
More Tina.
More Tina.
More Tina.
More—

Bill slid off the knife and crumbled onto the sidewalk like a marionette with its strings cut. After getting a towel on the lacerated girl's face, Tina rushed outside just in time to catch a glimpse of the naked boy running through the clearing across the street. Even without her glasses on, Tina could make out his white ass disappearing into the brush.

"Bill!" she cried.

THE CASE STAYED OPEN for nearly four months until Terry finally closed it with some rather unorthodox means. Ever since then, Tina Sullivan would put rat shit in the grinds for any cops that came into the café—minus Terry, of course. The only reason that she could stay in business after Bill's murder was because of the town's relentless addiction to her coffee. She could've retired comfortably after Bill's death—financially speaking—but working kept her busy, and a busy mind does not wander.

"Idle hands are the devil's playthings," Tina would often recall to herself after Bill died as she picked up a broom or wiped the counter. Bill used to frequently recite this excerpt from a book of Benjamin Franklin quotes that Tina gave him one year—on one of his brighter birthdays. He normally said it just to tease her—when he'd catch her taking a minute to stare out their café window at the marvelous snowcapped Tuqujuq mountain, which, like Denali, was tall enough to stay covered all year round.

"Oh, fuck yourself," she'd say to him turning around and reaching for a bottle of glass cleaner as he came over to her smirking. "I should've never gotten you that book—I didn't know Franklin was an asshole too. The two of you—"

Bill would grab her wrist before she could take hold of the blue spray bottle and he'd kiss her and they'd giggle until a straggler came in...

* * *

"T E R R Y!" Tina shouts amiably as the bell above her door jingles, but her smile promptly bends back into a frown as she approaches him—not because of whatever happened across the street, but because Terry has to be the one to fix it. *Her* Terry. She shuffles around the counter with a hot mug of coffee and greets him warmly.

"Hey, T," he says as she pulls the back of his neck down and kisses his cheek.

Terry has a habit of visualizing seniors in their younger personage. He's been doing it both consciously and unconsciously for as long as he can remember. It started when he found an old black and white photograph of his grandfather—a boy with a pompadour posing with a Boxer mutt. The boy's face he recognized as his own. From that point onward, Terry never saw his grandfather's grey hair and loose flesh, but instead, the tight skin of the boy with grease in his hair. Terry still does this every time that he stumbles across a photo of someone he knows from when they were young, and he's actually become quite accurate in doing it without a picture—even with strangers.

"I saw you coming across the street with one of those *piss-ants*," Tina's tone changes sharply, referring to Eddie—who stands outside oblivious. Behind them at a small round table, a man in a blue Municipal Department jacket spits his coffee with an involuntary chuckle.

"Kaz," Terry says with a sigh as he addresses the man. "You mind if I talk to Tina alone?"

"Oh, sure thing, Terry," Kazimir Panas says in his indefinable accent. As handy as Terry's face visualizing exercise is for remembering names, he struggles greatly with guessing ethnicities and always wonders where Kaz hails from.

"*Spasiqa*," Kaz says nodding to Tina and then places his empty mug on the counter. "*Paka-paka*."

"Paka, Kaz," Tina replies with a surprisingly close pronunciation. Terry waits for the store bell to ring again as the man leaves and then raises his eyebrows.

"*Paka*, eh?" he asks.

"Shut up," Tina says a bit abashed and Terry smiles. He found her little outburst as amusing as Kaz did, but Terry still feels the need to defend his detective-in-training.

"Eddie's alright, T," he says and then relishes in the caffeine.

"Oh, it looks like you have such a mess out there today," she whimpers, and the image in Terry's mind of a young Tina Sullivan—pigtailed and no glasses—abruptly immolates by a flash of the dissevered girl's pale frozen face. Her motionless eyes staring up at him particularly taunt him and he almost chokes and spills his mug as he wipes a dribble of coffee from his lip.

"I actually came in to ask you a little about that. Our blueboy over here thinks you might be holding out on us." Tina cocks her head around Terry to see through the large café window and her face twists at the sight of Eddie.

"Terry—"

"Please," he says solemnly before she can refuse. She looks wearily into his half empty mug, as if considering to change the subject to refilling it.

"For Bill," Terry adds, and she looks up to him and sighs—her eyes abandon their nature and become somber.

"Okay," she finally admits. "I did see *one* thing. Around 5'oclock, when I opened the doors…"

"What was it?" Terry presses.

"A black car sped by—that's all."

"What kind of car?"

"Oh, I don't know," Tina says and shrugs. "One of them fancy sports cars. Old looking—but nice. Something with *character*—that Bill would've liked; not like those damned things you see today."

"Did you catch a glimpse of the license plate?" Terry asks, unintentionally reverting to a cop-like tone.

"No," she says shaking her head.

"That's all?" Terry asks and glares at her with a dire look in his eyes. He assumes that this must be what a father feels when he's trying to get his daughter to snitch on her brother.

"That's all. Let me get you a cup to go—" she says, turning back to the counter.

"That's okay, T," Terry says, returning to the tone of a friend—or even a son. She nods and pinches his stomach.

"When did the station lose funding for its gym?" she asks. Terry smirks at her, even though he'd be embarrassed to admit how long it's been since he last worked out. "Maybe if the borough would hire some competent officers for once there wouldn't be so many cutbacks and you wouldn't be busy doing all of the work for these yellowbell—"

"Thanks, T," he says, cutting her off, but the defeated smile doesn't waver from his face as he takes one last gulp of coffee. He hands her the empty mug and walks back outside with another ring from the bell above the door which ends her ribbing.

"Stop playing with yourself and get back on the treadmi—" she jeers loudly as the door closes.

"Well?" Eddie asks, looking down to Terry's empty hands eagerly—as if asking for an update on coffee rather than for intel on the murder.

"We got a vehicle," Terry says hesitantly.

Eddie looks through the café window and sees Tina Sullivan giving him the finger.

CHAPTER IV:
Card House

NESTLED IN THE PINES across town, a large, odd shaped home stands on an unkempt estate. Tangled gnarls of trees twist upward around rusted out machinery and piles of various repurposed material make the grounds resemble an abandoned junkyard. Welded sculptures screech in the breeze. Many of them were designed to move with the wind and used to make pleasant chirps and simple melodies—opposed to the grating rasps and shrieks that they do now. Some of them even provided a small amount of turbine power to the house, but they're long overdue for some TLC. Though their functionalities have been ruined by rust, there's something still interesting about their towering appearances and the natural patinas they've accumulated from the elements.

A wide trail, the only part of the manor that receives active maintenance, snakes through the woods to the front of the house, which is a hodgepodge of construction—waiting in a veil of trees like Frankenstein's monster. All throughout the building, additions are continuously put on, altered or removed without any unifying element.

The outside, which only hints to the jumbled hysteria that goes on within, frequently ditches one material and continues with another. Brick walls meet up against stone and then change into wood and even steel. It can be assumed that when the mad architect runs out of one material, he simply continues with whatever he can get his calloused hands on next. But in contrast to this apparent carelessness, closer scrutiny reveals masterful and innovative craftsmanship.

A DARK MAZE of corridors and rooms wind throughout the basement. Most of the light switches don't work and the ones that do send sketchy surges of power to dusty burnt-out bulbs. The safest way to illuminate anything downstairs without getting shocked requires a flashlight.

A layer of caked dirt and cobwebs cover everything and a machine-like smell hangs in the air. Dank cardboard boxes containing pumps and motors, milk crates packed with miscellaneous old tools, and various black garbage bags stuffed with insulation, mulch and god knows what else, clutter every available space of the filthy floor.

At the end of the stone hallway which tunnels furthest from the main rooms of the cellar, stands a splintered door which leads nowhere—one of many throughout the house. An antique wheelchair sits halfway in a pool of stagnant water that leaked from an exposed and heavily oxidized pipe in the ceiling. Two old space heaters sit on the ground beside it and on top of them are stacks of cracked, foggy picture frames. The faces can't be made out, but they appear to be old family portraits. The hallway bends at ninety degrees and a pile of cement bags lie in the corner; the bottom ones have already been activated from floods that the basement undergoes every April when the snow melts.

The stone walls change to brick as the hallway wraps around in a circle. On the inside, the round room of the floor above drops down. There are many secret nooks and passages cut into the stone that allow candid peering of a spiral staircase in the center of this circular room. The architect, or artist, or inventor—or more commonly, "assholemotherfuckingjerk—" hasn't been up there in many, many years.

On the other side of this large round hallway, the corridor opens into another room where a half dozen shelves full of what can best be described as "shit" line the walls. A rusty metal shelf holds used cans of paint and stains and other chemicals. A leaning wood shelf houses opened boxes of tile and brick. Another shelf made of black pipe—a common material used all throughout the home—stores coils of hoses, wires and ropes.

None of these shelves can easily be accessed because long packages of fluorescent lights, rolled up carpets, and boxes and boxes full of stuff that never should've been kept are dropped all around them. At the far end of the room, another inoperable door stands and a grimy bathtub full of flowerpots rooted with dead plants. In front of the tub, new stacks of welding manuals, building codes, art magazines and Alaskan history texts take on their first layer of mouse droppings. They've recently been committed to their owner's memory and are waiting to be catalogued into his library beneath the round room with the staircase.

The heavy dust on the floor has trails beaten into it from regular traffic, but in the lesser traveled areas it gathers thickly. A fresh set of footprints lead from a crook that's barely wide enough to walk through and continue onto the beaten path of the final passage. The trodden dirt here is only stamped along one side because a stainless-steel operating table is pushed against the wall of the other.

A N   A N G R Y   V O I C E   E C H O E S down this last hall from where it opens into a large two door garage. It's substantially cleaner there, but still cluttered everywhere with something to catch your shin on or snag your elbow. An antique car with white wall tires and a small motorboat are parked inside, each filled and covered with bundles of clothes, dirty dishes, and plastic bins that overflow with what only looks to be more junk.

In the corner of the garage, a work bench with a single lamp glows in the dark. It shines on an old paraplegic man sitting in a motorized wheelchair. Various welding masks, acetylene torch goggles and other face shields hang on the wall above the bench. Behind the elderly man, a nineteen-year-old boy lies on his back.

One of the boy's dirty hands—which more resemble a man's—reaches around the chair and grabs a pair of pliers off the ground that is sprawled with other tools and wheelchair parts. He works feverishly, although he can't shake the thought of debauching the repair on purpose. If he only had another place to live and make some money, he'd reach into the back of the chair with the pliers, grasp down tightly and twist and yank until something cracked and the paralyzed man spilt onto the floor. He could make it seem like an accident, but that wouldn't spare him from an additional berating, and the current one is already enough.

"Do you *see* the piston?" the old man asks in an irritated French-Canadian accent. The boy has already clasped the piston with the pliers and is onto the delicate task of sliding its pin back through the hole in the barrel.

"What's going on?" the man croaks again, getting angrier by the boy's silence. "What do you see?"

"I see the piston!" the boy finally shouts but quickly lowers his voice. "It's twisted… I just need—"

"Goddamnit, Talon!" the man snaps, immediately assuming the boy is to blame as he always does. "I swear, if you fucked this up—"

"I just need another pair of pliers to hold the cuff in place."

"Then get them!"

The boy rises to his feet and steps into the darkness towards two red beat-up toolboxes. After the sound of a metal drawer opening and the rattling of some tools, he returns with an additional pair of pliers and stands at the edge of the light with only the toes of his boots lit.

"Come on! I don't have all night," the man yells.

"I think you need to recline back, Émile," Talon says softly from the shadows. "There's too much weight on it for me to turn it." The man raises his lower lip in contempt but nevertheless thumbs a switch on the armrest controls with one of his crooked hands and his chair begins to slowly tilt backwards. Talon casually reenters the light without glancing at the old man and stops when he reaches the back of the chair—out of sight.

43

Standing there behind him reminds Talon of the one and only time that he ever stood foot in a dentist's office. He was a child; young enough to still have some baby teeth, but old enough to know that it was wrong for him to bite down onto the probing finger and not let go—even after he tasted blood ooze from the latex glove and the dentist instinctually struck him.

He won't bite this finger though.

He'll take the abuse—his "medicine," as the architect calls it.

CHAPTER V:
Spartacus

T ERRY SITS BACK DOWN in his Bronco and watches the white coroner's van drive away with two frozen halves of an unidentified girl in it. As it turns off the Brig, his eyes shift to the glove compartment, but before he can lean over and pull out the dreaded papers, a nudge on the back of his elbow stops him.

From the back of the truck, a black dachshund with brown markings and a graying muzzle pokes his head through the large bundle of blankets and jabs Terry with his snout. His face is smushed to one side from burrowing below the warm covers—like the badger hound he was bred to be—and his eyes have not fully opened and adjusted to the rising sun.

"Spart," Terry says with a reluctant smile, "go back to sleep." But Spartacus is already climbing onto the console—his wagging tail now free enough to sway the top blanket back and forth. Defiantly, he continues to get into Terry's lap and raises his paws to Terry's chest so that he can lick his chin.

Hannah brought Spartacus home from a rescue shelter years ago as a surprise—back when things were still "good" between them. Terry wasn't particularly pleased about this; the real surprise to him was the new chore that he had to help keep up on. Still, the puppy made Hannah happy, so he expressed no grief. He played along and petted the dog and showed no anger towards him when he pissed on the rug and even took him for walks late at night in the cold without complaint.

After a while, Terry began to find himself thinking of Spartacus as a tiny Doberman pinscher or even a Rottweiler—mostly just because of the coloring of Spart's coat; his brown face and legs and shiny black body. But Terry also knows that despite being the smallest of all the hounds, dachshunds are bred for utility—they're hunters. Unlike yappy lap dogs that are bred to be toys rather than animals, Terry feels that dachshunds still have their pride.

T H E P U P P Y, which was understood to be *her* puppy, soon grew to be enamored with Terry. He followed him around the house wagging his tail, jumped into his lap whenever he sat down, and whined every time that he left. The dog would often lie on Terry's chest and push the top of his little head against Terry's chin with all his might. It seemed to him like Spartacus wanted to thrust himself under Terry's skin and he'd make exasperated grumbles of defeat every time that he couldn't.

Hannah found it all comical at first, because even though Terry never said it, she knew that he didn't care much for having a dog. Still, he'd come home from work, put his gun down on the table, and embrace Spartacus before her.

"Just to calm him down," he'd say.

One day, while Terry was putting on his jacket, which made Spartacus begin his incessant whimpering, all the humor that Hannah once found in it instantly turned to jealousy.

"Just take him with you!" she shouted. She was already up and making a bundle of blankets for him from their bed before Terry could say a word. She assured him that she wasn't upset; that the dog was *their* dog now.

After she left, Hannah only answered one of Terry's numerous calls—simply to ask for Spartacus. When he refused, she hung up the phone.

It wasn't out of spite that Terry did this, at least, not directly. At the time, he thought that if he gave up the dog, then it would be irrevocably over between them. As long as he held onto the dachshund—to Spartacus—there was still a chance to get her back.

Now, as the dog licks his stubble, Terry realizes that he keeps Spart because he loves him too much to part with the little shit.

S P A R T A C U S C U R L S into Terry's lap and rests his muzzle on his forearm. The papers will stay put for now. Tomorrow he can go over the terms of the divorce. They'll only cause him more pain—knowing that Hannah will inevitably get the dog—even if she has to bear seeing Terry again in court for a custody battle. The fact that he trained Spartacus as well as the precinct's K9 shepherd—at least, in terms of his nose work—will amount to nothing. He could try getting him certified as a service dog—

Emotional support animal, Terry thinks, but shakes it out of his head. He can fight all he wants—even show the judge how the dog prefers him—but the donation receipt from the animal shelter will easily prove Hannah to be Spart's legal owner when the time comes; when she's finally had enough with trying to be civil.

Terry sighs and looks out the window to the spot where the dead girl was found a few hours ago and then back across the street to Sullivan's café. As he stares, he notices that snowflakes are beginning to fall, and he watches them closely as they melt on the windshield...

* * *

CHAPTER VI:
Lonely Boys

TERRY WAS NEVER a huge drinker, and though Bill Sullivan's unsolved murder certainly stressed him, he didn't find himself sitting in The Buckaroo Club having a drink to get his mind off of it. No, Terry began doing his own sleuthing as soon as the case started to go cold—which was no fault of Rudd Hasson, the one officially assigned to Bill's case.

There were no cameras outside of Sullivan's Café, or the knife maker's, or the candy shop—or any of the nearby stores on the Brig. As for witness descriptions, the two assaulted girls couldn't have provided anything clearer in their testimonies—all the way down to the color of the perpetrator's pubic hair. The problem arose because there wasn't anything that stood out on the attacker that could be used to differentiate him from most of the young men in Bloodrun; *white, average height, early 20's...*

The only real evidence came from an abandoned pile of clothes, which were found in an alley not far from the crime scene; one sock, a pair of blue jeans, and boxer briefs. Some dead skin cells and a little sweat were able to be collected from the sock, but unfortunately, there weren't any DNA matches in any of the forensic databases. They'd prove to be useful once a suspect was apprehended, but until then, time ebbed away maddeningly.

As predicted, the pockets of the jeans provided no wallet or identification, but they did, however, present a likely clue for the cause of what happened—or at least part of it, anyway. Crumpled up inside the left side with a bit of dryer lint was a half-eaten strip of blotter acid.

No one was all that surprised when they discovered that the young man was likely high on LSD when he went on his rampage, but it was *something*. Everyone already suspected that some type of psychological disturbance must've been at the root of it. Bloodrun Borough might very well be a developing suburb that takes its fair share of oddities from Anchorage, but it didn't receive enough spillover for sane men to trudge naked through its streets.

THE ICE in Terry's gin nearly melted before he took his first sip. He was preoccupied with listening in on all the voices around him, hoping that he'd overhear one of them mention the word "acid' or "LSD."

And then what? he asked himself.

Yell "Freeze, motherfucker!" and go for your Walther?

If he raided another college party on his own, especially after the kids had already been formally questioned by Rudd, word would eventually get back to the station that Terry was working the case on his own. What Terry needed was hard physical evidence. If he could only find someone pushing blotters, he'd just have to somehow obtain one and get it back to the lab. Then they'd be able to analyze and compare it with the strip of psychedelic absorbed paper that they found with the dirty laundry in the alley.

AS TERRY SAT eavesdropping,

"—Jeannie's mother is coming up to visit next wee—"

"—I told him, 'If you ever talk to me like that agai—'"

"—Hey, can you put on the Golden Knights game? No one wants to watch this shi—"

his attention was pulled to one of the flat screens above the bar. A longtime had passed since Terry could sit down and follow his Flyguys, but as a result of Bill Sullivan's death, he was catching almost every one of their preseason games via bar televisions. A new kid on the team reminded him of the Legion of Doom days, and for a moment, he forgot all about the murder. The kid was dwarfed in size compared to the brutal trio that comprised LoD, yet he had no problem throwing the referee aside and giving a large brute on the Red Wings a run for their teeth.

He's a little beast, Terry thought and let out a cheer which promptly reminded him where he was. After inadvertently calling attention to himself, he self-consciously raised the drink to his lips—solely to keep an inconspicuous appearance up. Evidently, there were no other Flyers fans in attendance. A fair amount of people around town knew Terry, but the borough wasn't so small that anyone more than Chief Eddowes was really known from the precinct in the public eye. Still, Terry shaved off his mustache in a foolish attempt to secure more anonymity. He hardly thought of what he was doing as "going undercover"—he was just plain desperate to get a lead.

Terry took another sip of his increasingly diluted gin and stifled thoughts away of Hannah waiting for him at home while he pretended to be a detective when a man appeared beside him preceded by his smell. In retrospect, it would've seemed like destiny, if it weren't for the fact that the man was a regular—the proverbial townie of Bloodrun. The stinking man's name was Stephen James Albot, but he was more commonly known by his nickname.

CHAPTER VII:
"Fullsend Steve"

THE FIRST TIME that Terry encountered Albot, the man was leaning against a wall in the back of the Buckaroo with his eyes closed. Every so often, he'd slide over to one side but right before losing equilibrium and collapsing onto the hard wood floors—shattering the glass in his hand into shards—he'd jolt back to life, but then slowly start leaning over again. It reminded Terry of a poem that his grandmother used to read to him before tucking him in:

> I can sleep in the air with wind in my hair
> I can sleep standing up and not spill my cup
> I can sleep—

He couldn't remember how the rest went, only that the poet would go on boasting about all the precarious places that he could sleep in. After watching Albot regain consciousness two or three more times right before hitting the ground, Terry pointed him out to Hannah and they both began laughing and counting how long it'd take before he got kicked out—or finally dropped his drink.

Needless to say, Stephen James Albot habitually reeked of alcohol; well-whiskey, to be exact—and he always seemed to have a glass of it in the unfailing grip of one of his hairy hands. Albot drank the cheapest and most offensive tasting alcohols, not because he was poor, he told himself—and anyone who would listen—but because, "Some men drink things that put hair on their chests, and some men drink like baby girls." And perhaps this was true, for something had to be keeping him warm. The way he tramped across town through the snow—and occasionally slept in it—was remarkable.

At the end of the night, Albot could usually be seen in similar positions; sitting completely unconscious on a stool by the dartboards or leaning against the jukebox by the small stage—but always upright and holding his glass. Back when he was still earning the title of town drunk, other folks would also laugh at this spectacle of a man who never woke up at the command of bartenders or bouncers, but immediately sprang to life the second his grip loosened on whatever concoction he was drinking.

Having already received the "Fullsend" moniker, he amused no one.

A LBOT WASN'T FULLY INTOXICATED when he wandered over to Terry and slapped him on the back as he sat down, but Terry could see the glass forming on Albot's jaundiced eyes. He recognized Albot from his stench alone due to his frequent stays in the station's drunk tank. Terry brought him in a few times himself too—but always as *Officer* Volker—and he let Albot sit in the backseat of his cruiser without cuffs on because there was never any concern that he'd try to escape. Terry even picked him up once during a blizzard when he happened to spot Albot lying unconscious on the sidewalk collecting a blanket of snow. He always marveled at the man's flagrant alcoholism, which amazingly, he had yet to kill himself with.

Despite the town's frustration with him, they largely pitied Albot and accepted him as one of their quirks. He never caused much of a serious disturbance, and there were few who didn't have at least one story—or knew someone who did—where they overindulged and ended up going on a hell-ride with him. This usually involved closing the Buckaroo and waking up in a strange place—often a gutter.

His problem with the law mostly came about from repeatedly buying alcohol for minors and presuming to drink it with them out in the woods by Sedna's Crossing. Albot was such a valued commodity to these kids that when they'd get caught sneaking in through their bedroom windows at four in the morning covered in vomit, they'd tell their parents that some "Canadian with a red hat" bought them the booze to avoid ratting on the infamous Fullsend Steve.

Although he always managed to cause damage wherever he went, Albot never meant to hurt anyone. He was just a terribly lonely man who couldn't find people his own age to drink with, save for those occasional times of poor judgment or plain devilish curiosity—when someone joined him and awoke the next day to find their car smashed up on the lawn or their children screaming at the homeless-looking man passed out in the tub. He would ruckus with anyone willing to accept his invitation to drink wildly with him—as if it were the end of the world—and most often, this just happened to be thrill-seeking teenagers. Albot never once tried anything with any of the young girls and he treated the boys with admiration. In return, it was he who often ended up the victim—being beaten, robbed, and taken advantage of even by high schoolers (granted, he usually drank most of the alcohol that he bought for them). In spite of this, or perhaps from not being able to remember it, he'd wake up and do it again. All the while, Albot alienated himself from anyone his own age—largely through piss, puke and blood. He never did it to say, "Woe is me", nor did he drink for all the pity that was allotted to him. He simply wanted company.

Of course, this all made him a suspect early on. Detective Rudd Hasson brought Albot in for questioning, but he was quickly dismissed after it was determined that the drunkard was incapable of acquiring and distributing a Schedule I drug. None of Albot's prior arrests involved illicit substances and if he did happen to have something to do with it, Rudd assumed that it must've been during a bender which Albot had no recollection of.

Terry decided in that moment however, that he'd give Albot the no refunds ticket and go for the depraved ride. If nothing else, perhaps he'd gain an amusing anecdote to tell, like he and Fullsend Steve climbed the water tower or brought a stripper back to the holding cell—Hannah would love that.

"F LYERS FAN, EY?" Albot asked eagerly as he sat down on the empty stool beside Terry, evidently not recognizing him. Albot was an older man with far more grey hair than the few wisps that stood out on Terry's head. His nose was a jumbled wad of cartilage and bone from every time it was

53

used to break his fall—or someone's fist. To say that the man smelled like whiskey was an understatement—Albot smelled like a damn distillery. As Terry wondered how long it's been since the man last bathed, he noted a tiny jailhouse-looking tattoo on Albot's hand between his thumb and index finger. It appeared to be a small Egyptian sarcophagus—easy to miss because it was never necessary to handcuff him. As Terry observed the faded black lines of the little coffin, he also recalled how Albot's hands were quite easily the hairiest that he's ever seen on a human being. They reminded him of the wildman—

>the hair of his head grows thick as barley,
>he knows not a people, nor even a country
>
>always his tracks are found by the waterhole
>I am afraid and I dare not approach him

—from that story they forced on him in high school.

He's more animal than man, Terry thought and remarked how the hair even grew on the joints above Albot's fingernails.

But instead of being lured out of the woods by a naked woman, he's drawn by hard liquor.

"Broad Street Bullies," Terry replied with a smile, "you?" As he raised his glass to cheers, he thought again about that time when he and Hannah were getting a kick out of the old, inebriated fool. After losing count on how many times Albot nearly fell over, Terry and Hannah were invited to sit with a group of friendly Vietnamese tourists who didn't speak English. They continually raised their glasses over the center of the table to cheers every few minutes and then go back to talking amongst themselves. Hannah found it hilarious because it was the only time that she noticed any of them sipping their drinks. She couldn't determine if this was their custom for drinking, or if they just wanted Terry and her to feel like they hadn't forgotten about them.

"Oh, again," Terry would say and join Hannah in laughing. "Cheers, again."

"Is this how they drink in Vietnam?" she leaned over and whispered, still giggling.

"I don't know," Terry said and then decided to raise his glass and initiate the next toast himself. He tried his best to repeat what he heard them say before each round, "*Một, hai, ba,*" which he assumed meant "One, two, three," and then exclaimed, "Cheers!"

"*Dzô!*" they all shouted, dropping their heads back.

ALBOT CLINKED his glass against Terry's with a nod and gulped down the remaining whiskey in his glass.

"Well, let me buy you a drink then," Terry proposed, knowing Albot would be unable to refuse. "I don't think there's any way Detroit can come back now."

"Why not—what's one more drink?" Albot asked coolly.

"What's your poison?"

And by the way, do you have any acid?

"Seven & Seven," Albot answered. "Neat." This surprised Terry because he suspected that Albot would be drinking contemptible straight whiskies all night—but hey, if someone else was buying—

Albot noticed the difficulty which Terry had with finishing his watered-down gin—which may as well have been tap water to Albot—and reckoned that his new friend might be short-lived if he didn't intervene.

"Wait," Albot interrupted as Terry opened his mouth to order.

"Make that two Mind Erasers."

THE TWO OF THEM sucked the cold layered drinks up in suit through the straws in their tall narrow glasses until they were gone; first the Kahlúa, then the club soda, and finally the vodka. Terry felt relieved to discover how easily it went down, even with the brain freeze. He then remembered the Walther strapped above his ankle underneath his jeans and experienced some fleeting apprehension. It was one thing to get caught pursuing a case that he wasn't assigned to, but getting caught ripped with Fullsend Steve while carrying a personal firearm?—Chief Eddowes might have his badge for that. Terry was fully aware of Alaska's lenient gun laws and one's right to carry a concealed weapon, but the great state wasn't so lax when alcohol was added to the equation.

"Two pints of Guinness, please," Albot told the bartender when she came back for their empty glasses. It sounded strange hearing Albot speak without slurring his words, but what Terry found stranger, was what the man ordered.

First, Mind Erasers and now, stouts? Terry never knew Albot to drink anything but cheap whiskey and the Pabst Blue Ribbon that he supplied for high school keggers.

Either his tastes have unaccountably changed since his last arrest, or the cannery started paying him more than he knows what to—wait,

"Aren't we supposed to not mix alcohol?" Terry asked, trying not to sound too boyishly concerned.

"What for?" Albot asked earnestly. Terry found this to be a strange question which he didn't know how to answer.

What are we supposed to not mix alcohol for? he thought, furrowing his brows.

"Isn't the saying, 'Beer and liquor—never been sicker'?"

"Nonsense," Albot replied, as if he had great wisdom to bestow on this poor young wretch. "The Guinness will keep your stomach settled," he informed. Albot was under the impression that the creamy taste of the Irish stout resulted from actual cream that could in theory have the power to soothe a sour stomach. Nevertheless, Albot was on a remarkable streak for keeping his booze down. There was a method to his madness—he was like an alcoholic alchemist. Never mind how all the vomiting he suffered in his younger days had seared his esophagus and disintegrated much of the enamel on his remaining teeth. He was a man now, and throwing up was a shameful waste; a cardinal sin.

TERRY BEGAN to seriously wonder what exactly the cost would be if he continued with this. There was no way he'd be able to scale the water tower if he couldn't even walk, and in any case, Hasson *had* already questioned the drunkard.

"Ah, cheer up, son," Albot said, clinking his glass again against Terry's as he detected the hesitation on his face. "I can tell by your eyes that something's troubling you," he said and sipped the nitrogen-whipped head off his black elixir. For a moment, Terry worried that Albot was going to ask what this something was that troubled him.

Well Steve, for starters, my wife says I work too much and there's an unsolved murder that happened down the street in broad fucking daylight and instead of being home with her I'm out with you *at the fucking Bucka—*

"Right now's not the time for that," Albot continued and dunked his scarred-up lip into the foam and drank from its dark body. He returned the glass to the coaster and then brought his hand up to his face to examine his tiny tomb. It almost looked like he read from the very ink of it when next he spoke—like the words were microscopically needled into the lines of his little coffin.

"For I commend enjoyment, so we shall drink and be merry, as there's nothing better for the living, for tomorrow we may die—" but Albot was cut off from twisting and paraphrasing Ecclesiastes with other bible verses to validate his drinking—as many alcoholics who dabbled a bit in the program often do—when the Flyers' goal siren rang off exasperatingly from the television. The Red Wings scored their first goal of the game.

"God damn it!" Terry moaned and took a few small swigs from his glass—it was too cold on his throat to gulp it the way Albot did—but still, the alcohol was beginning to take its effect. In a few more rounds, they'd both be fit to swallow swords or breathe fire without any discomfort at all.

"Almost a shutout," Albot said shaking his head, abandoning Isaiah 22:13 and Luke 12:19.

Shutout... The word leaked out like a single drop of motor oil onto a rusty gear in Terry's mind. It started to turn slowly at first, grinding a bit here and there, but the alcohol helped fully lubricate it and the cog soon spun effortlessly. By the time Terry put his pint glass back down onto the bar, he could see the whole system turning. It wasn't a smooth-running machine by any means—Terry's ideas rarely were—but it was all he had.

A shutout, he thought again, *yeah.*

I N   O R D E R for Terry to bring up LSD inconspicuously, their conversation had to naturally turn to drugs. The rundown scheme machine that sputtered along in his mind, which would hopefully facilitate this turn, depended on Albot being a baseball fan. Particularly, it depended on if the old man had any recollection of the sport from the

70s—and even more so, of June 12, 1970, San Diego Stadium—when the Pittsburgh Pirates played the Padres.

It was hard to gauge Albot's age because of how mercilessly he cared for his body. The lines on his face were deep and the bones in his hands were knotted and twisted like tree roots. Terry was too young to remember this legendary game firsthand, but it was possible that Albot might. If he did, he'd certainly have it catalogued along with his repertoire of twisted bible verses for whenever the occasion might call for him to justify his indulgent lifestyle. He also had Hemingway, Buzz Aldrin, Warren Zevon and Elizabeth Bowes-Lyon—amongst many other notable alcoholics ready to cite—despite the fact that they all accomplished great things and Albot has done nothing.

"Nothing better than seeing a good no contest beating," Terry finally said, committing to his half-baked idea. He knew that he couldn't just come right out and say it—even a drunk might see through that—so instead, he tried to recall some other famous flawless victories that he could use to reel the man in before getting to San Diego, 1970.

There's always Iron Mike and Tiger, Terry thought and then tried to remember the score of a Patriots Titans game a few years back.

"Yes'sir," Albot agreed after knocking back the last of his Guinness. "Always love a good ass kicking."

Albot could talk extensively about sports, music, movies, cars, even women somehow—and perhaps more startling, politics. Not only could he croon along with almost anyone sitting next to him, but he did it all without having much of any inclination in the subject. All Albot really cared about was drinking and not being alone.

"How about that Rangers Red Wings game, 15-0 or something?" Terry asked in an inciting fashion, the way men do when they want to compete with one another in who knows more about something—a way for them to see whose penis was larger. Albot, who wasn't a true sports fan, was a professional when it came to this type of banter. He could rattle off far more than a list of top tier athletes with drinking problems. Sports were a popular topic of discussion in the bars that he frequented, so it was vital for him to be well versed in them. Conversation often led to strangers buying him drinks, but more importantly, it meant company—he could always get a top off from his flask.

"That's right," Albot said. "And if you're a real Philly fan, you must know about the Eagles first title match, right?" the drunk asked, leaving Terry completely emasculated and mind blown. He tried not to get thrown off course, but he couldn't believe that Fullsend Steve, of all the fucking people in Alaska, was familiar with *the Birds.*

"One and only touchdown of the game against," Albot put his glass down and pretended to think, "the Cardinals?"

"Yep—" Terry said and rushed past Serena Williams and Jordan. "Do you remember when Montreal took Washington, 11-0?" Terry asked quite pleased with himself, hoping that reference might get his balls back.

"Sure," Albot said. "Oh, and how about when the Phils crushed the Astros seven to nothing in game three of the World Series?"

This motherfucker.

"Of course, in game four they got it handed back to them when Houston threw a no hitter and won th—"

That's it! Terry's mind raged angrily and he gnashed his teeth.

"Speaking of no hitters," the words tripped over themselves out of Terry's mouth. "Let's not forget the greatest of all time—when Doc Ellis pitched a no hitter against the Padres."

"Haha, certainly not," Albot agreed with a laugh.

"You know, they say he was high on LSD when he did that," Terry said innocently.

"Oh, definitely," Albot agreed. "All of them should be taking acid before a game—baseball, football, even soccer. It'd allow them to really *zero in*, y'know? In their mind's eye, and *see* the ball." Terry wasn't sure at all what Albot meant by this, but he nodded his head.

"I bet Ellis could see where the batter was going to swing before he even wound up," Albot added.

"Man," Terry blurted, "I'd sure love to get my hands on some acid right now."

"Z'that right?" Albot asked.

"Oh yeah," Terry said assertively as he tapped his hands on the bar and leaned back uncomfortably. He had great difficulty with lying, even for a good cause, which conversely got him into a lot of trouble throughout his life. Most people make messes by not telling the truth, but with Terry, it was from being too honest.

"I haven't done any in, jeez," Terry paused and blew air through his lips, "I don't even know how long—but man, do I love it."

Come on you fuck.

Bite.

Albot polished off some foam from the bottom of his glass and then appeared to be contemplating something. Terry tried not to stare at him, but it was the longest Albot had gone all night without speaking.

Say it.

Say you have some fucking blotters on you so I can flash the brass and get the hell outa'here.

"Well," Albot teased, looking up to the ceiling.

If you're spending all this time thinking about what your next drink's going to be or another one of Philadelphia's iconic games, I'm going to fucking strangle you—

"I might be able to help with that—if you're so hell-bent on tripping tonight."

Dzô!

"How's that?" Terry asked eagerly.

Say it.

Say it, Terry repeated in his mind and tightened his grip on the badge inside of his pocket. He'd have to call an on-duty cop to make the arrest, but he'd be sure as shit that Fullsend Steve didn't go anywhere in the meantime. Albot laughed and flagged down the bartender.

"Don't worry about that, young fella. You lemme' take care of it. Two tequilas, please," Albot said when the bartender returned. "With limes and salt, darling. None of that lemon shit for me and my friend."

Friend? Terry could feel his face getting hot and thought that he might get sick. He knew that he wasn't going to throw up, but he was getting angry, and the anger stirred his gut.

Fearing that he might slam Albot's face into the bar and pull his hands behind his back before any acid was ever transacted, Terry slid off the barstool and took a wobbly step towards the bathroom. He unzipped his pants and pissed into the long stainless-steel basin full of ice chips. The urinal cake on the drain below gave off the distinct scent of Life Savers mints which he could nearly taste. It even possessed that characteristic tingling sensation, and he wondered if the owners were actually using Life Savers as air fresheners. It made his mouth water and he recollected how he never once in his life smelled such a pleasant public bathroo—

Shut the fuck up!

I'm losing it.

What if he doesn't have any on him?

What if he only knows where to get some?

Am I really going to be able to keep drinking Mind Erasers with this fucking degenerate all night to even make some shit canned bust on a crack head pal of his at three in the morning somewhere if I'm seeing double and holding onto the fucking walls?

Terry raised his hand to flush the toilet on the nonexistent handle and then took a long deep breath before zipping back up. He focused on the smell of the Life Savers scented urinal cake and it calmed him. A thought of Hannah yelling at him to control his anger during some fight—which always just made him fume more—tried to blindside him, but he stayed on the mint.

"Zero in, y'know?" he replayed Albot's words.

"See the ball."

Terry heard footsteps approaching through the wood paneled corridor and he opened his eyes and left without checking himself in the mirror.

"MY MAN, POTS AND PANS!" Albot exclaimed as Terry returned to his stool. "We won!" he shouted, pointing to the television with one hand and extending a salt rimmed shot glass with the other. Terry put his hand on Albot's shoulder and was instantly revolted by the oily feel of his jacket, but still slammed the bottom of the tiny glass down onto the bar, gulped it back and savagely bit into the lime.

"Sorry," Terry said, "I had to break the seal."

"No worries, my friend. Once that kicks in we won't have anymore need for booze."

The fuck did he just say?

"Once what kicks in?"

Albot peered around The Buckaroo Club and Terry followed his wandering eyes. Everyone who sat at the bar was talking amongst themselves or watching one of the games. Behind them, people sat at

61

tables laughing and slurping down the free soup du jour or dancing by the juke box to Thin Lizzy and throwing darts. On the little stage in the corner someone was setting up a drum set. When Albot felt convinced that no "squares" were watching them, he reached inside his gritty jacket and placed a clear vial on the varnished oak.

"What's this?" Terry asked. But he knew what it was. And all at once, he knew that it was now in his stomach.

You son of a bitch.

You fucking son of a bitch.

Albot laughed and snatched the vial away. It was all wrong. Terry needed blotted paper acid so that the lab could compare the fibers with the LSD they found in Bill's killer's pants. Acid chemists were rather proud and quite inventive with what they used to inscribe their creations on; vellum, maps, music scores, peculiar newspaper articles—even watercolor paintings and sugar cubes. Rudd had explained to him that if they did ever catch someone else in town on acid, this was how they could match it to the supplier and hopefully track down everyone they sold it to.

This was all for shit. Terry closed his eyes and gripped the wood counter, hoping that what he already knew was wrong.

"You said you wanted to trip—"

"Acid!?" Terry growled through his teeth.

"Whoa," Albot flinched and laughed again. "Keep it down, man." Terry could never call for backup now—even if he had been slipped a Mickey. Now he risked getting caught tripping with this deplorable bastard on top of whatever punishment he faced for taking it upon himself to pursue Bill's assailant alone.

"I'm just," Terry trailed off as he wondered how much time he had. He researched Lysergic Acid Diethylamide once when it was found with the young man's clothes and then again when he decided for sure that he'd start looking for the elusive hallucinogen on his own. He never planned to partake in ingesting it—he just wanted to know more about it than the shoddy information he gathered from movies and his grandmother's Beatles' records. He wondered if she even knew what "Lucy in the Sky with Diamonds" meant as she hummed along folding his underwear. All of his studies pertained to blotter acid though—he never anticipated getting his drink laced with it in its raw liquid form.

"I meant *blotters*," Terry said dejectedly.

"You don't want that shit, man; it takes forever to kick in. Plus, how do you know that you're not just getting ripped off with a fancy strip of paper? This is what Hendrix dripped into his headband before he went on stage at Berkley and lit his guitar on fire."

Great.

Terry looked around him and tried to focus on something to assess his perception. He didn't notice anything out of the ordinary yet, but he did feel an urge to laugh for some reason. The irony wasn't lost on him, and it was coupled with Albot's brazen audacity to drug a police officer—that he was doing Terry a favor—but that wasn't it. Terry found nothing funny about any of it. The urge to laugh felt more like the response to some bodily sensation—like something inside of him was being tickled with a feather but without any stimulus.

"Relax," Albot said. "All we need now's a Crimson." This strange impulse to laugh heightened at every word that Albot said and the difficulty with which Terry had at curbing it not only frustrated him, but scared him as well. He began to feel more and more like a child—carefree, enthusiastic, but deeply vulnerable.

With every breath that he took, something began to expand and radiate in his chest—filling him with an insurmountable amount of energy—which caused him to wonder if LSD was the only thing in Albot's dropper.

TERRY HAD "TRIED" cocaine once, back when he was just starting out as an evidence technician. Rudd Hasson brought it into the evidence closet, slapped the taped-up package down onto the counter and a fine white cloud puffed out from one of its corners. After Rudd trekked back upstairs, Terry stared at it curiously with a wet napkin for a whole minute before deciding to wipe his finger across it and taste it.

It was a good thing that he worked alone down there at the time because he immediately took up a new demeanor that would've caused suspicion in anyone who knew Terry's normal reserved conduct. No tall cup of Sullivan's could've been fit to blame for the way he paced through the shelves of bloody underwear, bullet casings, pocketknives, and other bundles of drugs. The sensation from the acid felt more like a reservoir of focus building up in him which he could use for whatever he desired—

Paper.

"I just... I really can't do this right now," Terry confessed as the waitress brought over two dark blood-colored cocktails and placed them on napkins. They made him think of Chief Eddowes' skin—rich obsidian, encasing all of his stone-like expressions—and Terry fantasized about spiking the Chief's morning coffee with Albot's eye dropper. Would his face continue to be so eternally carved if he found out that one of his officers was high on LSD with Bloodrun's most frequent delinquent? On the other hand, if Terry could still pull this off—if he could keep his mind straight and narrow and somehow still get a strip or two of paper blotter tabs from Albot back to the lab—there'd be a big promotion coming his way:

Detective.
So, that's why you're doing this? he questioned himself.
What about Tina?
What about Bill?

"You tell yourself you do it for other people, even for me," Hannah had said before, *"but you don't."*

"It's always all for y—"

"I have work tomorrow," Terry said, still looking into the maroon drink before him.

"Oh boy," Albot exclaimed. Terry couldn't tell if he said this out of concern, or if the drunkard had just begun to see the bottles behind the bar grow legs and begin dancing. "I'd call out if I were you," he advised, "this is potent shit."

Terry let go of the brass badge in his pocket and lightly wrapped his fingers around the new beverage. His fingertips felt like they were melding together with the glass and that soon he'd be able to suck up the contents through the alien tentacles where his fingers used to be. He dared not look down at them. In fact, he closed his eyes altogether.

Was this what happened to Bill's killer? Terry thought with a growing paranoia.

Did Fullsend spike his drink too?
Did the kid plunge into some... psychedelic rage?
A "bad trip", he remembered, *was what it was called.*
Is that what's in store for me now—insanity?

The reports that Terry came across in his research of college kids jumping out of their dorm windows and the manic flashbacks—*Hallucinogen Persisting Perception Disorder*—that acid users often experience later in life began to resurface in his mind. In place of the urge to laugh, came an impending fear for his fragile psyche—which was already disturbed enough when it was sober. He tried to think of things that would calm him; Hannah, Grandma Volker, the warm New Jersey sand back home—even the thick rolling blankets of unruffled Alaskan snow, which he came to love gazing at—but nothing worked. The snow froze into sharp shards of ice, the sand blew in his eyes, his grandmother lie dead in her casket, and Hannah—

How can the thought of Hannah's face not bring me peace?

He could see her clearly through his eyelids, as if she were sitting right next to him and not this madman, Steve fucking "Fullsend" Albot.

"W H A T ' S   Y O U R   D A M A G E?" Hannah's voice croaked and her angelic face twisted horribly. Terry felt like crying, but then thought of how he couldn't even bring himself to cry at Grandma Volker's funeral. He couldn't help but bawl beside her hospital bed when she died—but all he could gather in the small old graveyard where she was buried was a cold stone in his throat. He tried to swallow it, and not even the pain with which he struggled would grant him a single cathartic tear. The stone lodged itself there and he'd choke on it before he ever cried again.

"*What a* man *you are,*" Hannah's voice hissed, losing all semblance of her now.

"*Stone-safe, secure in your little cave,*" it mocked.

"*Don't let anything(one) scary come in, baby.*"

Is that what I'm doing? Terry thought and opened his eyes. His heart pounded. Sweat seeped through his pores. Behind him, a man was adjusting the microphones on the stage—perhaps getting ready to air Terry's thoughts over the barroom.

"*That's why you have these outbursts,*" Hannah's voice returned to its normal timbre. It played from the memory that Terry shooed away a moment ago in the bathroom.

"'*Cause you can't open up—*"

65

No, Terry thought, determined not to have an emotional breakdown in the Buckaroo with no one to console him but Fullsend Steve, who appeared to be in some type of trance, staring at all the liquor bottles with a shit-eating grin.

There's *a man in his cave not letting anything in*, Terry tried to reason.

"You're gonna die alone—just like him," the distorted voice came back and for the first time in ages, Terry thought of his parents. He was too young to have clear memories of either of them, but there were bits and pieces. One floated up of his mother passed out on the couch with a needle in her arm. Another followed of his father waving a gun around—

This is just the drug, he thought with a moment of clarity. He didn't know if it was true, but it helped get the images out of his head. Of course, it was more likely that he simply quelled the light that the drug cast on his newfound penchant to repress things—but he could feel himself regaining control—and that was more important. If he could just keep it all in the dark for a little longer, maybe he'd come back to it once Albot was behind bars—when he had time to sit down and cry.

TERRY'S HAND melded with more than just the glass containing the dark red drink, which, if he looked down, he'd see was becoming quite vibrant. The napkin that sopped up its condensation was also fusing with him.

There was a strip of paper in the pile of clothes that was blotted with LSD.

This son of a bitch must have some blotters too.

There's no one else.

Terry got enough nerve to look down and was relieved to see that there were no strange appendages in place of his fingers. He had a little more time before the acid fully took hold on the reins of his mind.

No hallucinations, yet, he thought and quickly looked away—not registering that his drink was glowing. He did notice a strange sensation in his eyes though and correctly assumed that his pupils were dilating.

"Steve," Terry mumbled and Albot looked up from his trance. Neither of them were aware of how long the passage of time had been since one of them last spoke. Albot raised up his glass in his customary fashion to clink it with whoever was foolish enough to sit next to him. Terry obliged, taking note of how the napkin came up with his hand holding the drink and that all three felt bonded together. He feared how he was going to peel them apart.

"You're not leaving, are ya?" Albot asked after they both sipped from their effervescent red glasses. Terry looked into Albot's eyes and saw that his pupils were nearly the size of two dimes. He suddenly felt an immense pity for the man—he could see right into Albot's soul through those giant black apertures and there was nothing inside but loneliness.

"No," Terry said uncertainly. He couldn't believe that he was feeling so much compassion for a man who only a few minutes ago had disgusted him. If the paranoia returned—or the hallucinations became too intense—he could always pretend to get up again for the bathroom and slip-on out the backdoor.

"Alright!" Albot exclaimed with joy. "All. Right," he emphasized with certainty that *all* was *right* and took another enthusiastic swig. Terry looked away from Albot's smiling face and discovered that he was beginning to see trails attached to anything that moved. The stride of the bartender persisted behind her—the trajectory of his hand lingered in the air as he lowered it to the bar. Albot's smile slowly faded above his shoulder when he turned his head. He needed to act fast.

"AND NOW, LADIES AND GENTLEMEN," a voice said over the PA system, "please welcome our first performance of tonight's Open-Mic Night: the wonderful, Elisheva." A young woman rose up onto the single step stage with a black guitar case which stowed a large semi-hollow guitar. She had a beautiful Israeli accent—sweet and humble—which she thanked the bartender with into the microphone. Terry stared hypnotically at the two F-holes that were carved into the top of her ruby red instrument. They looked like they were breathing.

"I am sorry the rest of the band could not be here tonight," she said to the few people paying attention. "I am here on vacation, you see," she continued. She was embarrassed by her voice, but she needn't be; she spoke well and it was lovely sounding. Especially to a man who was nearing another world. "Just give me a minute to make sure I'm not in tune."

"Tha's *all, right*," Albot repeated, and Terry heard the faintest indication that Albot was becoming intoxicated. His words reminded him of the way Porky Pig said, "B-dee-b-dee-b-dee—that's all, folks!"

"Because I just remembered," Albot added, speaking through a wide smile that he was unable to contain. "I have some blotters in my car. We can grab them later—"

"You do?!" Terry shouted, finally breaking the fusion between his hand and the cocktail. The girl looked up towards the direction of Terry's voice right as she was plugging in her guitar and it made a harsh crackle over the speakers that hurt his ears. He was so excited, drunk, and compromised by a psychoactive chemical that he wasn't even curious that Albot—who was also briefly known as "The Walking Man"—had somehow acquired a vehicle.

"Yessir, but you'll have to wait a day before you take'em—or double the dose—otherwi—"

"Let's go get them!" Terry exclaimed.

"We have plenty here," Albot said and patted his jacket. "Plus, we just took enough to make an Indian elephant see the eight rats—"

"No no no no no no no," Terry pleaded childishly. "Let's get them *now*, that way we'll have them before we get too fucked up—I'll pay whatever you want!" Albot considered this for a moment, but he was instantly rendered useless by the sound of a blistering guitar riff ripping through the air from the girl on stage. She was playing Stevie Ray Vaughan's lightning-fast instrumental "Scuttle Buttin'", and her fingers were ablaze over the rosewood fretboard. Albot was teleported into a world of his own from the first flurry of notes, which pierced through his soul like the whistling bullets of a revolver. His eyes closed and he watched each round burst into a blossom of colors as the girl performed as clean and poignant as the dead Texas bluesman himself—note for searing note.

TERRY COULDN'T HELP HIMSELF from being utterly engrossed by the music any more than Albot could. He even swore that he heard voices—lyrics, rather—within the streaks of melodies, which made synchronous arcs of electricity dance everywhere under his eyelids—that if he just listened more carefully, he could make them out. As Terry surrendered to the guitar, he tried to stabilize himself on Albot's shoulder, but touching the greasy jacket again made his eyes spring open with disgust; like touching the bottom of a stagnant pond—or reaching into a toilet.

"Come on, come on," Terry begged and tugged fiercely on Albot's sleeve.

"Goddamn it!" the old man yelled and opened his eyes as Terry dragged him to his feet and pulled him through the bar. The appearance of their breaths mesmerized them as they exited out into the cold—the way the acid warped them in the moonlight. Terry knew from his research that it wouldn't be long before the wild swirling visuals that he saw with his eyes closed would become full-blown eye open hallucinations. Albot pointed to a rusted-out clunker through a churning cloud of steam and stumbled awkwardly behind Terry as he guided him by the wrist.

"Man, we're missing it!" Albot groaned as the music faded behind them. They reached the passenger side door of Albot's beat-up car and he unlocked it with the key. From the glove compartment, he produced a small, folded square of tinfoil and turned to Terry.

"Let's see," Albot said, attempting simple arithmetic. "One strip of ten tabs—" but before he could begin adding, Terry snatched the LSD from his hand and began running away through the slush.

"Hey!" Albot yelled, "Come back! We didn't even get to climb the water tower yet!"

This created a startlingly detailed image to flare in Terry's mind, stopping him in his tracks. He pictured Albot slipping from the top of the water tower and doing cartwheels through the air every time his head smashed on one of the iron rungs below like a silver ball caught in the traps of a pinball machine. Terry took a deep breath and then lightly jogged back to Albot, laughing compulsively.

"For fuck's sake, man," Albot shouted as Terry took out his wallet. "You really had me going," he admitted and then joined in Terry's laughter. There was no way that Terry could make out the contents of his wallet in the dark—let alone high on acid—so he took hold of however much he had in between his thumb and index finger.

"As I was saying," Albot started again. "Ten dollars a hit puts you at—" but this time he was interrupted by a wad of bills which Terry flung in his face and dispersed on impact into green confetti. Terry then grabbed the keys from Albot's other hand and began sprinting away faster than before.

"What the fuck!" Albot yelled furiously as Terry hurled his keys into the dark and disappeared.

H AD ALBOT BEEN A LITTLE LESS DRUNK, or a little less high, or really, just a little less of an idiot, he could've found Terry easily after a short walk around the parking lot. Instead, he reached down, collected the scattered bills from the slush and followed a young couple back inside towards the sound of the wailing guitar.

"Mary had a little lamb," the open mic-er's voice leaked outside as the door opened. It sounded even sweeter than when she spoke. The juxtaposition of the old nursery rhyme with the booming electricity of her guitar made the bargoers inside of the Buckaroo go wild.

"Her fleece was white as coke, yeah

Everywhere the child went

The little lamb was sure to—"

The side door closed as Terry sat down in his truck and he stared at the small shiny square of tinfoil. His eyes blinked repeatedly, trying to clear themselves of the hallucinations, but the visions persisted. Carefully, he unfolded one of the delicate corners and beams of light shot out all over from the coveted strip of paper which undulated in his palm like a cicada larva. Fearing that it would slither away or grow wings, Terry wrapped it back up and put it in his glove compartment.

Stone-safe.

Secure.

Terry breathed a sigh of relief and leaned his head back onto the headrest. After what he believed was just a moment, he watched with fascination as snow began to fall onto his windshield and melt faster than he could focus his dilated eyes on. The unpredictability of it amazed him. The melting snowflakes looked like tiny Christmas lights that were turning off and on at random all over the glass. They reminded him of the fireflies that he used to catch back home as a child, which teased him with their sporadic glowing. His eyes couldn't anticipate where the next one would fall and disappear and it was spectacular. He sat there amused—in awe—and then without wondering if he should've thrown his own keys into the dark with Albot's, he turned on the ignition.

For most of the ride home, Terry stared out of his driver side window at the Talkeetna mountain ranges—particularly the high peaks of Mount Tuqujuq—which rolled as fluid as waves on the ocean. They were illuminated with a green glow from an immense aurora borealis which swirled all over the night sky. He rolled down his window to breathe in the fresh cool air and he heard voices in the wind. The same voices that he heard singing within the open mic-er's guitar—the magnificent droning of Inuit throat singers—thunderous, like Slavonic choir chants. They reverberated from the mountaintops themselves and they called to him.

"Cooooooooooooooooooooome," they hummed, in a language he couldn't understand, yet still divined the meaning. And he wanted to. He wanted to go and sit on top of them, but instead, Terry clicked on his blinker and turned towards home…

* * *

CHAPTER VIII:
Autopsy

THE SMELL of formaldehyde disgusts him, but he supposes it's better than rotting flesh. Upon reaching the end of the sterile turquoise hallway, he takes one last breath—like a child going through a tunnel on a road trip—and pushes open one of the double doors to the autopsy room.

His eyes go right to the severed body—he's been in this room enough to know exactly where she'd be lying. He scans around for something living and sees the pathologist's assistant coming to him wearing a surgical mask. He forces a quick awkward smile at her and she offers him a box of disposable masks which he accepts gratefully, though they have little effect on blocking the foul preservative's chemical odor. If anything, he feels like they merely introduce a new, faintly less offensive scent that can't quite cover the former.

"Fran will be right out, Ter," she says.

"Thanks, Patty," Terry says and she steps away. He hates talking to them through the masks, not because they obstruct their speech, but because he depends so heavily on his ability to read faces.

"Good God, Terry," the pathologist says and shakes his head as he makes his way over to him from the freezer. He removes a plastic apron and puts on a long white lab coat with "F. Helduser" stitched above the breast pocket in silver thread. Terry always feels particularly uncomfortable talking with him because the man's eyes are so unnervingly blank.

"Tell me you found something, Fran," Terry says as he moves slowly to the stainless-steel operating table which presents the two thawing halves of the dead girl. He looks down to her face and notices that the rime which previously frosted her eyes is melting and eerily gives the impression of tears. More shocking than this though, is the discovery of how vibrant her green eyes are—like jade—and Terry tries to recollect the last dead body that he's seen for comparison.

Was it Hannah's father? he wonders.

"I wish I could, but there's not a lot here, Ter," Francis Helduser replies. "Cause of death was exsanguination—excessive blood loss from a singular and uninterrupted bisection of the waist. Other than that—"

"What about the blow to the back of the head?"

"That could've killed her," Fran says, unintentionally giving Terry a moment of hope for the lesser of two horrible ways to be murdered. "But there are too many signs of healing here," he continues. "The clotting we found around the head wound indicates that she was alive for at least an hour or so after—it most likely gave her nothing more than a severe concussion. Left untreated long enough, it may've done the trick, but unfortunately, there was more to come before she was ever given that chance." Terry watches Francis Helduser's unexpressive eyes move above his face covering and then meet with his. "He must've wanted her alive for some reason—maybe she had information or—I don't know. That part of this nightmare is your department."

Terry takes a moment to process this information before speaking again.

"Wait, does that mean... Was she awake?"

"Impossible to tell for sure, but we believe so," Fran says as his assistant approaches with a box of gloves. "Do you see these marks around her orbitals? These are ruptured blood vessels; they appear commonly in people going through intensive strain; women giving birth; alcoholics recurrent vomiting; even extreme weightlifters—" he stops, seeing Terry nod his head.

73

"These ones here are fresh; they haven't fully bruised yet." Fran pauses as he considers what he believes to have happened. "She must have gone through hell, Ter." Terry takes a deep breath and Fran invites him to come closer, pointing with one of his gloved hands at the flesh around the top of the gaping wound through the girl's stomach.

"You can see the beginnings of inflammation here, which gradually decreases as the laceration makes its way towards her back. This tells us that he began cutting her in half from the front while she was still alive and exited through her spine. You wouldn't have swelling—even as minor as this is—if it was done postmortem. It must've been fairly quick, but there's nothing here that suggests he was in a rush to get this done; it's too neat—too careful. There's no doubt here that he intended to make her suffer."

Terry gets distracted from where Fran is pointing and he stares at the inside of the girl's exposed spinal cord.

"IT *IS* NEAT—steady all the way through—beginning here at the navel," the assistant says now and holds her hand in a chopping motion above the corpse, "and ending through the L4 and 5 lumbars—but we see no indication of it being done with any surgical precision, however. This is nowhere near the correct procedure that a real surgeon would use to perform a hemicorporectomy."

"Yes," Fran agrees. "From our perspective, it's unlikely that he chose this spot for any particular reason other than it being the easiest perform the act; she wasn't pregnant, there wasn't anything significant in her digestive tract, and none of her internal organs were altered or removed. The only significance we can see is that this is where the aorta bifurcates into a Y as it descends into the lower extremities—but this is most likely a coincidence, as this is simply what lies on the plane behind the belly button. This area would simply allow him to avoid the hip bones as well as the rib cage—making it the path of least resistance. That aside, I'd agree with Patty and say that it wasn't maneuvered with much more anatomical knowledge than that. If we were to aid in your profile at all, we'd only suspect that whoever it was has experience with using a chainsaw and a pipe."

"So, it *was* a chainsaw then?" Terry asks and Fran nods to his assistant.

"There's almost exactly a half inch of her missing," she says, "which is the standard width of most chainsaw blades. We were able to determine this without too much trouble because she was separated right at her navel—which gave us a good reference for measurement. This also coincides with the portion of bone absent from her two lumbars."

Aware that the nature of their work has a habit of desensitizing them to what may be considered gruesome for those outside of the morgue doors, they both stop—wanting to make sure that they aren't giving Terry too much too fast. While they wait, Terry's mind drifts and he begins to wonder how well a chainsaw would fare in cutting an ice fishing hole. He pictures pressing one down against a sheet of ice only to have blood spray out from under it instead of white shavings and water.

"Is that all?" Terry asks.

"Well, there's also extensive lividity—bruising and abrasions around her wrists and ankles that are uncommon to victims who are only tied up—further supporting the implications of the ruptured blood vessels. Ligature marks that are as pronounced as these would only appear if she was writhing. Unfortunately, the few signs that he did leave us all point to her being alive and conscious during the amputation. After her body was drained, he wiped her down with gasoline. No fingerprints, no residues, no foreign contaminants of any kind. Nothing in the toxicology report shows the presence of any unusual substances and there are no signs of rape. We might have something for you when the enzyme testing is finished, but I wouldn't hold my breath. All I can tell you is what you know already—you're dealing with a sick son of a bitch here, Ter. A complete psychopath."

CHAPTER IX:
Briefing

"AT THIS POINT we don't have much," Terry says honestly before a small room of Bloodrun's humble police department. Sitting in the back is a grey-suited Special Agent from the FBI who drove up from the Anchorage field office to assist in the investigation. The Bloodrun Borough Police Department manages well overall for its size, but it's no doubt limited in its resources. Unlike larger precincts, which have officers who operate under specific units, the officers of Bloodrun often switch hats when necessary. Today, everyone is Homicide.

"The girl was found dead this morning at Point Woronzof. She was severed in half through the waist and wiped clean. If she's one of ours, it shouldn't take long before she's identified and we can continue investigating. As of now, we have no leads, no witnesses, and no motive." Before continuing, Terry sees one of the patrolmen slowly raising his hand. "Yeah, Peery?" he asks.

"How was she—" Officer Peery pauses, embarrassed by his own morbid curiosity. Of course, it crossed all their minds, but none of them show any indication that he isn't alone.

"Cut in half?" Terry suggests bluntly. "The coroner sounds pretty confident that it was done with a chainsaw." Peery swallows and regrets asking.

"ON THAT NOTE, once the autopsy report is posted, I expect all of you to go over it in detail. I can tell you firsthand, it won't be pretty—you've been warned. In the meantime, if anyone sees anything suspicious on your patrols—do not hesitate to use your radios; it's why you got'em. If anyone has an idea or something strikes you, I want to hear it. The fact of the matter is we got nothing right now so, anything you can offer is gonna help—even if it's just to rule something out."

"Detective Volker," the grey suit says respectfully as he clears his throat, "if I could just interject really quick."

"Of course," Terry says. "Some of you may recognize Special Agent Liam Hollingsworth who helped us out before with the shooting at the Rod & Reel, as well as the murder of Bill Sullivan—"

"Please, *Liam* is fine," he says.

"Liam worked as a criminal profiler in Anchorage before joining the Bureau and he has more experience than anyone in this room with this type of thing so, let's all give him our attention."

"It's not much, but it may not be as bleak as it looks—if that's true about the murder weapon."

"Go on," Terry implores.

"Well, it just gives us an initial glimpse. It tells us that the killer has his own place—or at least, access to somewhere where the sound of a chainsaw could go on inconspicuous—if not totally unheard. Neighbors would remember hearing a chainsaw going off in the middle of the night. That means if he lives in town, we'll be looking for a guy who owns a house with a basement." Liam looks around the room hoping to restore some faith in the discouraged faces. "Also, in order to lift the body, he must be fairly strong and capable, assuming he worked alone. I wouldn't be surprised if he does some type of manual labor or skilled trade with his hands—certainly one not unaccustomed to… *dirty work*."

Terry nods his head appreciatively.

"That's not to say that any of you are to start banging on cabin doors and harassing our outskirts—or staking out the lumberyard for that matter and disturbing the workers. If we're going to catch this guy, we have to do the work right and go by the book."

What's the book on cutting girls in half? Terry catches himself thinking.

"Eddie, I expect you to send a copy of the autopsy and our police report out to every station across the country that's had similar crimes for any assistance. We're going to need all the help that we can get on this. There are two cases in particular that might be of some use to us that maybe Liam can go over himself; the Black Dahlia from Los Angeles and the Cleveland Torso Murders. I'll stress our urgency now by saying that both of these cases have gone on unsolved."

"Great," someone mumbles in the back.

"What was that?" Terry demands as he scans the room.

"What kind of help can they give us if they haven't even caught their own killers?"

"Wertman," Terry's voice becomes harsh as he identifies the patrolmen who blurted out. "Do you have a better idea, officer? Maybe we should just throw our hands up and call it quits?" Terry wants to lay into him further, but he knows better than to tear someone a new asshole before the entire station.

"A good leader will do that on their own time," Chief Eddowes once advised him. But still, something must be said.

"Look, I was as surprised as any of you to see that poor girl out there in the snow like that, but this sort of thing isn't unheard of. It isn't going to be easy by any means—this son of a bitch is meticulous—but we need to stay vigilant. Who knows what kind of insights LA or Ohio might have that could help lead us to our man."

"I'm sorry, sir, I jus—" but Terry leaves Wertman no room to finish.

"There are plenty of cases involving human dismemberment that *were* solved," he asserts.

"The Co-ed Killer, for one," Liam says. Terry raises his hand up as if to say '*ya-see?*' but before the point can be made, Eddie blurts:

"Didn't the Co-ed Killer turn himself in after his final vict—"

A grave and threatening look from Terry mows Eddie down in his tracks before he can expound on how serial killer Edmund Kemper was brought into custody.

CHAPTER X:
The Letter

"TER—DETECTIVE VOLKER," a female voice stumbles. The conference room is empty now except for Terry and he looks up from the podium in the corner toward the sound of the voice. It belongs to Joycie Kilbert, who works behind the front desk in the lobby. She also does various other things around the station— including watching Spartacus. Terry scrambles for the projector remote so he can spare her the image of the severed girl's lifeless face shining on the wall.

"Yes?" he asks as he finally finds the OFF button.

"I found this letter in the drop box earlier... I shouldn't have opened it—I'm sorry. Everyone was in such a rush this morning and all it said on it was 'BBPD'—"

"Slow down, slow down," Terry says reassuringly as he approaches her.

"I figured it was just an anonymous tip," her voice falls feebler now that she has his attention, "like they always are. 'I saw my neighbor beat his wife', or 'this license plate was in a hit and run'—you know, that sort of thing."

"What is it?" Terry asks as he looks at the folded papers in her hand and thinks dreadfully of his glove compartment.

"I—I don't know," Joycie stammers. "I wasn't sure what to think of it at first, but now—hearing about this girl—I should've just brought it right to Sheri so she could run it for prints, but... it scared me. I didn't feel safe unless I gave it right to you. It was stupid, I know—I'm sorry." She hands Terry the letter and walks away without giving him a chance to respond.

THE FIRST PAGE is blank—except for a single dark droplet placed neatly in the center. Terry stares at it, the color has nearly blackened as it dried, but he recognizes it for what it is—blood. He shuffles the tainted paper to the back, revealing handwriting on the page below scrawled from edge to edge.

> Split a piece of rotting wood and you shall find me. I am the nest of the roach. I am the prick of the thorn. Lift a sodden stone and there I am. I'm the scourging of the spore. I am the home of the worm. I have lived a thousand years just like an hour. I have felt the Earth rumble. I've heard the mountains reply. I was once one of the countless gods. I was there when their blood rained. I stayed while they have all died. I was swaddled in the skin of beasts now extinct. I cut their throats with the men. I have searched for another. Alone I'm free of death and rebirth. Could never make a pupil. Could never find a brother. As long as I'm alive I'll do the river's work. But the end is coming soon. My patience has broken time. The past will return and undo you. My real face is just a skull. It is all the things you hide. I can see you when you think that you are alone. You should keep your windows closed. I'll teach you to count your days. If light can get in so too will I. I'm the shade underneath you. I'm the monster in the maze. I will spread my insectile wings and find you. I will fill you with poison. I'll pin you down against claws. I'll extend my reptilian tongue. I'll maul you with sabre fangs. I'll grind you inside my jaws. The river, the river,

will come to deliver. Those who stay will not escape. I'm the bog where you will rot. You can run but you cannot stop me. Call upon your morning star. There is no light I can't blot. I'm even below the ink which you now incant. Don't you know all words are spells? A wise man would bite his tongue. A good man would've just gone right home. But there's no going back now. For spells cannot be unsung. The river, the river, your blood I will give her. This is my greatest work yet. The point of my favor waits. There is something in the blood she likes. It will darken with your lies. It will open up the gates. None can do as I've done without cutting their thumbs. They should be cutting their lips. For giving me many names. There's nothing that teaches like silence. Come and look me in the face. You will see it ends in flames. I'll leave them in daylight and still you'll defy me. There's nothing in you to save. I have opened up your bones. I have looked between your skin and ribs. Nothing waits for your false soul. Only death and death alone. This is your sentence and I will execute it. The river has chosen me. I will wave its blackened flag. There is still time for you all to flee. On every side I'll spill blood. And strip you of all those rags. While I roamed quietly my body did not waste. But I'm not here to prove this. I'm here to separate sides. Your cycle of life and death must end. I will cut you all apart. You will sink within the tides. The river, the river, will come to deliver. It flows while you grow tired. I know all your little schemes. You will have to lay your *head down soon. Toss and turn but do not sleep. Because I will eat your dreams. Open up a hillside and reach inside the hole. I am the rats within it. I am the ghost of shadows. Look into the storm clouds above you. I am the ancient of nights. I am the clasped beak of crows. You're like spiders caught within webs you weave yourselves. You try to cut your own threads. But it's me who has to rip. This'll be a drama in three acts. Next, comes your dissolution. In the end, your blood will drip.*

ACT II:
DISSOLUTION

CHAPTER I:
Joycie

JOYCIE SITS AT HER DESK biting her lip as she pulls up the surveillance footage from this morning. She fast-forwards through the motionless recording and feels both impatient and fearful to see the man responsible for delivering the letter and all its revolting contents.

She doesn't exactly agree that it's ethical for them to have a concealed camera facing the anonymous tip box, but she's been reassured by the men above her that it's only ever to be used for times as drastic as these—even for her own safety.

"What if someone put a bomb threat in there, Jodie?" Eddie asked once when she expressed concern.

"It's Joyc—"

"Or Jesus, even a real bomb?"

"Yeah, you remember the Unabomber, don't ya?" Rudd Hasson joined in.

Despite her hesitancy, this isn't the first time that she reviewed footage to find out an anonymous tipper's identity—not that there were many. Once, someone *did* threaten to blow up The Red River Museum. Another time, someone left a note that simply said, "the chick at the front desk has a nice ass."

The timestamp reads JAN12 5:17AM when a figure finally approaches the side of the building. A young boy on a bicycle rides up to the drop box and stops beside it. He leans on one foot, looks around to see if the coast is clear and then slides an envelope through the slot. Once it falls inside, he pedals away.

"Fuck," Joycie growls and rewinds. She's displeased with her findings—knowing the boy must've been put up to it—but some part of her is grateful. Some part of her doesn't want to see whoever wrote that letter.

WHILE JOYCIE CONTINUES reviewing the footage at her desk in the lobby, Terry has yet to move from the small conference room. He sits silent and motionless with his wrists in his lap—still holding the killer's letter. He stares past the blank projector screen but still sees the dead girl's face in every detail; the way her hair flowed on top of the snow; how her eyes gazed endlessly upward; her purple lips parted as if amidst a breath. He looks back down to the odd handwriting and a relentless urge to read it again hammers inside of him, but his eyes flit around aimlessly from line to line—memory to memory.

My real face is just a skull.
It is all the things you hide.
"What's your damage?"
...*he knows not a people, nor even a country...*
HANNAH VS. TERRANCE
A wise man would bite his tongue.
TEEN SHOT IN THE B—
A good man would've just gone right home.

Terry clenches his eyelids tight enough to make the crow's feet roll deep around his eyes and he hears the dripping from his showerhead like the second hand ticking away on a grandfather clock.

Drip-drip.
Drip—
"...*via an extremely large and rapid amount of—*"
—*drip.*
I am afraid and I dare not approach him

Terry can see the leaking water now below his eyelids and it turns to blood as it splashes into his tub.

"*Sick son of a bitch*," everyone moaned.

He turns away from the bathroom in his mind's eye—and the blood dripping from its shower—and faces the opposite direction. In front of him, he sees a closed door at the end of his hallway.

"Cooooooooooooooooooooome," a familiar voice drones deeply from behind it.

I've heard the mountains reply...

CHAPTER II:
Amarok

ON THE COMPUTER SCREEN in front of Eddie is an open .pdf of the first article that the *Herald-Express* made about Elizabeth Short—before she became better known as the "Black Dahlia." The headline boasts:

"WEREWOLF SLAYING"

but Eddie has hardly glanced at it. Instead, his eyes keep shifting to the other side of the office where Terry sits motionless. It bothers him tremendously to see Terry sitting down doing nothing, but he can't decide what to do about it. At first, he tries distracting himself by tapping the rhythm of a song he heard the other day on his empty coffee mug with a pencil. He can't remember who plays it or what it's called—he only knows that he loves hearing white boys play the blues.

But the tapping does nothing apart from annoying those around him. Eddie's focus quickly returns to the conference room window and the back of Terry's head. He begins to think about their conversation from this morning as Rudd Hasson snatches the wooden pencil from his hand, snaps it in two pieces and hobbles back to his desk on his bum hip. Eddie watches one half of the pencil roll to the floor without looking up.

"...one from somewhere else, maybe," he suggested earlier and then shifts his eyes back to the werewolf article.

> "The modern counterpart of a medieval torture chamber, in which a slim, attractive, young girl writhed for hours before her brutal murder by a maniacal 'werewolf' killer, was sought by homicide detectives today..."

Eddie remarks to himself how he considered the dead girl that they found to be attractive too—not his type per se—but good-looking all the same. She had a wholesome look about her that wasn't his taste—like the kind of girl that you were supposed to bring home to mom. He looks back to Terry again as he thinks about his mother's dismay over how he never brought girls like that home to her. While he pictures her frown, something else slowly turns over in his mind. It's a memory from when he was a boy—when they still lived up in Prospect Creek.

"I mean, this sort of thing doesn't happen here," he hears his voice again as the memory takes form.

H IS MOTHER WAS TUCKING HIM INTO BED and—at Eddie's request—was retelling him the story of why her mother moved up to Prospect Creek from the small fishing village they lived in in the Kenai Peninsula. In 1950, the year his grandmother became pregnant with her, hunters from the village began disappearing and washing up dead in the lagoon. But they weren't just dead. All of them had been mutilated in some horrific way, and he remembers his mother saying that some were even torn in half.

Within a week of the first murder, five others had been found and four were still missing. When a child washed up on the fifth day, the village was abandoned overnight, and the mystery was never fully investigated. All that remains of it now are some dilapidated shacks and the rusted and crumbling cannery equipment that once sustained it.

"Couldn't it have been a bear, *anaana*?" Eddie asked after she explained to him what the village suspected was responsible for the killings.

"No, *pui*. Bears do not kill men like that, and they especially do not target them over and over. That is why the gods put fish in the streams—" his mother continued. She then told him again about the tracks that they found—ones that her anaana claimed to have seen herself. They were bigger than a bear's, yet unmistakably canine.

"They could only be from an *amarok*," she said.

ACCORDING TO THE VILLAGE LEGENDS, an amarok was a shrewd creature that first appeared in a story they told about the domestication of dogs. They believed that wolves came to the first people with a proposition—a covenant, really. They'd agree to pull the people's sleds for them if they were given a turn inside of their bodies—leaving the people free to don the wolves'. Eddie can't remember the details of this transaction, only that it usually worked out well for both parties. Many of the humans made better animals, and likewise, many of the wolves made better people. But an exception occurred with lone wolves. A lone wolf would invariably trick the human and instead of jumping into the sled reins, it would leap inside the human's skin and become an amarok.

Eddie looks back to the computer and squints his eyes at the words "maniacal werewolf." He's proud of his native Alaskan heritage, and though werewolves and other mythical creatures are rooted in his culture, he never thinks more of these fables than as cautionary tales. All of the stories that he's heard around bonfires late at night about shapeshifters and bestial mermaids lurking below the frozen water—waiting to snatch you up and pull you under—were only meant to scare children from venturing too far out on the ice or walking alone through the woods.

He minimizes the old article and pulls up a new one titled, "The Nemesis of Neglect." This one focuses on the idea that serial killers—Jack the Ripper in particular—are products of their environment. Eddie counts how many times he comes across the word "apathy" in it and without finishing, he opens another. This one—"The Clinical 4%"—correlates the brutality observed in the wild amongst warring chimpanzees with an evolutionary reason for why psychopaths exist. It's best summarized as: men must occasionally kill.

Eddie looks up from the monitor—unable to read another article on serial murder—and sees that Terry still hasn't moved. His frustration finally forces him to stand up and he walks across the office to the open doorway of the conference room. He half expects to see Terry sitting there with his eyes closed and his head falling forward—even hopes for it a little—but when he sees that Terry is awake—just sitting there staring—the frustration melts away into concern.

"Ter?" Eddie asks softly, fearing that his voice might startle him. Terry shows no sign of acknowledgement and remains fixed on the projector screen. "Are you okay?" Eddie asks a bit louder and then notices the papers in Terry's hands. Without any indication of snapping out of it, Terry slowly raises his eyes up to Eddie and then lowers his head back down to the drop of blood.

"WHY WOULD THE GODS put an amarok in the village?" Eddie asked his anaana one night after she kissed his forehead and turned off the light.

"The gods did not put it there, pui," she said. "The devil did."

CHAPTER III:
The Unipqaaq of the Quiet People

IN THE BEGINNING, there was only silence
> But the people desired to speak like the magpies and crows
> They wanted to squawk and sing like the birds
> Who flew from all ends of the Earth
> Imitating the sounds that they heard;
> Moose and bears and the barking seals
> Even the cracking of ice
> And the howling of wolves

> The sounds confused the people
> And they became tired of their silence
> So they went to the great white gull and beat their drums
> But Gull and the other gods were not sentimental
> They looked at the people like straw-dogs

CHAPTER IV:
The Thompsons

"J E S U S," Special Agent Liam says after reading the digital scan of the letter. The original was sent to the lab and is now under the microscope for fingerprint testing and further analysis.

"I'm not exactly sure what to make of it, yet," he continues. "It's certainly not like anything that I've ever worked on down in Anchorage—or in any of the other cases I've studied for that matter. *But* he sent it for a reason." Liam narrows his eyes as he reads the last line over again and then looks away. He decides not to expound on any of his initial interpretations and only focuses on what he gathers is clear. As someone who has studied gang graffiti, ransom notes and ciphers by other killers, the phrase "*all words are spells*" particularly pangs him.

"For starters, we can throw out any hope we may've had that this was just a crime of passion. He clearly plans to do this again and has no intention of ever stopping." Liam then goes on citing: "*As long as I'm alive... you cannot stop me... I'll spill blood—I'm here to separate sides—I'll cut you all apar—*"

"Enough," Terry says, getting the point. He's already figured this, but it's still agonizing to hear.

"The words seem to have some kind of meter to them too, but I'm not sure what to make of it yet."

"Like a poem?"

"Yeah," Liam says and reads a portion over to himself while counting on one of his hands. "It appears to be broken up into 16 sections. Each section begins with a line containing 12 syllables, followed by two lines of 7. A line of 9 syllables comes after that, which he then follows with two more lines of 7—ending with a rhyme. See here; '*I was swaddled in the skin of beasts now extinct*'—that's 12 syllables. '*I cut their throats with the men. And I searched for another*'—that's two lines of 7. Next comes the line of 9; '*Alone I'm free of death and rebirth.*' And after that, he ends with two more lines of 7, '*Could never make a pupil. Could never find a brother.*' 12-7-7-9-7-7—over and over again."

"Any ideas?" Terry asks.

"Not at the moment," Liam confesses. "If it's some kind of code, I'll have to sit on it for a while. I was hoping that this was just going to be some lunatic's raving, but it looks like he put as much care into writing this letter as he did to killing the girl. A lunatic will make mistakes. Might even accidentally tip himself off, like Dennis Rader, but—"

"You're saying he's *not* a lunatic?" Eddie asks.

"Oh, he's 110% percent out of his mind," Liam says. "I just mean I think he's too smart to try and lure us or give anything away. What's really strange is that all of the serial killers we have in custody who've written stuff like this all admit to doing it for the thrill of seeing their taunts in the newspapers—but this guy never once mentions anything about it being published."

"Maybe he just forgot?" Eddie asks.

"I don't think so. I don't think this guy forgets anything."

"Then why send it?" Terry asks.

"I don't know," Liam says shaking his head. "But you might want to consider it."

"Publishing this shit?" Terry barks. "And get the whole town stirred up?"

"This town is going to get stirred up regardless," Liam says. "It's only a matter of time before word spreads or," he pauses, knowing that what he's about to say will be further upsetting, "it happens again."

"And what are we to gain from the hysteria that ensues in the meantime?"

"Someone might see something familiar that maybe we're overlooking—they might even recognize the handwriting or," Liam pauses. "I know we all want it to be, but this isn't one of your tourists or some drifter."

Terry's ears prick at the word *tourists* and he pulls the mouse from Liam's hand and begins scrolling.

...insectile wings, he reads.

"The river is mentioned eight times in the letter," Liam says.

...reptilian tongue...

"And alluded to a handful more—why?" Liam asks rhetorically.

...sabre fangs...

Motherfuckers, Terry thinks.

"Because it's someone who—"

"Would profit from the publicity," Terry interrupts.

"I don't follow," Liam says.

"The Thompsons," Terry starts to explain—wondering if it's truly plausible for the owners of Bloodrun's bogus tourist attraction to commit murder or if it's just his abhorrence towards them that's drawing the connection. "They attempted this... *publicity stunt*—years ago." Terry stands up and grabs his jacket as if the point was made clear. "*Insectile wings,*" he mutters, "—assholes. Come on, Eddie."

"Wait, I don't understand—where are you guys going?" Liam asks.

"The Red River Museum," Terry says, causing Eddie to close his eyes. "Care to join us?" he asks, turning back to Liam.

"I've heard of that place. Do you really think there might be something there?"

"I don't know," Terry says. "But we got nothing else right now."

"I think I'll just stay here and work on the code—unless you need me?"

"We'll manage," Terry says motioning for the door.

"Ter," Liam says. "I'm not here to take your case—only offering the Bureau's resources—just like before."

97

"I know," Terry says.
But this is nothing like before.

JOYCIE WAVES TO TERRY AND EDDIE as they enter the lobby and then quickly signs the "come here" gesture. Before they can say anything, she presses a finger to her lips and points down at Spartacus who lies napping in her lap. They stand there for a moment a bit confused until she points forcefully at her computer screen. As Terry and Eddie make their way over to Joycie's desk, she clicks the green PLAY button on the surveillance footage for them to see the boy on the bike. When it's over, Terry nods to her and they exit the lobby quietly.

"You know she likes you, right?" Terry asks once he hears the doors close behind them.

"Who?"

"Joycie," Terry says and rolls his eyes as Eddie acts like he doesn't know whose name this is. "The pretty girl at the front desk."

"Oh," Eddie says dully and continues walking across the parking lot.

"What?"

"Nothing," Eddie says and raises his lower lip, attempting to brush it off.

"What do you mean 'nothing'? What's wrong with Joycie? She's cute, smart, nice—" but as Terry lists all of her appealing attributes, he realizes that they are the problem. "Oh, I see."

"See what?" Eddie demands.

"She's not your type, that's all," Terry says pulling out his keys.

"What's that supposed to mean?"

"She's not like the girls over at Good Time Charlie's."

Eddie waits outside for the passenger side door of Terry's Bronco to be unlocked, unsure if he's supposed to be offended.

"S O, Y O U ' R E   S A Y I N G," Eddie says, changing the subject as Terry turns out of the station, "Greg and Clara—that's their names, right?"

"Yeah," Terry says, letting the wheel roll back under his hands.

"Greg and Clara Thompson could've killed the girl, or at least wrote the letter, in hopes that all of the madness and publicity would help draw freaks back to their business?"

"She appears to have been drained," Terry remembers someone saying earlier.

"Haven't you heard about when Rudd caught them trying to dye the river red?" Terry asks. "They anticipated that we'd have the water tested if they just used colorants, so Greg and his hunting buddies started storing moose blood in 50-gallon drums in their basement. Who knows what they did with the carcasses, they damn well didn't eat them all. The dumb fucks actually thought dumping a few barrels of blood in the river was going to do something—like it was the greening of the East Race Waterway. *Sabre fangs*. They might not be smart enough to have written that letter, but they're sure as shit sick enough to. Half of their barrels turned into black rotting slime when we found them."

"So, you think the girl was intentionally drained?"

"Maybe—I don't know... If they really wanted to cause pandemonium before, they could be planning something even worse this time."

"Like what?"

"I don't know, Eddie. That body, this letter. It's got me thinking all sorts of messed up shit." Once more, a chainsaw being pressed against a sheet of ice with blood spurting out from under it flashes before Terry's eyes.

"But then why not demand that the letter be printed?" Eddie asks. "Wouldn't that help them get more attention?"

"I don't know," Terry says again as he shakes the grim image from his mind. "Maybe they thought it'd be incriminating to ask for publicity when that was all they really wanted."

CHAPTER V:
Herod

THE RED RIVER MUSEUM, owned by Greg and Clara Thompson—which shouldn't be confused with the quaint and well-regarded Bloodrun Museum—is nothing but an eyesore on the otherwise beautiful small town of Bloodrun, Alaska. The people here cherish their charming mountain town for all the reasons one would expect; it's quiet, peaceful and surrounded with natural beauty. The scenic views of its massive river flowing below Mount Tuqujuq—encompassed in a sea of snow powdered pines and alders—draw in tourists from all over as one of Alaska's best kept secrets. The last thing that any of the residents want are these two maniacs who portray their town as a hotspot for paranormal activity and spout insane claims of the coming "doomsday."

The little-known history of the Bloodrun River is certainly odd and even carries with it a bit of mystique, but what the Thompsons try to pass off for a "museum" is scarcely more than a ghoulish sideshow attraction. Its walls are lined with old, misconstrued newspaper clippings, proposed artifacts, tasteless reproductions, and numerous glass cases filled with slews of sick bullshit that Greg Thompson has quite literally stitched together himself. Painted on its floors are trails of red footprints which alternate shapes between human and beast as they lead through each eerie exhibit to an enormous gift shop stocked with scarlet vials of "Real Water from the Bloodrun."

I N 2 0 0 7, when the Thompson's mad house really started gaining traction, the borough reluctantly allowed the Discovery Channel to run a special on the town—so long as they stuck strictly to facts and made no mention of extraterrestrials or evil spirits. Six months later, an innocent and amiable documentary aired, which surprised many, considering the network ran programs on Skin Walker Ranch and Amish "mafias." In truth, the frozen remains of the Ice Age man found on Mount Tuqujuq were all that the Discovery Channel really cared to cover.

"Located two hours north of Anchorage, this handsome fishing town sits along the mystifying Bloodrun River," the narrator said as aerial footage followed the marvelous view up from Cook Inlet. "Nestled in between the Chugach and Talkeetna Mountain ranges, Bloodrun Borough is easy to miss and lacks many of the sought after amenities of a typical ski resort town. Its distance from such places, however, allows it to fall somewhere quite comfortably in the middle of a desolate fishing village and an up-and-coming tourist attraction. But take caution if you ever plan on journeying up to Bloodrun because there's no stop for it on the Alaskan Railroad and only a single airstrip and a winding road off Glenn Highway allow visitors access to this large but lesser-known tributary of the Matanuska. One wrong turn could leave you stranded like their legendary iceman, or as archaeologists call him—"

The documentary did much in helping to deter Bloodrun from becoming the next Salem or Roswell, but it also inadvertently helped Alaska's best kept secret to spread. Not long after the premiere, many locals began selling their homes to the influx of vacationers who were seduced by Bloodrun's striking landscape. In fact, until a few years ago, most of the homes in the borough were small and modest, but sturdy and well-made. Today, many of these original cabins still stand, but they're sandwiched between impossibly expensive, yet cheaply made condominiums.

W ITH THE BUDGET AND RESOURCES of a major network behind them, which had no problem funding shows like

Ghost Lab and *Ancient Aliens*, they were able to uncover geological evidence for how the Bloodrun River likely received its name.

"Technically," the narrator explained, "it originates from a point upstream in the Wrangell Mountains known in Ahtna as, '*K'ełt'aeni.*' Through various core samplings, it was discovered that roughly a few thousand years ago, this location had an unusually high percentage of 'watermelon snow', or *chlamydomonas nivalis*; a red pigmented algae that thrives in the cold. It's assumed that back when this algae grew rampant, the melted snow would carry it downstream and dye the Bloodrun red—creating a marvelous and terrifying illusion of a river running red with blood."

Unfortunately, not much else could be excavated besides some arrowheads and ivory tools. Aside from a few recently unearthed boneyards, archaeological evidence is hard to find in general north of the Yukon. The only thing that the documentary couldn't explain was why K'ełt'aeni became so prone to this arctic fungus, but they claim it was related to the Wrangells' volcanic activity during the Pleistocene.

The real town museum, the rightful Bloodrun Museum, begins its exhibit with these findings and devotes the rest of the tour to the town's definitive history—which began with the construction of the antimony mine.

"H A V E Y O U E V E R actually gone in?" Eddie asks.

"And give those lying fuckwits my business? Hell no," Terry says. "Have you?"

"I think my anaana would kill me just for standing here."

The two of them stare at the black glass of the double door entrance and grimace at the thought of entering. It reminds Terry of the time Grandma Volker took him to see the Ripley's Believe It or Not Odditorium on the Atlantic City Boardwalk—where "truth is stranger than fiction." He remembers the shrunken heads with their eyes sewn shut, the Mandan men hanging from hooks in their skin, and the iron maiden and other medieval torture devices. He exhales deeply and clenches his fists.

"We're just going in to talk to them," Terry says aloud, more to himself than to Eddie. "See how they respond."

"Of course," Eddie agrees. Terry glares at the dark one-way glass and Eddie gives him an inquisitive look, unsure of what's about to happen. "You really don't like these people, huh?" he asks.

The question causes Terry to think about the barrels of blood—*black rotting slime.*

"This is our home," Terry says and turns to Eddie. "There aren't any vampires or witch doctors here to blame for that girl's death. *Somebody* cut her up. Somebody *wanted* her to be found like that. And that letter sounds an awfully lot like it could be framed and hung up inside this place with whatever other bullshit they have in there... There are no monsters lurking out in the pines, Eddie," Terry says looking back to the tinted glass. "People are the only monsters. And *these* people, they're fucking—"

One of the front doors swings open before Terry can finish and a posh-looking family exits. The mother and father are both putting sunglasses on as their son follows behind them. From inside, Terry and Eddie can hear the menacing hum of an *igil huur* bow, which Eddie notes, is played in Siberia—not Alaska.

"I can't believe those people told us not to waste our time checking this place out, that was creepy!" the woman exclaims. The boy steps out into the dim gray light and removes a chintzy red devil mask. His face looks tired and disappointed. In his other hand, he holds a bag from the gift shop like the limp leash of a lame dog, but his eyes light up when he sees the gun on Eddie's hip and he waves enthusiastically.

"—freaks."

A POLAR BEAR SKIN rug is stretched out on the floor inside the doorway and the still attached head snarls up at them as they enter. Looking down at it—seeing its once white coat now filthy with black street slush from foot traffic—Eddie realizes just how little these people care for animal life.

Directly across from where they stand is a large glass case that sits low enough to also serve as the counter for a cash register. The inside is filled with various skulls, most of which are leftovers from Greg's abominations.

A large dark oil painting of the Bloodrun River—apparently in its proposed heyday, suggested by the nearly glowing red water—hangs on the wall behind the register. Its style imitates an Andrew Wyeth landscape, only more gothic and desolate. At the end of the tour hangs a similar painting; the only difference is that the modern borough is added to this one, indicated by a few twinkling light pillars from the riverbank—the water still red with blood.

To the right of the painting, a black curtain divides the welcome area from the rest of the museum, not unlike the ones in a theater which separate the audience from the scenes of *Hamlet* or *Arsenic and Old Lace*. For a moment, Terry and Eddie stand there alone gazing around the dimly lit room as the droning sound of the igil huur fades.

"Welcome," Clara Thompson says as she splits open the curtain and stands in the corridor. "Come on in, Herod doesn't bite… anymore," she snickers.

It has a name, Terry thinks.

Cute.

He takes an unwilling step forward onto Herod's soiled fur and expects it to move or growl once he puts his weight on it, but it stays dead. Eddie walks around him so that he can remain on the polished cement floors—as if any dignity or respect can still be given to the animal.

C L A R A   T H O M P S O N   L O O K S far more like a witch than any of the images Tina Sullivan's customers envision while they wait in line for coffee. A black bandana is pulled low on her forehead with its long ends draping down one side of her pale neck. A black silk shawl hangs loosely around her shoulders and her tight black leather pants remind Terry of the Elvis '68 Comeback Special that Grandma Volker used to love watching over and over on VHS until it broke. Her large gold hoop earrings also remind him of the gypsy fortune teller boxes you'd see at a carnival—the only thing she's missing is a crystal ball.

"Officer... *Volker*, isn't it?" she asks as the three of them draw together around the counter.

"Detective," Terry corrects.

"*Detective*," she repeats nodding her head. "I have to say, I'm surprised to see you've finally come in for a tour."

"We're not here for a tour. We're here to talk to the *ghost*," Terry says and searches her face.

"I don't know what that's supposed to mean," she says blankly. "No ghosts here—everything on display is dead."

"Isn't this the *home of the worm*?" Terry asks. "Or what was it—*nest of roaches*?" Clara stares at them almost amusedly before speaking.

"My, your little dog has grown into quite a big boy," she finally says, turning to Eddie.

"Clara," Terry says before Eddie can open his mouth.

"So, one adult and one child?" she asks, smiling wider.

"Save it," Terry says. "You know why we're here."

"Okay then," she says and presses a couple of buttons on the register. "Will that be the self-guided tour, or shall I call Gre—?"

"We're not here for a fucking tour, Clara. This is serious."

"I'm sorry, paying customers only. No cash, no pass."

"But we have an invitation," Terry says reaching into his coat and produces a copy of the ominous letter which lead them here. He slaps it down onto the glass counter and his wedding band clangs loud enough to wake the skulls below it. Clara's face stays blank for a moment as she stares at him and then finally drops her eyes down to examine the papers.

"What's this?" she asks lifting it up. As she reads, the igil croaks again as the front door opens and two smiling faces enter from the street. They're both bundled up to their necks like they're about to go on an arctic expedition or summit Denali. Dark salty slush drips from their boots and one points excitedly at Herod with a gasp.

"Recognize your handwriting?" Terry asks. "Or is that Greg's?"

"Who wrote this?" she asks and looks up to Terry with an alarmed face.

"You know who wrote it, Clara."

"I don't know anything! What is this? What happened?"

"You know damn well what happened!" Terry snatches the letter back from her so quickly that she flinches.

"Greg!" Clara calls towards the curtain, but Greg Thompson was already on his way in from the moment he heard the bang on the counter.

"What's going on here?" he asks as he slips through the curtains.

"We're not publishing this shit, you hear me?" Terry says holding up the letter. Eddie feels the need to stand in between the two men but he stays at Terry's side—ready to pounce.

"You," Greg says with disdain and steps forward without even looking at what Terry's holding.

"Who was the girl, Greg?"

"What girl?"

"The girl that you killed and drained just like those fucking animals. Did you pour her into the river yet or are you and your hunting buddies going to figure out how to properly seal a barrel this time?"

"Get the hell out of here. I don't know what idea the two of you got in your heads," Greg pauses, and his eyes shift to the couple who entered a moment ago. They're no longer gawking at the small display case on the other side of the room that has a grotesque looking dog in it. The placard on the glass says that it leapt into the river during a full moon and crawled out mutated like this, as if the moon could radiate the great river like the fallout of Chernobyl. Six eyes run up its head like a spider and a spiky iguana spine lines its back and tail. The couple, Greg can see, look concerned by the raised voices. It's against everything Greg Thompson stands for to let people leave without buying something first—but it's even worse to have them scared off by a cop. It's *his* job to send them scurrying.

"Perhaps you've seen one too many horror movies. This is a reputable business," Greg says. It's the only time that he's ever referred to their venue as anything less than a *historical establishment* in front of patrons. "For paying customers only."

"*Reputable*? The only people who ever come in here to look at your lying fuckery are out-of-state dipshits," Terry snaps impulsively—loud enough for the roving duo behind him to hear—but he no longer cares. Terry likes his small town the way it is and he wants it to stay that way. If he offends some tourists he doesn't know, so be it.

"Whatever it is you *think* Clara and I are a part of must really be terrible if you've come here like this," Greg says calmly. "Which tells me that you must not have the first clue for how to go about fixing it—*that's* the scary part. If you want to see some *real* horror, folks," Greg says addressing the couple now, "go down to our precinct and see how these blue-boys operate." Before Terry has a chance to respond, Greg leans over the counter and says, "Your Chief is going to love hearing about this, Acid Cop. Now, get out."

"Come on, Ter," Eddie whispers as he finally takes a step between the two red faced men. "It's not worth it. We'll be back."

As they exit, Eddie catches a glimpse of the grey slush melting beneath the couple's feet as it pools towards Herod's snarling mouth.

CHAPTER VI:
Kynikós

SPARTACUS LEAPS DOWN off of Joycie's lap and comes running and yelping at Terry's ankles the moment that he enters the station—tail whipping with every bark.

"Stop it!" Terry snaps and Spart drops his head submissively.

"Aw, come here, Sport," Eddie says snapping his fingers encouragingly, but Spartacus ignores him. "How come he won't ever come to me?"

"'Cause he doesn't like you."

"Why not?—he likes Joycie."

"Joycie knows his name."

"I know he's a *dash-hound*. I bet she doesn't know that," Eddie says looking up to her. "Weiner dog—"

"Don't say, 'dash-hound' like a fucking yahoo," Terry says stopping in his tracks. "They're bred in Germany—it's *dahks-huhnt*. There is no dash-hound. Dash-hound doesn't fucking exist—"

"Alright, jeez." Spartacus sniffs Eddie's hand as he reaches down to pet him but then runs back to Terry's side. "I'll never understand what that dog sees in you," Eddie mumbles as he kicks off snow from his boots...

* * *

"IT'S BECAUSE THEY'RE KIN," Hannah said to herself a moment after Spartacus scrambled away from her and began trying to hop into bed with Terry.

"Pick him up before he hurts himself," she said, and Terry obeyed, catching the flying sausage on his next heroic leap. Spart then climbed onto Terry's chest and the two of them began taking turns showing each other their teeth. Spart would lick Terry's chin, Terry would bare his teeth at him, Spart would get frightened and bare his teeth back, but then after a second or two, his tail would begin wagging and he'd lick Terry's chin again. Hannah watched them repeat this a few times amusedly and then pulled one of Terry's warm t-shirts over her head from the laundry fresh out of the dryer. When she could see again, Terry was holding Spart's ears straight up and pretending that they were cropped like a Doberman.

"Stop doing that," she said, knowing what he was thinking from the last time that she caught him doing it. "We're not chopping up his little elephant ears like a guard dog," she said, and they both turned to face her as she came closer. When she reached the edge of the bed, Terry released Spart's ears and they flopped down onto the sides of his tiny head.

"I figured out why he likes you so much," Hannah said as she lifted the covers. Terry scratched the back of Spart's neck and stared at Hannah's thighs before they slipped under the sheets.

"Oh yeah? Why's that?" Terry asked, pretending to be interested.

"Because, you *are* a dog," she said. Terry rolled his eyes and then flashed his teeth at her in a teasing snarl.

"I can't keep my eyes off of your legs so that makes me a dog?" he asked and turned his body over towards hers, dumping Spartacus in between them in the process. "It's your fault, y'know. You shouldn't have put those tattoos on them—that's what it is." But it wasn't. There wasn't a spot on Hannah's body that Terry didn't enjoy staring at, inked up or not.

"That's not what I mean," she said giggling and helped the squirming puppy get back to his feet. Terry was only familiar with what it meant to be called a "dog" in regards to a man obsessed with sex. He couldn't imagine how else she could've meant it.

Reincarnation was the furthest thing from his mind.

"Good," he said and kissed her on the lips. Upon doing this, Spartacus stood up on his wobbly hind legs and tried to climb onto Hannah's face, all the while licking at the air in front of Terry. She groaned, lifted Spart up by his belly and put him down by the foot of the bed.

"I meant," she said, grabbing one of Terry's hands and placing it between her thighs, "you *were* a dog. In your past life. People always talk about coming back as birds, or dolphins, or whatever-the-fuck after they die—human souls born again but subject to the limitations of an animal." She could tell that she was losing him, so she began sliding his hand further up her leg; the one with a Hindu deity tattooed on it.

Terry never liked to talk about religion—especially, the afterlife—but what started out as more-or-less a joke was becoming exceptionally important to her; skin deep. "But the same is true for all life. When animals die, they come back as *us*. You have the soul of a dog that's living inside the body of a man."

"Is this more of that Hindu shit?" Terry asked. He meant it teasingly, but it stung her. It shouldn't have come as such a surprise to her that just like a dog, Terry had no shame.

"Yeah, Terry, it's more of that 'Hindu shit,'" Hannah said and tossed his hand away. As she rolled over, Spartacus clumsily made his way back in between them…

* * *

"I *A M A D O G*," Terry says over his shoulder as he picks up Spartacus and walks across the lobby to Joycie. Eddie stops, taken aback by the strange statement and puts on an unsure smirk.

"Any news on the delivery boy?" Terry asks.

"Not yet—" Joycie says, but Terry cuts her off—still hot from the Thompsons.

"Get Peery or Wertman on it. Tell them to head over to Ralph's with a picture from the footage and see if he can recognize him. Kids that age still bring their bikes to Ralph whenever they jam their chains or get a flat—"

"Ter," Joycie tries to interrupt politely, "we have an ID on the body."

CHAPTER VII:
Paige

"I WAS TRYING to get a hold of her Tuesday night, but she wouldn't pick up. I tried not to let my maternal instincts go wild and told myself that she must've just been tired or busy. Maybe even sick or out making friends," Eileen Glore says with a sad smile, her eyes still puffy and red from her breakdown in the autopsy room where she was called to identify a body.

"When she didn't answer again this morning, I used a spare key to get into her apartment, but she wasn't there and nothing looked out of place. That's when I decided to drive over to the station and file a report. But, as I'm sure the two of you are aware, a missing person's file can't be processed until 48 hours have passed, so, all I could do was wait and pray she'd answer her phone."

"I'm sorry, Eileen, there's a procedure in place to avoid—"

"It's okay, Terry," she says. "It wouldn't have changed anything."

"I APOLOGIZE we had to put you through that again, Mrs. Glore," Special Agent Liam says after she finishes recounting the timeline leading up to her daughter's disappearance. "We find it's best to do these interviews while it's still fresh in your mind," he adds. "Memories have an interesting way of changing as time goes on and we want to make sure that we have every detail."

"A lot of that may've seemed trivial right now," Terry says, "but a minor detail somewhere in there could actually be the thing that helps us catch this bastard."

—like a crumpled strip of paper in a boy's deserted jeans.

"Could you tell us the names of any of her friends?" Liam asks rolling his pen. "Or where she worked—what she liked to do." Eileen sniffles and wipes her eyes before answering.

"Paige didn't really have any friends, so far as I could tell. I remember her saying that she was going to go out for pizza with some coworkers once, but I don't think she ever did. I always tried to encourage that sort of thing with her, but she never showed any sign of interest."

"And where was that," Liam asks, "that she worked?"

"At the library. All she ever liked to do was read. She was such a good gir—" but Eileen Glore's voice cracks and she sobs uncontrollably again.

E D D I E I S L I N G E R I N G in the lobby while Terry and Liam are finishing up with Paige Glore's mother in the interrogation room. He's pretending to inspect the framed photographs of Bloodrun's past police squadrons, but he's really just trying to inspect Joycie without her knowing.

"—cute, smart, nice—" Terry's words replay in Eddie's ear.

She is *cute*, Eddie admits to himself as he takes what he believes to be another unnoticed glance at her.

Joycie looks up suspiciously as Eddie strolls a bit closer, but she tries to stay focused on her work. She's already typed up a description of the boy from the grainy surveillance footage and is now trying to determine the make and model of his bike. She begins with researching the difference between mountain bikes and beach cruisers as Eddie sneaks beside her desk where the original Bloodrun blue-boy photo hangs on the wall in black and white. From the corner of her eye, Joycie notices Eddie turning to her when Terry's voice shatters the silence from behind them.

"Junior!" he barks and grins with satisfaction as they both jump. "Quit bothering Joycie, she has work to do," Terry adds as Eddie whirls around.

"I'm not—"

"He's not—" they say in unison.

"Come on," Terry says, pushing open the front door. Joycie and Eddie smile and blush as Spartacus comes running around the corner, ears bouncing, following Terry's trail.

"I better get him," Joycie says as Spart scratches helplessly at the door. Eddie tries to think of something smooth to say, but all he comes up with is:

"Yeah, you better."

"S UCH A SWEET, SWEET GIRL," the town librarian says as Terry and Eddie follow her into a room with a large glass window overlooking aisles of bookshelves and computer desks. They both reflect how this soundproof room for study groups feels quite similar to the interrogation room back at the station.

"Paige was quiet, which was great for the library—but sweet," she says again and tries to smile. "I can't think of anyone who'd want to harm her."

"Have Greg or Clara Thompson ever come in here?" Terry asks as he and Eddie take a seat across from her.

"Are you kidding?" the woman asks audaciously. "Do you think either of them actually research real literature when putting together their—" she breaks off, trying to find a polite word for *bullshit*.

"What about anyone else?" Terry asks. "Anyone come in and check out any strange books?"

"*Strange* books?" the librarian asks defensively, recalling the outrage she receives from the parents of budding bookworms who see her display cases filled with *strange* books every Banned Books Week. "Such as what?" she asks. "*Federal Mafia* or *Cobalt Red*? I don't believe that *The Anarchist's Cookbook* even has instructions on human bisection."

"Who told you she was bisected?" Terry asks.

"I'm sorry—I won't spread the rumor any further—but it's going around. Is it true?"

It's only a matter of time, Liam's voice plays in Terry's ear.

Terry rubs his forehead and confesses that he doesn't know what a "strange" book might be before reshaping the question. "Did you ever notice anything at all that was out of the ordinary with her? Maybe she wasn't herself one day or you saw her helping someone that didn't fit in?"

"Well," the woman says, thinking for a moment, "I *did* see her talking with Émile Lepus not long ago, actually." Terry sighs contemptuously, recognizing the name. "He *is* a rather nasty—but, do you think he could—I mean—he's in a wheelchair."

"When was this?" Terry asks.

"Hm, let's see," the librarian says, turning to the window, "about a week or so, I suppose." Eddie writes this down in his notepad as she continues. "That man is a menace. Every time he comes in here, he—"

"Do you know what they talked about?" Terry asks.

"No," she says, shaking her head. "Paige hardly spoke to anyone aside from helping them find a book—that's why it was so odd seeing her talk to *him*. Do you really think he could be the one responsible for this?"

"We're going to look into it," Terry says. "In the meantime, we'd appreciate it if you kept all of this between us."

No more talk of anyone being bisected, please, he hopes his face says.

"Of course... That miserable old shit," she mutters and turns red. "Oh, forgive me, it's such a shame what happened to him."

"Who's Émile Lepus?" Eddie asks when they get outside...

* * *

CHAPTER VIII:
The Tuquji Iceman

IT WAS BACK IN COLLEGE—where Terry and Hannah met—when Terry first heard of Émile Lepus. They were both enrolled in the same beginner level drawing class at the University of Anchorage—for Terry, it was an elective, for Hannah, a prerequisite. Terry did well enough in the class—he had steady hands and an eye for detail—but he found himself perplexed by all the strange things that he saw hanging in the hallways on his way to class. He knew that he wasn't an authority on whether or not art was any good, but he did feel that he could at least tell what art was and wasn't—and this, to him, was bullshit.

He was unable to idly abide the Mark Rothkos and Damien Hirsts of the art world—who made millions of dollars from smearing paint around and bejeweling skulls—and thus, entered many harsh arguments with his classmates. He could tell that it amused Hannah though, who was working on her BFA in painting—*real* painting Terry fancied. The way that he'd compare the classical arts with what he referred to as, "the crap made by Kooning and Pollock," always made her smile.

TERRY FOUND HANNAH attractive from the first glance, but he never initiated conversation with her. After the first week of class, when it was clear to him that he stood for the minority, he gave up all attempts at conversing with anyone—whenever he did, it always ended in a fight.

But more importantly, Terry feared discovering what Hannah's position was on this new thing called "art." It was better not knowing; there was no risk of her beauty being tainted—even though he caught her holding back laughter a few times while he rolled off insults at some unfortunate student majoring in Product Design. This way Terry could go on supposing that Hannah was what he considered to be a *genuine* artist when he thought about her while he masturbated.

Class discussions often got tangled up in the topic of socioeconomic status among artists, and though Terry didn't have the words to articulate it, he believed that the role of art was inherently anti-bourgeois. Instead of attempting to gather his thoughts and make this point clearly though, he'd frequently just erupt on the other students.

"You're an Art History major—you have no frame of reference here," Terry would assert.

"*I* have no frame of reference? What does studying Art History have to do with it, copper?"

"Look around—there isn't a single person majoring in Art History who isn't some rich stuck-up white girl who's never held a paint bru—"

"Terry," the instructor said lowly—the same tone one says a dog's name when it's right about to get into something it shouldn't. Hannah cringed at the sharp remark, but she couldn't help cracking a smirk from having thought the same thing.

After one of their "morning critiques"—the words made Hannah laugh because they referred to the class' daily task of evaluating each other's homework, not Terry's outbursts—they were given instructions for a figure drawing. A nude model posed in the center of the room and everyone moved their stools and easels around for their desired view. Hannah decided right then and there that she was going to sit next to Terry—in spite of the fact that this meant she'd be starring at some stranger's bare-naked ass for the rest of the week.

As Hannah tried to salvage something resembling a decent composition, she noticed a small tattoo on the topside of Terry's forearm as he adjusted his easel. It was the same tattoo that marked the underside of hers.

"S WEET TATTOO, BRO," Hannah heard herself blurt in some over-characterized voice she imagined frat boys using. She restrained herself from clenching her eyes shut in embarrassment and tried her best to commit to the ruse.

Terry finished tightening his easel before looking down to his tattoo, unsure of what to say. He felt like he ought to have an explanation rehearsed from every time that someone has asked about it, but yet—

"Oh, um, it's... uh—" As he stumbled over his words, Hannah rolled her wrist over and presented the mirror image that she had inked into her own skin.

"Tuquji," she said, trying to save him from explaining—she knew all too well how stupid it felt.

Terry's eyes darted up to hers enthusiastically and he fought an overwhelming compulsion to examine the cut of her shirt as his eyes travelled down to her overturned arm.

"Well, no shit," rolled clumsily out of his mouth when he registered that not only did she know what it was, but that she had one too. "This is a first."

"I know!" Hannah exclaimed. "How do you know about the Iceman?" she asked, referring again to the Ice Age man discovered on Mount Tuqujuq, mummified in ice. His frozen body was so well preserved that a unique tattoo remained visible on his flesh.

"That documentary," Terry said scratching the back of his head, trying to resist the urge to let his eyes wander again.

"Oh, duh. I didn't think anyone actually watched that."

"*Chlamy-dom-o—*" he tried.

"Yeah-yeah, 'watermelon snow,'" Hannah said, turning her arm back over onto her thigh. "I can't believe I finally met someone who actually knows what it is."

"And what is it?" Terry roused.

"Well, it's the oldest tattoo ever discovered, for one."

"The oldest unsolved murder case too," Terry added, as the Iceman was found naked with his limbs bound together in rope—but Hannah knew these grim details and didn't bat an eye.

S CREAMING JAY HAWKINS sang incoherently over the classroom speakers—muffling Hannah and Terry's voices as they drew—but their laughter had to occasionally be stifled by the instructor's shushing. Terry learned about Hannah's interest in all things tribal—art, religion, tattooing—and she learned about his aspiration to become a detective.

"So, what's your damage?" she asked mischievously.

"*My* damage?" Terry asked. "You're the artist—don't you all drink turpentine and cut your ears off?" Hannah pulled back her hair to reveal her ears and then threw her eraser at him.

"What about Bruce Wayne and Travis Bickle, huh?" she asked. "I thought all the bravest have some kind of troubled past?" Hannah stopped drawing as Terry considered it for a moment that was far too long for her. "I'm sorry, I didn't—"

"No," Terry replied indifferently, trying to stop the roses from blooming in her cheeks. "I don't think I have any damage," he said. Unlike Bruce and Travis, Terry's parents were still alive—albeit long gone—but he never thought much about them.

"I don't believe in waiting around for tragedy to occur before doing the right thing," he started again. "There's already enough to be angry about in the world without having damage, but no one wants to get involved until it happens to them; *then* they throw their capes on—when it's too late. Fuck Bruce Wayne."

"Fuck Bruce Wayne?" Hannah asked giggling.

"Fuck'em," Terry said and returned her smile.

"So, are you going to solve Tuquji's case then?" she asked playfully, not believing how enamored she felt already with this strange spitfire who disturbed Drawing 101.

"Unlikely," Terry said. "I think that the Iceman will be forgotten about again before anyone really knows why he was frozen up there in the first place."

"Maybe we should freeze ourselves," Hannah suggested jokingly. "That way they can find our bodies in another couple thousand years and carry on Tuquji's legacy…"

* * *

"HE'S THIS…" Terry says after the memory finishes with him, "*artist.*" It still greatly annoys him to grant Émile Lepus the esteem of being called an 'artist'—but for far more reasons than Terry had when he first learned about him with Hannah. "He built that estate out on Hilldrum Road—*Card House*. He's a real bastard. Makes Tina Sullivan look like a girl scout."

"Can't wait to meet him," Eddie says merrily as the passenger side door to Terry's Bronco screeches open.

"We got a domestic disturbance call from up there a few years ago," Terry says as he turns his key in the ignition. "An argument had escalated, that sort of thing. But as soon as we pulled up, someone inside let Émile's dogs out—two *huge* scarred up beasts. 'Funeral' and 'Hearse' were their names," Terry says shaking his head as he rolls out onto the Brig. "One was a giant Bernese mountain dog and the other was some kind of nasty looking mutt—wouldn't be surprised if it had some wolf in it. We thought the intention was for the dogs to attack us or at least, dissuade us from going in but... The moment the two of them realized that they were outside alone, they just started going at it with each other—*viciously*. I mean, they were ready to kill one another. Barking and snapping—hackles up—slamming and ripping into each other. I can remember hearing their paws pounding on the ground." Terry pauses for a second and lets his foot off the gas as Eddie follows his gaze through the windshield to catch an orange sign reading:

ROAD WORK AHEAD
1 MILE

"At any rate, they did deter us, at least, for a few minutes. We didn't have our tranquilizers ready of course because no one said anything about animals, and we weren't about to risk getting out and breaking them up by hand. They way they kept making each other yelp made me want to just roll down my window and euthanize the damn things right then and there." Up ahead, Terry sees yellow caution lights flashing as well as a small line of cars waiting for their turn to use the only open lane.

"Someone eventually came around the side of the house with a hose and started spraying them," Terry continues. "Red water was splashing all over. Luckily, it distracted the dogs long enough for Hasson to shuffle out to his trunk and put two bear darts in them." A man in a hardhat spins the sign he's holding and nearly dances as he points emphatically for them to follow the orange traffic cones.

"So, what happened?" Eddie asks.

"Well, obviously Émile couldn't do much but holler and break things; push over shelves, sweep off tabletops—petty bullshit. From the outside, we could hear a lot of shouting and glass breaking. Once we finally got in, we found blood all over the kitchen floor. His girlfriend claimed that she knocked something over and stepped on it. That it was all a misunderstanding—an *accident*. At that point, there wasn't a whole lot more that we could've done—but Émile wouldn't let up. The more we tried to calm him down, the worse he got. If it weren't for him, we probably would've just taken the girl to the ER and reported him to animal control and it would've ended right there."

"What did you do?" Eddie asks and looks out his window as they approach the roadblock; an enormous mound of jagged ice which fell and smashed onto the road from the sharp cliffs above.

"We had to arrest him; had to take him out of his chair." Terry pauses and watches other heaping chunks of ice float faintly down the Bloodrun—which seems to ooze more than it flows—and he's surprised that the river isn't completely frozen over yet for this time of year. "The arresting officers had to put cuffs on him and that *really* blew his lid. It was horrible."

"*Ajurnamat*," Eddie says in his mother's tongue but then glances back to Terry confused. "Wait… So, how does he make his artwork then?"

Terry blinks his eyes and tries to remember the slideshow that one of the other students had presented on Émile Lepus long ago, but finds that he paid more attention to Hannah's legs that day. He sighs heavily and tries to recollect the best he can.

"The house itself *is* the artwork. It's constantly changing; additions are put on, old ones are ripped out. 'Impermanence' is one of his many *themes*… I mean, the kids who live there are the only ones who really know what goes on inside." Terry nods his head to the man on the other side of the ice barricade who's waving them forward as they pass.

"Kids?" Eddie asks.

"There's this group of misfits living with him; runaways and delinquents that might know some carpentry; art school dropouts. All the ones that get turned away, he takes them in and puts a hammer in their hands."

"Like a halfway house?"

"Not exactly." Terry sighs again before going on. "If he was anyone else it'd actually be really great what he's doing." He pauses, finally able to recall one of the slides from the presentation:

"Local artist teaches underprivileged youth new trades
in his new large-scale evolving sculpture,
'Card House.'"

But the image is soon engulfed by the puddle of blood that Terry saw in Émile's kitchen.

"They live scattered throughout the property in exchange for labor; knocking down walls and what not to put up his latest 'installations.'"

"Installations?" Eddie asks.

"He designs these mechanical sculptures that all function and integrate with the house—solar panels; floating staircases; all kinds of clever heating systems. As much as it pains me to admit, he's not completely full of shit. Hasson says that Émile could park his wheelchair next to the hood of your car and talk you through changing the engine without even looking at it."

"Do you think it could be him?" Eddie asks, looking back to Terry. "I mean, do you think he's behind it?"

"I don't know," Terry confesses. "Who knows what those poor kids might be driven to with him?"

Eddie produces a toothpick from his back pocket and grips it lightly between his teeth as he adjusts the radio. Between the static, a familiar chord rings out—a strange track from War & Peace Party's first album—and Eddie turns it up.

♪ *...I really wanna see the light*

*Is tonight just another
autumn white night?
It's just a little bitter going down
Oooooo ooooo oooo ooo
You don't believe unless you're
willing to hit
the ground
Yeah
Have you talked with Father Jim?
He'll get you right, you know
He'll tell you that the best way to escape is just to go and fade
away
There's no tomorrow, yeah
They come
for us
today... ♪*

CHAPTER IX:
The Architect

"E D D I E," Terry says, lowering the volume as he parks beside the curved path that leads up to Card House. "When we get inside, don't touch anything."

"Aye-aye, round-eye."

"And don't say anything either for that matter."

"You da boss, applesauce."

"I'm serious, Eddie," Terry says as they slam their doors shut. "There's gonna be crap all over the place in there and Émile's got short enough fuse as it is. What might look like a bucket of shit could very well be his latest gallery piece that some idiot in New York will pay your salary for."

"I promise not to touch any buckets of shit," Eddie says, holding his hand up like a boy scout. Terry rolls his eyes and starts walking up the driveway.

W ELDED STRIPS OF STAINLESS STEEL roller chain and other variegated metals run down the middle of the path through the woods around the Lepus Estate. They allow Émile to maneuver his wheelchair outside in the summer mud without getting stuck, but are slick with frost for anyone walking on foot in the winter. The landscaping—or lack there of—allows the undergrowth around the property to grow thick. In between all the trees and bushes are overgrown weeds that twist up through the snow and are well on their way to rising as tall and knotted as the trees that surround them. Below the snow lies a thick layer of pine needles and pithy cottonwood seeds.

"Jesus!" Eddie groans indignantly as he slips on the icy roller chain.

Scattered in the brush, they see empty oil drums and rusted out car parts protruding through the blanket of snow. A stone bird bath sits on its side and behind it, someone has unsuccessfully chipped away the ice from an old radiator.

Terry slips this time but regains his balance before crashing onto a pile of red bricks that were dumped beside the path. Up ahead, they see the tip of a chimney poking up through the trees above a bend in the path and begin to hear murmuring.

"Audrey!" a panicky voice whispers. "Someone's coming."

"Shit—put it out," another flusters, but the smell of pot is already heavy in the air.

When Terry and Eddie turn around the corner, they see a teenage girl standing like a deer in headlights beside a large shit-hammered crane—its yellow paint mostly devoured by rust.

"Burning down Babylon, eh?" Eddie calls to her smiling.

"Hey man," the other girl gets the courage to say as she steps into view from the rear of the crane. "This is legal now!"

"We're not here for that, darling," Terry says calmly and narrows his eyes at Eddie. "Is Émile home?" he asks, taking an unimposing step closer to them. The girls stay quiet and look at each other uncertain of what to do—

Like puppies, Terry thinks.

"Why don't you two finish," he says raising his hands, "you'll be more relaxed to talk then, right?" The girl with half of a joint in her hand looks down, already feeling paranoid.

"He's up there," she says, pointing towards the direction of the house. "In the garage."

"Thank you," Terry says and leads the way on the path of assorted steel linkage up to the two stoned teenagers. Both girls keep their eyes averted as the men approach, but Terry makes sure to examine their faces for signs of abuse. They're both pretty girls, he thinks; one with green hair and a septum ring; the other plain with her hair pulled back in a ponytail—reminiscent of how Paige Glore looked when she was still alive.

"Y'know, I bet you could be lieutenant by now if you were that nice to everyone," Eddie says in passing.

"We don't have a lieutenant—shut up," Terry says all at once, nodding his head forward. "Look."

Parked in front of an open two door garage up ahead is a black 1968 Dodge Charger and a white van which has been gutted and rigged to facilitate Émile's wheelchair. Eddie wipes the smirk off his face and rests his palm on the handle of his Beretta.

As they near the back of the pristine black car, they hear music coming from within the garage. A live performance of "Love Me Forever" by Motörhead plays at a volume not nearly loud enough to keep the band's late frontman from rolling in his grave—clearly, not Émile's choice. Before they can make their presence known, an extremely bright flash emits from inside the garage and they smell a new aroma of smoke. Sparks escape from the source of the piercing light and Terry shields his eyes with his hand.

"The wire speed is too high!" Émile Lepus shouts from his wheelchair. "I can hear it sizzling!" he snaps again with his pointed French tongue.

Beside him, lying belly down on the garage floor, someone wearing a welding hood is working on what appears to be the base of a giant birdcage. A plume of blue smoke glows from the blinding light of the welding gun and Émile sits watching it, apparently unaffected by the harsh flashes and fumes.

When the machine cuts off, Talon Warth flips up the hood to inspect his molten seam of steel. He has on well-seasoned tin jeans that he no doubt waxed and oiled himself, and a Morakniv clipped to his hip that Terry pays special attention to. The sleeves of the boy's flannel are so tattered from spatter burns that he hardly has protection from the sparks, even with the oversized motorcycle gloves he's wearing. As the weld cools, the slag begins separating and he taps it off in a single stroke with the sharp tip of his chipping hammer—the wire speed was perfect.

"Good afternoon, Émile," Terry says as he and Eddie reach the hood of the Charger. The wheelchair turns slowly around and Émile greets them with his customary scowl. When he says nothing in return, Terry is forced to continue.

"Mind if we ask you a few questions?" he asks and looks away from the old man to the boy. For a second, Terry's stomach drops as he notices a streak of soot that's smeared under one of Talon's eyes. Before Terry gets lost in the dreadful memory that it harks back to, Émile rolls in front of him through the lingering clouds of smoke.

"Yes, I do," he croaks. He then turns his back to them and rolls away as if it were settled.

"Well, we're going to ask them anyway, Émile," Terry says, and fans smoke away from his face as he steps into the garage. "How are the pups doing?"

"Locked up in cages somewhere, if not dead—thanks to you," Émile says sharply. Terry doubts that the ferocious dogs were put down, but he isn't sure. Ordinarily, shelters try to rehome the abused animals that they recover, but Funeral and Hearse may've been unfit for adoption.

"I'll go get some angle iron from the yard," Talon says to Émile as he gets to his feet, "—while the welds cool." Terry detects a hint of fear in the boy's forbiddingly familiar face, but he isn't sure if he sees any guilt—at least, for the severed girl. He assumes that the boy just had too many run-ins with police and that Eddie's uniform probably makes him uneasy.

"No, you'll finish welding *now*," Émile says.

"Why don't you let the boy go kick rocks while we talk?" Terry suggests, taking another step into the garage with Eddie following behind him now. Talon stands still, unsure who to listen to.

"Do you have a warrant?" Émile asks, zipping his chair back around to them.

"We don't need a warrant to ask questions," Terry says as Eddie's eyes wander—hoping a giant Bernese won't leap out from behind somewhere and rip out his throat.

"Oh, is that so?" Émile asks, wheeling towards them.

"If there's something we need a warrant for, we can happily come back with one and tear this place apart," Terry threatens idly. "I'll have my guys down here in fifteen minutes, dumping every box of crap you got in here out onto the driveway. We won't leave so much as a box of nails unturned. But I thought you migh—"

"What's this about?" Émile Lepus—older and easier to intimidate than the Thompsons—asks begrudgingly. Despite his seemingly haphazard cataloguing of possessions, Émile knows exactly where everything is at all times and hates more than anything to have it touched without his instruction.

"Where were you this morning, Émile?" Terry asks.

"Asleep," the old man says and wheels away again.

"Well, we have an eyewitness who says she saw your pretty Charger speed down the Brig around 5 o'clock," Terry embellishes.

"Who said that?" Émile demands.

"Where were you going?" Terry asks, emphasizing every word.

"I needed some things from my storage unit," he says, making Eddie burst at the seams—the thought of there being even more shit stored away somewhere else is too much for him. "You're making house calls to write speeding tickets on tittle-tattle now, Volker? The borough doesn't have anything els—"

"Were you driving?" Terry asks, turning to Talon who has still yet to move.

"Me?" the boy asks.

"Why—what has he done now?" Émile nearly shouts.

"Were you driving?" Terry repeats, looking harder into Talon's soot smeared eyes.

"Like hell I'd let him drive that car. *I* was driving," Émile says.

"I thought you were aslee—" Terry begins to say, but Eddie—quite cavalier—blurts:

"You can drive?"

After being cooped up all day—rolling slowly along in his wheelchair, the only thing that faintly raises Émile Lepus' dark spirits is roaring a V8 through the winding hills. It's not as thrilling as the manual transmission that the car once had of course, but the paraplegic modifications it was replaced with are better than nothing.

"How do you know Paige Glore?" Terry asks quickly, before Émile can erupt on Eddie.

"Who?" he growls.

"Come on, Émile. Enough with the shit. Her body was found this morning at Point Woronzof, and we know that you were seen with her a week ago. Unless you want to take another ride down to the station, I suggest—"

"She was supposed to come work for me—never showed up. Kids these days have no work ethic," he says, narrowing his eyes at Talon.

"When did you last see her?" Terry asks.

"Let's see," Émile says and tilts his head back. The undeviating frown on his face makes it difficult for Terry to tell if the man is really trying to think, or if he's just fucking with him more.

"We went to the library last Thursday," Talon speaks up meekly, only to have Émile shoot him another piercing glare.

"So, neither of you have seen her in almost a week?" Terry asks.

"Get away from that!" Émile yells over Terry's shoulder to Eddie, who has left the conversation in embarrassment from his last remark and is now examining the large birdcage more closely. The bones of it are a simple enough design; a wide steel plate for the base with segments of curved rebar arranged around its edges which all meet at a single point about six feet in the air.

"What's it for, anyway—an emu?" Eddie asks, backing away.

"It's going to be my elevator," Émile says through his teeth.

"An *elevator*?" Eddie asks with a stupid grin on his face. "You got a death wish or something?" he jokes, taking a step back over to them. "I wouldn't get in that thing if you paid me a—"

Terry doesn't bother cutting in to divert Émile this time. Instead, Terry just turns around and starts walking—leaving Émile to roar French obscenities as Eddie rushes out after him.

T H E W O R S T P A R T in dealing with Émile Lepus—for Terry, at least—isn't the old man's volatile temper and bizarre pretentious artwork, but that Terry has to grapple both with a furtive soft spot for the ornery old man.

After Émile's first arrest following the incident in the kitchen, Terry learned how Émile was paralyzed. In his early twenties, Émile fell madly in love with a woman who loved someone else. His solution was to slip a noose around his neck and jump from the banister on the second floor. In his despair, however, Émile failed to calculate the strength of his gallows. The fall broke the banister in half upon impact, and as a result, broke his neck just enough for it to not kill him. This makes the face that Terry visualizes of Émile in his younger countenance even more difficult to look at than the twisted glower of the real assholemotherfuckingjerk.

T H E Y D R I V E A W A Y in silence as Terry's rage subsides. Once Eddie senses that the rebuking he's expecting isn't coming after all, he finally ventures to speak.

"I *didn't* touch anything," he says. Terry turns his head to him and feels himself smiling despite his anger.

"No," he agrees, "but you opened your goddamn mouth."

"I didn't know he tried to—"

"Forget about it, fuck him."

"You think the Chief is going to have two counts of harassment pinned on us now when we get back?" Eddie asks nervously.

Terry shrugs and adjusts his grip on the steering wheel.

"What was up with you and that kid—you know him or something?" Eddie asks a moment later, recalling the look on Terry's face when Talon flipped up his hood—like he'd seen a ghost. Terry takes his time visualizing the black smear of soot on Talon's cheek before answering.

"He reminded me of someone."

"Who?"

"You've heard about the shooting at the Rod & Reel, right?"

"I have," Eddie says softly. He's even read the police reports, as well as the defaming articles, and heard all about it from Rudd Hasson and the others back at the station—but still, he wants to hear Terry talk about it in his own words.

"So, you know I was there when it happened?" Terry asks.

"Of course. You—"

"Shot a teenage boy," Terry says flatly. "In the back."

"You *had* to, Ter," Eddie says. "Imagine many more people would've been killed if you hadn't?" but Terry disregarded that question long ago—he knows the answer is zero.

"It was purely coincidence that I was even there that night in the first place, but... I knew what was about to happen," Terry tries to say humbly. "Well, I knew *something* was about to happen. There was this weird kid standing outside and Hannah had just stormed out—I really pissed her off good—and a moment later, bullets were spraying everywhere. It was all happening so slowly up until that point, but then it just flew by like I wasn't even there. I guess training kicked in instinctively so I wouldn't have to think about it."

Eddie nods his head as if to say, "Go on."

"I dropped to the ground and crawled under something for cover and when I finally had a grip on my gun, the shooting stopped. I thought he was reloading—people were still screaming and falling all over. He was prowling from room to room and when he finally appeared in front of me, I..."

"Terry," Eddie says, "it had to be done. Ajurnamat."

"I had no way of knowing he was out of bullets."

"He was probably counting on that, Ter. I bet the son of a bitch accidentally overshot and didn't have one left for himself..."

* * *

CHAPTER X:
The Boy with No Shoes

I can sleep on a bench in the city's stench
I can sleep in the street with dirt at my feet

"CAN WE PLEASE go somewhere else?" Hannah asked one last time as Terry tugged her along the sidewalk towards The Rod & Reel Tavern.

"Come on," he said as they walked up the boardwalk-style ramp that led to the outside deck where they were greeted by the same bouncer who used to pretend to check their IDs when they were underage. When the roads were clear enough, they'd venture the drive up from school to visit Hannah's hometown and would usually find themselves here or the Buckaroo.

After graduation, Terry put in a request to transfer from his lowly evidence technician position in the Anchorage Police Department to a lowly evidence tech in Bloodrun so that he and Hannah could continue dating. On Terry's first night in town as an official resident, he celebrated by ordering a round of drinks for everyone at The Rod & Reel that he couldn't afford. After the bouncer was forced to kick him out for the grossly unpayable tab, Terry and Hannah stumbled back to the apartment that Terry had just moved all his stuff into. It was only four blocks away, but they restlessly kissed each other and laughed the whole time.

When they reached the second floor—after stopping in both stairwell landings for more necking—they made a wrong turn into a vacant efficiency across the hall that was accidentally left open. Most of their clothes were already pulled off and discarded into the dark before either of them noticed that something wasn't right.

Terry opened his eyes when he realized that he should've backed into the foot of his bed already, but he hardly had a second to see that all of his things had evidently disappeared before Hannah pushed him forcefully—expecting him to fall safely onto his mattress. Instead, Terry flew backwards onto the floor with nothing to catch the back of his head except the wall.

They made love laughing in the empty room down on the rug and passed out there until the next morning when the building manager brought in a prospective tenant. When the little old lady that came in to see the apartment got a good look at Terry's morning wood instead—which stood upright at full attention as he slept—he was evicted on the spot and had until the end of the day to move anything he wanted to keep into Hannah's place. It was too soon for them to be living together, but hung-over and still amused at being caught red-handed, it seemed like a good idea.

Plus, in typical young love fashion, it was too tempting to not see it as fate.

T HE ROD & REEL CAME TO FEEL HOLLOW to Hannah though, like a joke she heard too many times. It was always loud and crowded and not the sort of place that she had in mind when she told Terry that she wanted to talk—even outside on the deck in the summer air.

By this point in their relationship, Hannah knew that Terry was in need of some anger management—but that was a whole other discussion. On this night, she just wanted to talk about the overtime, the coming home late—the never letting go. She didn't want him all to herself—she just wanted him there for her when he was home. And if not for her, but for the day when they were ready to have a—

"Terry," Hannah said quietly once they found a table by the wooden balustrade that overlooked the Brig. Terry's brows were furrowed and he was staring intently, but not at her. "*Terry*," she said louder this time, trying to get his attention. He opened his mouth to say something, but nothing came out. Hannah followed his gaze and found his narrow eyes locked on someone standing across the street.

"Who's that?" she asked patiently, hoping that they could address them quickly and move on.

"I don't know," he answered curiously. She waited another moment as it looked like Terry was going to ask her something but then changed his mind.

"Terry, can you please listen to me?"

But there was a strange looking man across the street. Terry honestly set out the night with every intention of having this long-dreaded conversation that he knew was coming, but the moment that the man began walking towards the bar, he tuned Hannah out.

THE MAN'S DARK hair was slicked back and disconnected tattoos covered his pale skinny arms. He wore a pair of blue jeans that were rolled up around the ankles and a white tucked in t-shirt that had one sleeve pulled over a pack of cigarettes—reminding Terry of a bygone greaser; like someone who may've drawn a switchblade on his grandfather—or tried to sell him heroin.

As the man came closer, Terry could see that he was actually quite young—perhaps only in his early 20s. He took deep drags from one of his cigarettes and blew out cloud after cloud of smoke, all the while staring at the bar from the middle of the street. Terry could also see that a black band streaked across the boy's eyes from ear to ear like tribal war paint. When he finished the cigarette, it merely slipped from his fingers to the asphalt, where Terry noticed the most disturbing thing of all—the boy was barefoot.

"Babe, *this* is what I want to talk about." Hannah put her hand on Terry's cheek and pulled his face towards hers. "You have to stop this. You're always taking it home with you."

Terry pushed her hand away and turned back to the street, but the boy was walking away—soon behind Terry's line of sight—towards a bus stop at the end of the block.

"Look, he's leaving," Hannah said in a more playful tone. For a moment, she naively thought that Terry dropped it, but he was only waiting to turn around until the boy with no shoes was far enough away to not catch him spying on him. When the bus came and the boy didn't get on, Terry finally turned back to Hannah.

"Something's going on. That fucking kid. He's gonna *do* something," he blurted.

"Not tonight—he's waiting for the bus."

"The bus just came."

"What's he going to do, Terry?" Hannah asked, switching tones back to annoyance. "He wasn't armed—even I could see that. Those Fonzie jeans were too tight to conceal anything. He's just some weirdo."

Hannah still loved Terry, even when he irritated her. Hell, she was fucking crazy about him—but she could feel him slipping away. She wanted to tell him that, but instead, she just laid her hand over his and forced a smile. Although Terry didn't want to admit that she was right, it did appear as if the boy had lost interest in the bar.

"Now," Hannah said, "I wanted to—" but before she could steer the conversation back to their relationship, the waitress popped over to take their orders.

"Hey guys!" she said cheerfully and clamped a drink tray under her elbow. She always recognized her regulars and often busted their chops in a jocular manner that didn't reek of tip-seeking. It's one of the only reasons why Hannah still agreed to come to the Rod & Reel and ordinarily, she would've shot the shit with her. "What can I get yaz?"

"Just a water for me tonight," Hannah said dismissively.

"Uh-oh, girl," the waitress teased, trying to insinuate that Hannah might be pregnant. She shifted her weight to one leg and giggled as she looked to Terry for any sign that her joke landed, but found nothing. Her cheeks blushed though she knew that both of them had made similar gags before.

"And a Modello or gin for you tonight, Ter?" the waitress asked.

"Modello's fine," he said.

Hannah sighed as she watched the waitress walk away and Terry took the opportunity to steal a glance back at the bus stop while she wasn't looking. To his dismay, the boy was still there. He stood up from the bench and was ready to cross the intersection when a cop car pulled up slowly in front of him. Terry could tell from the young man's gestures that there was an exchange of words going on between them—far too congenial for his liking—and shortly after, the cruiser's brake lights released and the patrolling officer rolled along.

Come on, damnit, Terry thought, and the young man turned back for the bar.

THE SIDEWALKS UNDER THE BRIGHT midnight sun were becoming animated with night crawlers—couples heading home, drunks switching bars, people walking dogs—but the boy paid no attention to any of them. A group of skateboarders turned around the corner ahead of him and stopped to point and laugh at his strange appearance.

He doesn't want that, Terry caught himself thinking as the boy walked through them with no reply.

He wants to be feared.

"Terry, would you please just listen to me?" Hannah begged at the back of his head.

"Hold on," Terry said and held his hand up in her direction.

Before the boy could resume his post in the middle of the street, a man with a Vizsla emerged out of an alley. The dog was wagging its tail as it sniffed along the pavement when it saw the boy coming and suddenly went wild—barking and snapping at him as he stood before it indifferently. Terry was unaware that a Vizsla's sense of smell was unmatched by any other breed, but he could tell in that moment that it got a foul whiff of the boy's soul.

"Kenai!" the man yelled at his crazed companion and tugged back on her leash as they tried to pass. "What's gotten into you?—I'm sorry!" he shouted over the dog's snarling as he struggled to keep her snapping jaws away—evidently too concerned with her sudden outburst to take any stock of the stranger's painted face and bare feet. When they were far enough down the Brig to continue their late-night walk unperturbed, a final figure approached.

A man dressed entirely in black.

THERE WAS NO apparent greeting between them—no handshake or even a nod—but somehow Terry knew that they were together. That the boy had been waiting for him. Or more specifically, he was waiting for what the man in black was holding by his side; a guitar case.

"Han—" Terry yelled as he swung around, but she was gone. "Hannah!" he shouted again, not wasting another second to look back at the street—he knew immediately what the man in black had delivered.

He jumped up from his seat, startling the table behind him, and searched the crowded deck for Hannah's auburn hair. His eyes scanned feverishly over all the laughing faces; his ears heard every voice in the conversations around him; his nose even smelled the stale beer that had long stained the deck, but there was no sign of her. Darting over to the railing with his heart pounding in his chest to see if Hannah was stomping down the boardwalk like she had done many times before, Terry locked eyes with the boy with no shoes...

* * *

T E R R Y G A S P S as he bolts upright in bed, sheets wet with sweat.

He saw my fear, Terry thinks, still hearing the boy's submachine tearing through the walls of the Rod & Reel.

He saw my fear and then he was ready—

"I had no way of knowing he was out of bullets," the words he had previously told Eddie repeat in his ears—the same line that he rehearsed for the DA's office when he was sworn in to give his formal statement.

—and then I was ready.

It isn't the guilt of killing a teenage boy that disturbs Terry so much after all these years, it's that he'd do it again. The exact same way.

Right in the back of his fucking head.

Before he ever had a chance to hurt Hannah.

The pipes creak again in Terry's bathroom and the tub begins filling with cold water.

CHAPTER XI:
Black Glass

H IS C L O T H I N G has become exceptionally important to him; fitting better than his own skin—or any of the other skins he's worn. Each piece appears darker than the last; black boots, black jeans, black bomber jacket, and of course, a black mask and gloves. But he's not—as his pursuers consider him time and again—a man in black. He's a man *of* the black. Of the pitch. Of the soot and the soil. Of death and decay—*the home of the worm.*

He's spent years—
just like an hour
watching them—learning how they talk, how they dress—to mimic them perfectly. He's learned the hard way that they'll stop at nothing if he doesn't—even chase him up the peaks. But with the right attire, he can blend in anywhere—become anyone; sometimes appearing like a neighbor, sometimes like a friend. Sometimes a *god.* Because under his mask, he is, in fact—
Come and look me in the—
faceless.

N AILED TO THE WALL before him is a handmade scry mirror which reflects his muscular silhouette in the orange glow of a candle. He has no use for scrying though—or any other method of divination—the foretelling of the future is irrelevant to him. He *is* the future. He's the past, the present, and all time. The black glass simply suits him; the same way that his clothing and masks do. It's clear enough for him to see his graven image, yet obscure enough to see himself as he envisions; as a shadow—as a *ghost*.

At one time, the mirror hung in the dank cellar of St. Herman's Russian Orthodox Ministry—a rundown stone structure that marked Bloodrun's original site. Back then, it was nothing more than a dusty picture frame which housed a reproduction of da Vinci's *Savior of the World* painting—where Christ stands holding up two fingers on one hand and a celestial orb in the other. At the bottom it read:

"Альфа и Омега"

before he burned it and carefully held its glass above the smoke to collect all the blackening soot without cracking it.

A N   U N C O N S C I O U S   Y O U N G   W O M A N lies naked on the other side of the flickering candle. She has blunt force trauma to the back of her head from the strike of a steel pipe. Her pelvis rests on one half of a custom operating table with her rib cage on the other—her spine crossing like a perilous tightrope above an empty space between two slabs of butcher block. Both her hands and feet are lashed with rope and an empty plastic barrel is positioned on the dirt floor below a crude drain.

The first sign of life comes when the faceless man pulls the start cord on his chainsaw—a quick burping sound. The woman's eyes open upon hearing it but her vision is hazy, doubled, and spinning from the blow over her head. She tries to focus on the black figure above her, but there aren't any features to anchor onto. Savior or slayer, she can't tell—until the motor roars with a second pull.

Her limbs yank and jerk frantically against the taught ropes, but her hysteric screams of terror are drowned out by the growling buzz of the saw. A scarlet cloud sprays off the spinning chain as it's pressed against her belly and thick spurts of blood gorge from the opening wound as the faceless man pushes the saw further through her navel.

Though the pain is tremendous, it's not so much the ripping and tearing that makes her scream and repel, rather it's due to the knowledge of what's happening and her lack of control over it. Her life is being slowly, yet swiftly taken away with no hope of escape. Even if she could pull one of her hands free, there's nothing for her to grab onto to stop him but whirling blades. What's being done to her is implacable and irreparable; like the harsh words of quarreling lovers.

Or a falling guillotine.

Blood rains down everywhere and she knows that she'll soon die, but this gives her no solace. She clings to life in a desperate frenzy until the very end—writhing down to her last instinctual twist as the chainsaw vibrates through her spine and splashes blood onto the candle, extinguishing the light with a wisp of smoke.

T E R R Y L U M B E R S numbly out of the freezing bathwater and stares into the mirror shivering. His teeth clatter, his shoulders sting, his body tenses and twitches all over—desperate to generate heat—but his mind is clear. He's cold enough now to not think about Talon Warth or the teenage boy that he shot long ago.

He draws in a deep breath of relief and closes his eyes as he rests his palms on the sink. Behind his eyelids, Terry sees a long dark hallway with a closed door at the end of it. Something beckons him from within it—something familiar, but alien—welcoming, yet menacing—and he staggers forward. With every step, he feels more soothed than afraid, and he reaches out for the doorknob. As he takes hold of it, the calming effect that emits from it turns heavily to fatigue. Terry feels his knees buckling but his eyes flash open before he can enter.

He looks up from the sink and sees Talon Warth's face glaring back at him in the mirror; the soot still smeared across his cheek like the black paint over the eyes of the boy with no shoes. Terry can't tell if he's dreaming again or just having a latent hallucination—courtesy of Fullsend Steve—and submerges back into the tub. As cold-water rushes over his body and he begins to lose consciousness, lines from the killer's letter begin taunting him like an alarm clock that he can't wake up from:

The past will return and undo you...

...It will open up the gates...

...The past... will return...

...It will open...

...The past...

...the gates...

...The...

* * *

CHAPTER XII:
Papa and the Wolf

"'Tell that city boy husband of yours I want to take him hunting'," Hannah playfully repeated what her father had told her. It didn't matter much to Terry; he had no desire to go hunting, but he wasn't opposed to it. It was important to Hannah that the two of them got along though—or at least pretended to—so Terry tried to impress the man by buying a small freezer for whatever nature might provide two men with rifles.

Terry was grateful for an officer's salary and Hannah's tattoo shop was starting to take off, but neither afforded them the luxury to go out and buy expensive appliances that they'd never use—most of their savings went into the down payment for their home. But it was unthinkable for Hannah's father to waste anything—let alone fresh meat that he toiled for with his own hands—and he'd be insulted if Terry didn't take some of it.

"Oh, this little thing won't hold a moose," her father said patting the lid of Terry's freezer. He pulled up their driveway in his beaten-up Chevy and entered the house without knocking. It always bothered Terry that her father drove that old S10 flatbed for 13 years without ever having a problem and yet, every car that Terry ever owned had something go wrong with it at some point.

It was the entering without knocking that really bothered him though. It wasn't necessary of course, they were expecting him and they *were* nevertheless family. Still, it irritated him because he knew that the man felt like he could walk in unannounced at anytime—unlikely as that'd

141

be. Hannah's father generally avoided coming into town as much as possible and if it weren't for his daughter, he would've packed up for Nome or Utqiagvik long ago. He was an old *Cossack*, as they'd say in the Buckaroo—a real SOB.

"Are we hunting moose, Roy?" Terry asked, knowing that his father-in-law previously had said that they were only going to shoot some ptarmigan—maybe track a few small-game trails, if Terry could keep up.

"You city boys," the old man replied with a chuckle. According to Roy Lindskog, any man who didn't live in a log cabin was a 'city boy.' It was meant as a joke, but Terry swore that he heard something accusatory in his voice and he was tired of the man's gags. He almost retorted back by asking if his daughter had become a city girl when she moved in, but he bit his tongue—Terry knew that it broke Roy's heart when Hannah decided to ditch homesteading with him to go to college. Plus, Terry *was* born in Philadelphia after all.

"Just because we're not huntin'em doesn't mean one won't come out of the woodwork and charge at us. More people get attacked by moose than by bear up here," Roy informed, as if he were a tour guide—like Terry hadn't spent half of his life north of Canada.

"And you, *working for the state*," Roy added sordidly, "ought'a know that we're obliged to salvage all edible meat—even from unintended kills."

Terry was familiar with this commonly misconstrued law, but he wasn't about to waste time explaining it to Roy Lindskog. With any luck, he could be the one to arrest Roy for harvesting a moose that ran out into the road and finally demolished his fucking truck.

Terry also knew that more people in Alaska accidentally shoot and kill themselves than get attacked by wildlife. In fact, he knew that there were on average less than 5 fatalities every year attributed to bear and moose attacks combined, and over 150 due to the mishandling of firearms—most of which were on hunting trips. But, he decided to keep his thoughts—

I guess we'll fucking fill the freezer with pizza and dog foo—

to himself when Hannah unexpectedly appeared in the doorway holding his sleeping bag.

The sight of her immediately calmed his nerves.

"Y O U G U Y S picked a great weekend; it's beautiful out," she said. She heard the two of them talking from upstairs and could tell that Terry's patience was wearing thin. Despite how badly she wanted her father to like Terry, she wasn't blind to the fact that the old man could be difficult to please. But she also wasn't overlooking the fact that Terry could easily incite his own brand of aggravation. In order for father and son-in-law bonding time to work, she'd have to put the two men in their places herself.

She was wearing one of Terry's old faded long john tops that had a Flyers' emblem printed on the front. It was too big for her, but it clung to her breasts and scarcely covered the two tattoos on her upper thighs. On the left was a black and white sailboat, and the right displayed a vibrantly colored rendering of Ganesh—both of which she had done herself while practicing for her apprenticeship. They were ambitious for a novice, but she maneuvered the needles with such natural dexterity that they were nothing short of extraordinary, even after scabbing.

Terry smiled as Hannah walked over to them, but Roy averted his eyes. He could live with the fact that his daughter was free to walk around with no bra on—in a *Flyers* thermal no less—but the sight of her tattoos pained him greatly. He didn't attend any church gatherings or even ascribe to a particular faith, but he still fervently believed that the body was the temple of the Lord.

Hannah pressed the sleeping bag into Terry's stomach, kissed him on the cheek and then gave her father a hug which said, "He may be a boy from the city who frustrates the hell out of me, but he's *mine*."

Without needing her to say another word, the two grown men took their orders.

T R U E A S I T M A Y ' V E B E E N that Terry was inexperienced in hunting—and that it may've been at least partly due to where he was from—this *city boy* was certainly familiar with guns. After his graduation from the police academy, Terry contended a few times in the "The Shoot"—an international marksmen competition alongside Alaskan State Troopers and Canadian Mounties. He even took home a minor place trophy that Roy glanced at but never acknowledged. It was no display of supremacy, but it did at least prove that Terry was competent with a firearm—which was more than Roy would ever care to admit. For a boy who grew up playing Wall Ball and Kick-the-Can in the narrow streets of South Philly, while his father-in-law learned how to tie knots and field dress wild game, Terry was quite proud of this achievement.

But he never thought to use this prowess for hunting. Terry had no interest in killing anything---or anyone—unless his survival, or more importantly, the survival of those around him depended on it. He believed that firing a gun just meant a different thing to hunters than it did to law enforcement—joy and sorrow.

Terry thought about all of this and still had to stifle thoughts away that there wasn't a chance in hell that Roy Lindskog could outshoot him. He found himself delighted in the challenge, but this just made him wish that they were going ice fishing instead. But the ice was all melted.

The Bloodrun flowed.

S WEAT BEGAN TO FORM on Roy's brow as they loaded the bed of his pickup. It was nothing profuse, but Terry was surprised to see any labor slow the man down at all. He always knew him to be remarkably fit for his age; he even caught himself thinking that Roy would've made an exceptional cop in another life. He couldn't wait to see how well the man would fare hiking through the woods in the heat if packing up his truck was already gassing him.

Terry tried to insist that he'd load the rest of the bed up himself, but Roy wouldn't have it. There wasn't all that much left anyway; a cooler full of Pabst—Roy enjoyed having "two" (twelve) Blue Ribbons after a long day by a rip-roaring fire—which meant some wood as well. Terry spent the larger portion of the previous day splitting some dead spruce that fell in their backyard—Hannah had been complaining that it was going to end up rotting there. Plus, Roy would never let him hear the end of it if they stopped and bought some on the way out of town.

"Where girl?" Terry called up the stairs in a low buffoonish voice.

"I'm in the bathroom!" Hannah called back giggling. Speaking to each other like cavemen had become their love language. Terry ran up the steps snorting as oafishly as possible, which he presumed must've been how Neanderthals ran. She continued laughing even as she heard the lout's thumping return to a civilized gait.

"We're gonna head out now," he said as he passed the bathroom door.

"Okay, I'll be right out."

"I take old man out to wood. We kill deer for girl eat."

"Shut the fuck up!" she hollered.

Terry walked over to their bedroom window with a satisfied smile—it was never enough for him to just make her laugh; he had to annoy her with it.

"Girl stay here. Dog protect her," he called and listened for more giggles, but she held it back—the more of a rise that he got out of her, the more he'd go on.

Terry looked down on the street and saw Roy leaning against his truck, glaring impatiently at his watch. For a second, he thought about cracking the window open and yelling, "Five more minutes!" when Roy suddenly grabbed at his chest and lurched forward. He tottered towards the house but quickly fell down onto one knee. Then the other. Right as Terry was about to turn back for the stairs, he caught an unmistakable glimpse of a grey timber wolf trotting out of the woods behind Roy's truck.

You gotta be fucking kidding me, he thought as his eyes darted all over.

ROY CRAWLED HALFWAY up the driveway and was lying on his back when Terry got outside. The wolf had its snout down and was investigating the motionless man; first his crotch—then his neck. Terry hoped that the sound of the front door swinging open would've caused it to scurry, but it only looked up casually. It didn't bare its teeth at him or so much as raise its hackles—even as Terry took a step toward it with his gun drawn. It just stood there and watched him until Hannah burst through the door carrying Spartacus.

"Oh my god—shoot it!" she yelled as Spart began growling in her arms. Terry took another step forward and this time the wolf retreated a pace.

"Go inside and call 9-1-1," Terry said calmly, keeping his eyes locked onto the wolf.

"Just shoot it!" Hannah screamed hysterically and Spartacus barked along with her. Terry's fingers tightened around his gun as he advanced again and the wolf took another step back.

"It doesn't mean us any harm," he said, but Hannah continued crying madly and reached out for the gun herself. "I said go inside and call an ambulance!" Terry yelled, turning his head to her and sending her scrambling. When he focused back towards the direction of the wolf, it was gone.

Across the street, the bushes swayed and all Terry saw was a flash of its tail…

* * *

COLD BATH WATER forms a puddle around Terry's feet as he stands naked in his garage shivering and staring down at his inadequate freezer. He takes a deep breath as he slides his palm over the lid and then flips it open. There's no game meat packaged up and stored away for the winter—or frozen pizza or dog food. It's completely empty, save a thick layer of frost which has accumulated from disuse. He stares motionlessly into the frozen box until he hears his phone buzzing from the kitchen.

"Ter—" Eddie's voice, hardly audible.

"What is it? Speak up," Terry says, but only silence follows. "Eddie? Are you there?"

CHAPTER XIII:
The Unipqaaq of the Quiet People

"Y OU MUST teach and learn without speaking,"
    The great white gull said to them through his clasped beak
    "Weaken your desires, and toughen your bones
    This speech you seek creates curses
    Words become flesh
    Leave alone the crows and wolverines and caribou—

    If you break this tie between us,
    The gods will not return to help you
    And you will be alone forever
    Stay quiet and you will become the strongest creatures on Earth
    For you were made of earth
    And when the Earth dies and gets covered
    You too will die and be covered in earth
    And then the Earth itself will change—
    Take power from this!"
    And the men put away their drums and heeded

B UT SEDNA REMAINED RESTLESS and sought to defy the
    great white gull
    "I won't take a husband," she protested
    She was tired of being treated like a doll
    So she abandoned the quiet people and went into the woods
    And she climbed the mountain made of bones

But the bears dared not teach
The magpies would not instruct
And the pines refused to guide
They all feared Gull and the rest of the countless gods

But eventually, Sedna met a wolf
And he taught her how to howl

CHAPTER XIV:
Miss Meliss

T H E S E C O N D B O D Y was spotted this morning in the headlights of the 6:10 Denali Star leaving Anchorage for Fairbanks. As the train approached the bend at Sedna's Crossing, the engineer operating the barreling locomotive noticed what he presumed to be a dead animal on the side of the tracks.

Normally when they inadvertently hit wildlife—even Alaska's behemoth land mammals—the body either bursts into a cloud of red mist or goes somersaulting into the trees like a mosquito flicked away by a finger. Still, it's not uncommon for them to occasionally see a carcass lying by the rails being picked apart by crows—or at least, the red splattered snow from where the animal previously stood, or thus, splashed. What the engineer did find unusual was that no explosion of blood and entrails marking either of these spots could be seen anywhere around this one.

When the train drew close enough for the engineer to take a better look, he leaned over the controls and knew immediately that it wasn't an animal.

"No goddamn way," he uttered in disbelief, even after catching a clear glimpse of the naked body and its markedly human face.

"B I S E C T E D A G A I N through the waist," the woman with the camera says as she clicks off another shot. It isn't easy, but she forces herself to review the images on her digital display screen purely in terms of light and shadow. When her eyes get caught onto the sickening details, she lifts the viewfinder back up and tries to find something else. She has a doggedness that Eddie would appreciate if he could only remember her name.

"Once more, the victim appears to be drained and wiped clean," Sheri says and clicks her shutter again before moving. Terry can smell the gasoline this time.

"If only this one was dumped over the weekend," Rudd Hasson begins and chews angrily on his lower lip as Sheri continues around the body. She used to enjoy using real film—measuring out her chemicals under the red light—but she's glad that she won't have to stand alone in the darkroom and develop any of these.

"...ligature marks again around the wrists and ankles..."
Click-click.

"Those little chickenshits that party out here could've caught a glimpse of him," Rudd says releasing his lip. Terry blinks, not quite listening to either of them and looks over to Eddie who appears unusually distraught.

"Ed?" he asks, but Eddie makes no response. "*Eddie—*you alright?"

"Miss Meliss," he whispers.

"What?"

"That's Mel Nestor," Eddie speaks up, but doesn't move his eyes away from the new body that's ripped in half before them on the snow.

"You knew her?" Terry asks, taking a step closer to him. Eddie swallows and looks up from the red windows.

"She danced at Good Time Charlie's."

"Were you guys...?"

"No. I mean, yeah. But we—we were just friends," Eddie struggles.

"*Just* friends? Tell me more, Eddie."

"I don't know, Ter," Eddie says growing frustrated. "She was too young for me, but... She liked me and I liked to watch her dance, so, y'know."

"Jesus, Eddie. How many times?"

"Maybe five."

"Five?" Terry asks.

"Or six," Eddie says louder. "Dozens—I don't know, fuck! What're you my father now?"

"Eddie," Terry pauses and closes his eyes. "In case you haven't realized this yet, the *FBI* is involved with this now and they're going to want to know a lot more than what I'm trying to—"

"We were fuck buddies, alright?" Eddie shouts. "But it was different. We were friends. She told me things."

"Like what?" Terry asks. Eddie rolls his eyes as he catalogues through their banal conversations.

"Well, her name's spelled with two L's instead of two S's. It's not a clerical error or anything—her father was just stoned and wrote 'Melissa' wrong on her birth certificate forms. She showed me her ID—I thought she may've been making it up, you know how strippers—"

"Go on, Eddie," Terry says, trying to remain patient.

"She's from Bethel. Graduated high school with a 4.0—I don't think she made that up either, she sounded smart. She was always using words I didn't understand. She got a scholarship for college, but dropped out after half a semester to take care of her mother when she got sick. In the meantime, she started stripping—popped out two kids. When her mom eventually died, she packed up and moved to Bloodrun because she 'wanted to be near the water'—"

A fresh start, Terry thinks as his grandmother's casket flickers in his mind. It was plain, simple and closed—all at her request.

"I don't want anyone seeing me lying there looking like shit, kid," she told Terry from her hospital bed and they both laughed.

"Save the money for Alaska—don't bury it with me," Grandma Volker went on, not quite ready to die yet.

"Now, go home and get my make-up; that sexy doctor will be poking his head in here again tomorrow." But tomorrow never came.

"—Been working at Good Time Charlie's ever since," Eddie says.

"When was the last time you saw her?" Terry asks.

"Two days in a fucking row," Rudd mumbles behind them as he struggles to listen to Sheri—the composed way in which she describes what she's photographing infuriates him.

"...small blunt force trauma to the back of the head..."

Click-click.

"I saw her... Monday—after her shift. She seemed fine; nothing out of the ordinary," he says and begins to feel shame as a thought crosses his mind.

Mellisa Nestor's face used to beam at him whenever he came into Charlie's. She'd whimper and laugh and whispered things into his ear while she danced on his lap and teased him. She didn't deserve to be killed like this. She didn't even consider it an inherent risk of the job—but still, it makes sense to him. Strippers, prostitutes, girls just walking alone at night—none of them have it coming, but they're the ones that men like they're after prey on.

"Sick son of a bitch," Rudd Hasson says.

Click-click.

"I suppose it's the FBI's case now?" Eddie asks and looks over to Special Agent Liam—who's been on his cell phone the whole morning and yet to step foot under the yellow tape.

"Fuck that," Rudd says and shakes his head. "These are *our* girls."

"We don't have a choice," Terry says. "This is out of our hands."

Click-click.
Click-click.

CHAPTER XV:
THE BLOODRUN BUTCHER

"YESTERDAY MORNING, a young girl (Paige Glore, 19) was found dead on the side of the road by Point Woronzof. Police Chief Derrick Eddowes has informed *The Crest* that BBPD currently has no leads as to who her murderer may be and have requested that we publish a sinister message that was received in connection with her body. Anyone who may recognize anything at all from this letter is advised to call the FBI hotline number below.

Split a piece of rotting wood and you shall find me. I am the nest of the roach. I am the prick of the thorn. Lift a sodden stone and there I am. I am the scourge of the spore. I am the home of the worm—"

"Working on the investigation is one of my best guys, Detective Terrance Volker," Eddowes says, and Terry lowers the newspaper at the sound of his name. Above him stands a new agent, this one in a black suit, extending his hand over Terry's desk. "And Eddie," the Chief adds dryly. They shake hands without saying anything and Terry leads them into the interrogation room to discuss the case in private.

T E R R Y R E M E M B E R S how the FBI headquarters in Anchorage looked the last time that he was there. Red bare brick. A couple boarded up windows. Milkshakes splashed on the walls. Homeless men and women shivering along the sidewalk. He wonders if the windows still have boards over them as he slides the newspaper over to the agent in the black suit.

"It was a smart move to publish this," the agent says after giving it a quick scan. "Now that it's clear you have a serial killer on your hands. I suspect that even a small town like this will start getting its prank call confessions—especially after the national news takes it up—but you'll be able to weed them out when they can't provide any specifics that you've kept from the paper. Having said that, was there any physical evidence from the letter or the dumpsites?"

"No," Terry replies and presents some of Sheri's photographs.

"This is... impressive work," the black suit says after a moment of inspection. "He's no novice, that's for sure. When we spoke on the phone and Eddowes said 'chainsaw', I admit, I was hoping this would be, well—sloppier."

"You think he's done this before?" Eddie asks.

"Oh, definitely," the agent says nodding his head. "Once we catch him, you can bet he'll jump for a plea bargain by telling us where the rest of the bodies are that lead to these two."

"But we've never seen anything remotely like this before," Terry says.

"That's only because he *wants* these ones to be seen. These are his '*greatest works yet*', to quote the letter. Of course, he does say something about being a thousand years old and hearing mountains speak—but we shouldn't discount the letter entirely. Especially the part about slashing men's throats and what not. The others, if we're right, were just..."

"'Practice'—you could say," Special Agent Liam finishes. "Serial killers don't start out like this. They arrive at this level of proficiency the same way anyone else does—through experience. Now, the common theme of his letter gives us a good place to start looking for those additional bodies—once the weather breaks, that is."

"The river," Terry whispers.

"You got it," the black suit chimes back in. "Either there or up in these mountains you have here. We've found bodies in our stretch of the Chugachs that were from missing persons cases as far back as the 1930's. But there's no sense in wasting time and resources on such a substantial search—your man is moving way too fast for that to be of much use to us right now."

"The fact that he's not waiting a single day between kills tells us that he's done this a lot," Liam says. "Kill periods for serial killers usually get closer and closer together the longer that they're able to keep getting away with it. Killing is like a drug for them and they need it more and more until they, well—disappear altogether. It's terribly alarming that he's already on a two-day streak; it tells us that he's nearing his *crescendo*—I believe is how Edmund Kemper put it after his last victim."

"What do you mean *disappear*?" Terry asks.

"The Zodiac, The Eastbound Strangler, the Axeman of New Orleans, and several others who've evaded detection long enough—The Sleepy Hollow Killer—they all need a 'cooling off' period or... *hibernation*—a hiatus of sorts—before striking again."

"Believe it or not, BTK took a ten-year vacation, so to speak," the black suit says. "That is, if he wasn't just killing in some other way before returning to his bind-torture-kill pattern. Some of them do that too—especially if they see us coming."

"There are a number of reasons why they do this, but none of them are very reassuring—" Liam says.

"Take Jack the Ripper for instance," the black suit talks over him. "Even though he was never caught, the Bureau has learned as much about the psychology of a murderer from him as we did from John Wayne Gacy. Each of Jack's kills grew more grisly and frequent until he ripped up his last victim unrecognizable, and then—*poof*—never to be seen again. On one occasion, Jack was interrupted before he could finish his sick fantasy and had to slaughter another victim on the same night just to fully get his rocks off."

"We caught Gacy though, didn't we?" Eddie asks.

"Yes," the black suit replies. "We did."

Terry thinks that he heard a slight emphasis on the way the man said "we."

"Do you have any suspects?" the black suit asks as he laces his fingers on top of the case files.

"No one promising," Terry says. "None with anything that'll stick."

"Tell me about them, no matter how unlikely."

"The first two that we questioned are a married couple, Greg and Clara Thompson. They own a... *museum* in town. Just like the letter, the museum exploits the river and highlights ritual sacrifice and other macabre and paranormal folly. There was an incident in the past where they were collecting animal blood for this publicity stunt. I had a thought that maybe these bodies aren't just devoid of their blood because of how they're being killed but—maybe it's intentional."

"Like they're collecting human blood now?" the black suit asks.

"Yeah."

"That's interesting," he says, already dismissing it. "But we've had the unfortunate opportunity to learn from past cases that there are far better ways of doing that." He decides not to elaborate, assuming that no one cares to hear about the more effective methods of draining a body.

"We're not saying the blood doesn't play a part in this," Liam adds, "but if it's as important to him as he makes out in his letter, he wouldn't be carelessly tearing through his victims with a chainsaw. This fantasy he vaguely describes—"

"It's nothing more than something he has to tell himself because at the end of the day, he knows that he's just another freak that gets off on killing women. It's one of the two ways that these types of killers are able to turn off their empathy. Enacting some type of purpose, or—"

"Delusions of grandeur," Eddie suggests.

"Exactly," the black suit says.

"What's the other?" Terry asks.

"Reverse anthropomorphosis," Liam says. "If they can see their victims as mere puppets or toys, then they can disconnect from any feelings of compassion or remorse for them."

"Is there anyone else?" the black suit asks and sips his cup of station coffee with a grimace. "Besides this couple."

"An artist," Terry says scratching his eyebrow. "His name's Émile Lepus—"

"Ah, I know that name," the black suit says. "My wife has one of his sculptures in our yard."

"My condolences," Terry says. "Émile has a bit of a history with violence. He was also seen with the first victim a week before she was murdered."

"These types of killers," Liam says, "who make lavish displays of their victims—it's not uncommon for them to believe that they are in some way... 'artists.'"

"Or even just the presenters of art—like curators," the black suit says.

"So, you're saying we should stay on Lepus and the Thompsons?" Terry asks skeptically.

"We're just saying, don't throw anything out yet. Everything is still worth exploring at this point."

"Terry," Liam says solemnly, "if were going to catch this guy, it's either going to be now or never. These men are fleeting; we have to strike iron while it's hot—catch him off-guard."

"And how do we do that?"

"There are usually only two types of serial killers: the Robert Hansen and David Berkowitz type, y'know, 'Son of Sam'—for them, killing is more about the thrill of the hunt, like a sport. Think *The Most Dangerous Game*. The other is a psychosexual or *paraphilic*—the Ted Bundy and Jeffrey Dahmer types. We believe the person that you're after here will fit the profile of the latter. The young white females—both nude—indicate that he's most likely a local, middle aged, Caucasian—"

"You think these murders were *sexually* motivated just because they were naked?" Terry asks. "He wiped them down with *gasoline*, why would he bother putting their clothes back on just to dump th—"

"We know this is shocking and hard to understand—believe me, it's still hard for us to fully wrap our heads around. But even if the bodies weren't found nude, the way in which he's killing them takes tremendous privacy and care. For him, it's an intimate situation. The fact that he *is* wiping them down and not just spraying them with a hose or dunking them in a lye bath is indicative of—"

"It's also worth noting here that your latest victim was a topless dancer," the black suit says. "Sex workers and the like are the number one choice for—"

"And what about the first?" Terry snaps. "Paige Glore was a library assistant. And neither of them showed any signs of being raped."

"Often they won't," Liam says calmly. "In many cases, it satisfies them enough just to inflict pain on someone. With sadists, you can forget everything you know about traditional sexual gratification, which makes this perversion so bewildering—but that's how the serial killers we have in custody describe it. The grotesqueness is completely lost on them." Liam takes a deep breath before continuing. "We find that somewhere along the way in their sexual development, something traumatic happens to them that causes them to equate sex with violence. The necessity of privacy, even for the act of torture—"

"The victims may not all be *strippers* here," the agent in the black suit cuts back in. "But you can bet that they'll all continue to be young attractive girls. *That's* how we catch him. These aren't random hitchhikers or opportune people he's targeting, like the hunter profile searches for. For them, there's always a thrill that their prey might get away. *This* killer's thrill, as difficult as it may be to digest, derives from his twisted desire for intimacy—and of course, *dominance* and *control*. He won't risk anyone getting away. He *can't*." The black suit pauses for a moment. "Now, we're highly unlikely to ever discover what exactly this sick fantasy is that he keeps trying to recreate, but we *can* find the connection between the girls. *That's* how we catch him; it's the only way to stop him before—"

Poof?

Joycie knocks lightly on the door and the two Special Agents look up.

"Ter—uh, Detective Volker," she says stepping into the room. "Sorry, you know that little bait shop on the way out of town?"

"Carney's Hooks?" Terry asks, gladly turning his attention away from the topic of sexual deviancy.

"That's the one," Joycie says. "The owner just called—Willow Carney—she says her son is the... *Bloodrun Butcher.* She says she has evidence."

"See that?" the black suit says. "Small town folk, huh? You probably won't even need us."

"Thanks Joycie. We'll go talk to her right now—I think we're done here," Terry says standing up.

"You and Eddie go," Liam says, remaining seated with his partner. "No need for us all to barrage her. Plus, it'll give Special Agent Bressi and I a chance to go over these reports more thoroughly."

"That's right. And get a better feel for your town," Bressi adds, adjusting his black tie. "Which reminds me, is there anywhere around here that we can get some coffee?" he asks, diverting his eyes from the paper cup that he sipped from earlier but hasn't touched since.

Eddie is about to tell them to steer clear of Tina's—she'd sniff the two of them out the second they stepped through her door—but Terry blurts:

"Sullivan's Café. It's the best coffee in the state. Right in town on Brigantine Boulevard—across from where the first body was found."

"Perfect," Bressi says. "That's exactly what I wanted to see next."

I bet, Terry thinks, and feels himself giving Liam a dirty look.

159

"I'm not here to take your case," Liam told him the other day.

"Go, run along," Terry imagines him saying as he and Eddie turn to leave.

"The Federal Bureau of Investigation is here."

CHAPTER XVI:
Lashes and Lips

"*SEXUAL,* HUH?" Terry asks, startling Eddie, who looks up from deleting nude photos of Mellisa Nestor off his cellphone. "Do they think Émile Lepus is getting out of his wheelchair when no one's looking and having sex?"

Unsure how to respond, Eddie considers swiping a nude selfie of Miss Meliss getting into the shower off his screen and pulling up the *Nemesis of Neglect* article from the day before—or better yet, the one on the disturbing violence amongst chimpanzees—but instead, he attempts to wing it himself.

"Do you remember Jane Goodall?" Eddie asks, putting his phone down.

"The ape lady?"

"Chimp, yeah."

"What about her?" Terry asks.

"I read some articles yesterday," Eddie says, "about psychopaths. They didn't really fit into the mold the feds were just giving us, so I didn't bring'em up."

"I don't blame ya. What'd they say?"

"One claimed that psychos aren't born, they're made—y'know, products of their environment; family, school, work, society—whatever. They're not even all killers. Lots of them just become CEOs and athletes or religious leaders, yada-yada."

"Okay," Terry says unsurely.

"But the other one said that psychopaths are a natural occurrence."

"Natural?"

"Imagine if you're living out in the jungle and you're at war with another tribe. You're gonna want as many Walter Filipeks on your side as possible."

"Who?"

"Guys that can go handle the messy shit and come back undisturbed. It said that the basis of the argument came from observing wild chimpanzees. Jane Goodall first noticed it back in the 70s, but apparently other researchers have witnessed the same thing. A new leader rises up, forms a posse and then takes them all to war. If the troop is unwilling to kill, they die. It sounded awful—ripping each other apart, limb from limb. It ended by saying that the chimps often cannibalize each other afterwards. How would you like to pet one of those things at the zoo?"

"So, you've become one of those freaks obsessed with serial killers now?" Terry asks.

"Like a Night Stalker groupie?"

"A what?"

"Some of them have fans—like, *real* fans. They write'em letters and shit. You'd think it's just a weird morbid fascination or something, but according to that article, it's an unconscious tendency we developed long ago for self-preservation. If your tribe is going down, not only would it benefit you to follow someone willing to commit murder—it'd benefit you more to do it yourself. Maintain order. Survive."

Eddie's words provoke Terry to reflect again on the shooting at the Rod & Reel and he sees the boy with no shoes lying on the floor beside him—a halo of blood forming around his head.

"Ter," Eddie says.

"What?"

"If it comes down to it, I'll put a fucking bullet in this guy's head."

"Well, junior, I guess you're a psychopath then, huh?"

"Comes with the uniform," Eddie says.

"You don't want to shoot anyone—"

"I know," Eddie says. "But if I *had* to—"

"Even then," Terry says. "If we have to, we have to—but that's how they win. I prefer that we don't give this one the satisfaction—let him fucking rot behind bars."

TERRY AND EDDIE SIT QUIETLY on a sofa across from Willow Carney. A log cracks as it burns in her fireplace and Terry unconsciously visualizes how the old bait shop owner may have looked when she was young. She leans over her coffee table and pushes a folded piece of paper towards them. It's a page torn out of an old spiral notebook, and minus a few wrinkles and creases from where she folded it, it's still in decent shape. Terry lifts it up as Eddie peers over and they both furrow their brows.

"Mrs. Carney," Terry tries to say as patiently as possible. "...What is this?"

In his hands is a child's drawing—a crude single page comic strip in #2 pencil. The first cell begins with two circles that have rudimentary faces drawn on them and simple lines that jut out for their limbs. One portrays a male and the other is presumably a female, denoted by her exaggerated eyelashes and lips. In the next frame, the circle-people run toward one another at full speed and crash together in a large cloud of scribbles. When the dust settles, indicated by some dissipating squiggles and dots, only one circle-person remains. This new figure who stands in their stead has a wavy line drawn down its middle. On one half, it has the man's eye—on the other, the eye with lashes and lips. It bounces around for a few more frames doing menial tasks; eating, farting and dancing. At the end, for no discernable reason, the amalgamated circle-person takes out what appears to be a chainsaw—an oval with tiny triangles all around it—and presumes to cut itself in half. The two semicircles cry for the last few frames and then go their separate ways with a final cell that says, "The End."

"How true," Eddie's face says, but he quickly furrows his brows again—not wanting to be caught looking like the artistic genius of a child has resonated with him.

"My son drew that when he was *eight*," Willow says. Her voice is so virile that Terry is unable to hold onto the image that he summoned of her as a child.

"I could've guessed that," Terry says. "But why are we looking at it?"

"Isn't it obvious?" she shouts. "That's a *chainsaw* that he's using to cut the girl in half there! That *is* how they're being killed, isn't it? I heard all about it—"

"Actually, if I may," Eddie says, "I think that the man and woman here are—" but before Eddie can expound on his interpretation, Terry's eyes burn a hole through the side of his head.

"Mrs. Carney," Terry says turning back to her, "you said you had evidence that links your son to the recent murders."

"Six months after he drew this, I had to start taking him to see a therapist. Do you know how much that cost me?"

"A therapist for what?" Terry asks.

"He started bringing dolls home," Willow says hesitantly and reaches for the drawing back.

"Dolls?" Eddie asks.

"Yes, *dolls*," she says nastily as her cheeks redden. "I don't know where he was getting them, but he'd bring them out back behind the shed, break them apart and reassemble them with chewing gum and pieces of his army men." She stops for a moment, assuming that they're judging her parenting, but both of them just stare blankly at her not knowing what to think at all.

"If his father caught him playing with *dolls*," she says disapprovingly. "A boy shouldn't be playing with dolls. He shouldn't be drawing people being cut up," her voice becomes sharper as her humiliation turns to fury. "And they most certainly shouldn't be living at home in their twenties!"

"What did the therapist say?" Terry asks, trying to get back to the point.

"That Joshua is antisocial and has a learning disability. I could've told them that from the start and saved a lot of money," she says turning to the fireplace. "When he was 13, I started getting the calls. The only homework assignments he ever completed were ones that involved drawing—which he always managed to make disturbing. His illustration of the first Thanksgiving was a particular delight," she says with a scornful smile. "He drew a bunch of Indians chopping up a live turkey."

"Wampanoag Native Amer—" Eddie couldn't resist trying to correct her, but she pays no attention and talks over him.

"First, they tried holding him back a year," she says. "Then another. Then, the calls took on a more troubling nature altogether. His teachers said that Joshua was to be removed from the other students and put into a classroom for... 'special' children," she says with much distaste. "So that he couldn't *harm* them anymore."

"Harm them?" Terry asks, finally a bit interested in what it is they're doing here.

"Apparently, Joshua began harassing the girls. Pinching and pushing at first—that sort of thing. But then he began cutting their hair and..." Willow's cheeks are now blistering with embarrassment. "*Pantsing* them."

"This is all," Terry says after a deep exhale and tries to find the right words, "very upsetting for us to hear." He glances over to Eddie who nods his head in agreement before continuing. "Your son sounds like a real cause for concern, but—"

"Last week, I woke up in the middle of the night—in my nightgown—and found him standing beside my bed staring at me! I have to lock the door to my own bedroom now to keep the filthy pervert out."

"Mrs. Carney," Eddie says. "Has Josh ever shown any aggression towards animals? Maybe a neighbor's cat or—"

"Not under my roof—he knows better," Willow says shifting her eyes to Eddie. "But he could be doing anything when he's not home."

"Where is he now?" Terry asks.

"At work. He washes dishes at Charlie's."

"Good Time Charlie's has dishes?" Eddie asks preposterously.

"Charlie's *Hamburger*," Terry says and bites his tongue. "Mrs. Carney, the man that we're after, not only is he very...

sophisticated," he tries putting it delicately, though he knows that she'd have no problem calling her son an imbecile. "But he's also extremely violent. Do you really believe that your son is capable of doing something like this?"

"Yes."

HELEN LEADS THEM through her rancher to the back bedroom which serves as Joshua's quarters.

"You'll have to excuse the mess," she says before creaking the door open. "I quit cleaning up after him years ago."

The first thing that Terry and Eddie notice is the overdue laundry strewn carelessly across the room—and the smell—both of which they expected for a twenty-year-old living at home. What they didn't expect were all of his toys.

No neatly arranged model trains or rare collectibles sitting safely on shelves. No sought-after figurines in original blister packs or other prized playthings of any kind. Not even a toy box to throw it all in. Instead, miscellaneous playthings line the windowsill, poke out from under the dirty clothes, and might even fall from the dust covered ceiling fan if it was turned on. Two masked wrestlers—Big Van Vader and Papa Shango—clash with a fleet of army men beside Joshua's bureau while two masked murderers—Michael Myers and Jason Voorhees—tie up a posse of cowboys at the foot of the boy's unmade bed.

Terry treads over some random dice and discarded Clue weapons—noticing no game board in sight—and makes his way over to the closet. He lightly kicks a few LEGO blocks out of the way from jamming the door before opening it and steps back. An uncatalogued stack of comic books and graphic novels spill out from beneath empty coat hangers. The covers of Charles Burns' *Black Hole* and *From Hell* by Alan Moore catch his attention as he scans the horde of ominous titles. He lifts up an old, tattered adaptation of Poe's *Masque of the Red Death* and flips through the illustrations—stopping once to read:

"...No pestilence had ever been so fatal, or so hideous. Blood was its avatar and its seal—the redness and the horror of blood—"

He closes it and gives the bleeding skull on the front cover a good look before tossing it back onto the heap alongside *Swamp Thing* and *The Dark Tower*.

A messy desk—made from an old wooden door and two stacks of empty milk crates—rests against the wall adjacent to the closet. Playing cards, pocketknives, colored pencils, crumpled papers—drawings hardly more advanced than the one Willow had already shown them—and a multitude of half full soda cans litter its surface. Terry spots a dusty laptop tagged with stickers and suspects that it hasn't been opened in ages due to a mortal infection of porn viruses. A plate of buttered spaghetti sits precariously close to one edge of the cluttered desk and is heavily dusted from an open bag of granulated sugar. Terry prods the bag disgustedly with his index finger and continues looking around, becoming more and more disinterested.

Mounted on the wall above the desk is an immense flat screen television—the kind that would've taken Joshua the entire summer to save up for. An assortment of survival-horror video games are thrown in a plastic bin underneath—the cases for Resident Evil, Siren, and Dead Space are on top and missing their discs. Terry frowns as he turns back to Willow and notices a poster taped to the bedroom door behind her. It depicts a scene from Goya's *Disasters of War* series with the words, "Y HAY NO REMEDIO," printed below it.

"Any idea what that means?" Terry asks stepping closer, taking care to not step on any Matchbox cars or dirty underwear.

"'It can't be helped', I believe," Willow sighs.

"*Ajurnamat*," Eddie says enthusiastically.

"Well," Terry says, taking a final look around. "Your son is evidently very into the macabre, Mrs. Carney. But there's nothing here that indicates that he's a murderer."

"Won't you at least talk to him?" she begs. Terry considers this as he looks down to an unmasked Spawn figure between his feet—Al Simmons' burnt face twists in agony.

"Hey Ter," Eddie calls over his shoulder before he can answer. "You want to come look at this?" Eddie holds up a faded vintage *Playboy* that Terry overlooked amongst Joshua's library and Willow's face flushes red when she sees the cover.

"I thought I threw all of those filthy things out," she says through her teeth.

Between the pages that aren't stuck together, nude women pose with sections of them torn from the defiled pages. Some are missing heads, others limbs, but all of them have been ripped apart in some way. When Eddie turns to the centerfold of Darine Stern, they discover that she's been ripped cleanly in half—right through her navel.

NEITHER TERRY NOR EDDIE are much convinced that Joshua Carney could actually be the Bloodrun Butcher, but they use him as an excuse to grab burgers at Charlie's. Sure, Eddie's might have some punk kid's spit in it, but neither of them had a bite all day.

"Two singles!" the manager of Charlie's calls into the kitchen window. "Anything to drink?"

"No, thank you," Terry says.

"And what can I get for you, Officer?"

"Six doubles with cheese," Eddie says.

"Six?"

"And a black and white shake."

"Alright, six doubles and a shake—is that all?"

"That's it. Company card?" Eddie asks looking to Terry.

"Funny."

"I'll have Josh come right out," the man says and disappears into the back.

Terry looks up to a sign above the register that says "Closed All Holidays" as the kitchen door swings open and a boy in a dirty apron steps through.

"Joshua Carney?" Eddie asks, tucking his wallet away. The boy nods wearily and lowers his eyes. "We're from the police department. Do you mind if we talk to you outside?"

"Am I in trouble?" he asks without looking up.

"Why would you be in trouble?" Terry asks as Joshua begins scratching his arm nervously.

"Because... I did it again."

"Did *what* again?" Terry asks, exchanging glances with Eddie.

"Mama says it's bad—but I didn't hurt'em. I just wanted to see what was inside!"

...I have opened up your bones...
...I have looked between your skin and ribs...

IN THE ALLEY behind Charlie's Hamburger is a green dumpster with Joshua's bicycle leaning against it.

"They left her here, I swear," the boy says pointing to the plastic crate strapped to his seat which previously held gallons of milk for Charlie's famous malt shakes. Inside of it lies a naked doll—broken apart and reassembled with pieces of Juicy Fruit and Government Issue Joe.

"Mama said if I ever did it again, she was going to send me away, but I was gonna give it back once they came in again—please, don't tell mama. I swear, they left it here. Once they come back, I'll give it to them!"

"Josh," Terry says, trying to calm him down. "We're not going to tell your mother." Lies

"You're not?" he asks, finally raising his eyes to them.

"As long as you tell us the complete truth."

"I swear, I swear, I swear! I didn't steal it! I didn't—"

"Josh," Terry repeats louder. "Have you ever done this to a human?" he asks, and the boy's face wrinkles in confusion.

"Like, to a *real* girl," Eddie says. As soon as Joshua understands what they're asking, he hunches over and pukes up what looks like a half-digested Charlie burger with everything on it and a liter of Dr. Pepper all over Eddie's boots.

CHAPTER XVII:
Tashira

"I THINK I may've finally gotten a lead on the kid who dropped off the letter yesterday," Joycie says.

"It's Joycie," Eddie says lowering his phone. "She says she has an ID on the delivery boy."

"So," Terry says, "talk to her."

"Talk to me."

"Peery brought a still shot from the drop box footage over to Ralph's to see if he recognized the kid—no luck. Ralph told him he couldn't be sure because of the hood. I was hoping that the Mongoose would've been enough to jog his memory; it's a trick bike—not a lot of kids ride those around here. Anyway, afterwards, Peery went over to Bayshor—"

"Joycie, Joycie, Joycie—" Eddie says, making a chatty puppet gesture with his freehand, but Terry ignores him. "Did you get a name or not?"

For a second, Joycie considers hanging up on him, but she reminds herself that this is about young girls being murdered and torn apart—hanging up on him won't do anything to stop that. She also realizes in that second that it was much easier to have a crush on Eddie Koyukuk back when he wasn't paying any attention to her.

"Tashira Roddy," she says coolly.

"Tashira? That sounds like a girl's name."

"It is. She goes by 'Rod.'" Joycie pauses for a moment to see if he'll allow her to finish this time. "As I was saying, after Peery left Ralph's, he went over to Bayshore Skatepark but couldn't get any of the kids to talk to him—apparently Old Sully's influence has spread to children now." This makes Eddie smile as he remembers how the old coffee brewing witch flipped him off the day before. "So, I decided to use my lunch break today to go over and try myself. I figured it was his uniform that was to blame; or maybe because he's a man—"

"Alright Joycie, thanks—we'll handle it from here," Eddie says and abruptly ends the call. "What a sneak! She got it herself," he tells Terry, unsure if he spoke accusatorily or admiringly. "We ought'a remember to send a pretty girl out next time we need info from little boys."

"So, she's pretty now?"

"Shut up."

As they drive to Inlet View Elementary school, Terry remembers how all the schools in his neighborhood growing up would've had a snow day if they got anything more than an inch or two—the news would even tell the elderly to stay inside. Here in Alaska, it's just another day.

The children are having recess as they arrive—many are stomping paths through the snow towards the slide and other play equipment. Others brought their sleds, opting to ride down the enormous pile of snow from when the parking lot was plowed. Another group innocently battle against one another's poorly made igloos. Terry watches a kid jump up and down on the top of one while his opponents pelt him with snowballs until the dome roof breaks and he falls in up to his armpits. This is how he envisioned the child that he and Hannah planned to have would grow up.

"Turn left here," Eddie says, "the entrance is on the other side. We can park behind the school buses, so the kids don't get excited."

"Oh okay, boss, anything else?" Terry asks.

"Yeah, *I'm* doing the talking this time," Eddie says confidently and burps up some of his milkshake.

After Eddie speaks with the principal, who in turn speaks with Rod's parents, one of the recess ladies calls Tashira Roddy away from leading her battalion of girls into the imminent decimation of the boys' snow forts.

"Hey Rodney," Eddie says like a dimwit when the three of them are alone in one of the empty classrooms. "I'm Officer Koyukuk and this is Detective Volker. We'd like to ask you about that letter you dropped off to us the other day." She just got done whitewashing the tallest boy in her grade and outsmarted the rest of them into near surrender—she can handle the likes of these two idiots too.

"It wasn't mine," she says.

"We know that—" Eddie says snarkily and Terry immediately intervenes. The last thing that he needs right now is to watch his trainee get into an argument with an eleven-year-old.

"Rod, can you please tell us about the man that gave it to you?"

"How do you know it was a man?" she asks.

"Was it a woman?" Eddie cuts back in.

"...No," she admits with some annoyance.

"Do you know his name?" Eddie continues.

"No."

"What did he look like?"

"I don't know—like you," she says and almost sticks her tongue out at him.

"What did he say to you?" Eddie asks.

"He said, if I dropped that letter in the box and didn't tell no one he'd give me $20.00."

"And did he?"

"I'm telling you about it, ain't I?" she asks, raising an eyebrow.

"So, what happened then?" Eddie asks.

"I rode up and dropped it in and when I turned around, he was gone."

"Gone?"

"He drove away."

"What was he driving?"

"A white van," she says and turns her head away from Eddie, evidently having enough with helping the police for today. She stares at the window that looks down onto the playground where her friends are all still playing in the snow.

"Tashira," Eddie says, trying to draw her attention back.

"One of you smells like shit," she says without turning from the window. Eddie looks down to his boots—still wet from Joshua Carney's vomit—and then up to Terry who nods his head in agreement.

"She's right," Terry says. "Why don't you go stand in the hallway?"

Tashira Roddy smiles and wrinkles her nose at Eddie as he's dismissed from the classroom like a disruptive child sent to the principal's office.

CHAPTER XVIII:
The Unipqaaq of the Quiet People

SEDNA BECAME STRONGER THAN ANY OF THE MEN
    And this made her father weary
    She could climb the mountains barefoot,
    Eat raw meat off the bone,
    And was unaffected by the stints of both Malina and Igaluk;
    The sun and moon gods

    When Sedna's father learned of her treachery,
    He took her on his kayak and threw her into the crests
    The waves crashed over her head and still she tried to climb back aboard
    But her fingers froze to the gunwales
    Her father pleaded for mercy from the great white gull,
    But Gull was merciless.

CHAPTER XIX:
Brass

AS EDDIE LEAVES the room, Terry fishes through his pockets for something to bribe the girl with but only finds some kibble and his badge.

Kids like dog food, right? he asks himself, but then slides his badge across the desk with a calculated glance, watching her eyes widen.

"You're not in trouble, Rod," he says. "Do you know what this badge means?" She looks up from the brass shield and shakes her head. "It means," Terry says, leaving the badge in front of her, "I'm here to protect you."

"Can I...?" she asks, looking down.

"Go ahead," he says, and she lifts it up and rubs her cold fingertips—which are still numb from making snowballs—all over the metallic engravings: the bald eagle holding a banner displaying the Bloodrun Police motto; "Peace. Bravery. Justice." The two totem poles, one with an American flag hanging from it and the other with Alaska's. In the center, a simplified depiction of Mount Tuqujuq with the Bloodrun River swirling below. Terry would have no problem giving it to her to flash at her snow fort friends if it weren't for Chief Eddowes wringing his neck.

"How do you become a detective?" she asks.

Oh, simple, Rod, just take some mind-altering substances at a dive bar with a suspect in an unsolved murder case.

Killing a mass shooter also looks good on the old resume—

"By catching bad men," Terry says, "like the one who wrote that letter." Her eyes drop and she rubs her thumbs over the raised impressions again—still feeling the warmth from Terry's pocket—and then places the badge back on the desk. "I need to know what he looked like, Rod. No more games."

SHE TRIES TO COOPERATE. She even wants to. Holding Terry's badge gave her a little confidence, but the more she tries to remember the man's face, the more it eludes her. It flickers away, fading out like a candle deprived of air. The memory is blurry somehow—difficult to retrieve—like it happened long ago. Their exchange of words sounds muffled, like they were talking through thick planes of glass. When she tries to concentrate on any of the details—the color of the man's hair, the tone of his voice—the face that she conjures of him in her mind begins to morph into a human skull.

But that couldn't be. She'd remember talking to a skeleton, especially one that could drive. It's more unsettling than when her mind replays images from the horror movies that her sister warns her about. She's convinced herself before that she saw shapes moving in the shadows; heard sounds coming from under her bed; even felt something reach out and grab—

"Rod," Terry tries again. "I get that you don't want to be a snitch, but this man isn't the type of person that you want to help."

She frowns and closes her eyes this time to really envision what happened.

"Hey, you!" she can just make out. It's the man's voice—garbled as if he were underwater—calling to her as she pedaled down the Brig. "*Makchit*!"

She turns her head in her mind's eye to locate the source of the voice and for a split second, she can see the man sitting inside his van waving to her. In the instant that her eyes focus on him, his face splits away in ribbons like a thin plastic produce bag that's been stretched beyond its limit. The sudden burst and rippling noise that it makes—like the flaps of his skin were sucked up by a jet engine—turns her stomach even more than the rotting bloody skull that leans toward her.

"Rod?" Terry asks, jumping a little when the girl's eyes flash open. "What is it?"

"I can't remember!" she shouts.

No, it isn't anything at all like the scenes she glimpsed at in *Nightmare on Elm Street* or *The Thing*. She still remembers how the sound of Tim Curry's voice used to haunt her every time that she rode past a sewer drain, and the week that she wouldn't bathe because Anthony Perkins stabbed a lady to death in the shower. Even though they terrified her, a part of her has always known that they weren't real—but this is different. This is her own memory, yet she can't account for it. She knows that there wasn't anything frightening about the encounter when it happened—odd maybe, but nothing that made her afraid. No worm covered skull. So, why is she seeing it now? If this damn copper hadn't forced her to think about it, she never would've even thought anything of it.

"Please, Rod," Terry begs.

"I can't," she whimpers, and defeated tears form in the little girl's eyes.

"This man... He's done terrible things to women, but I can catch him if you—"

As she wipes her face, a swarm of roaches fly out from the decaying skull's open jaw and she breaks down in a deluge of tears.

"THE GIRL SAYS he was driving a white van," Terry says into his walkie.

"Like Émile's?" Joycie radios back.

"Yeah—maybe," Terry replies. "She thinks she can point it out if she sees it again, but doesn't recall any insignia—probably unmarked."

"But what about the guy? If we find a suspect, she'll be able to identify him, right?"

"Unlikely," Terry says angrily.

"What—why? She saw him, didn't she?" Joycie asks and releases the call button to listen for Terry's response, but his signal returns nothing but oppressive silence.

"One would think that," he finally calls back, "but she wouldn't give us anything useful. *Couldn't*, she claims. Doesn't recall a mustache, eye color, or even what ethnicity he was—could've been Native, maybe half," Terry says looking over to Eddie. "She couldn't even tell us what color hair he had. Only thing she remembers was a black hat—like a rolled-up ski mask."

"How can she not remember? It was *yesterday*."

"I don't know, Joycie," Terry says, tightening his grip on the steering wheel. "She said that she didn't get a good look at him—that he's '*hard to look at.*' Once he offered her the money, she lost interest in who he was and pedaled away. When she turned back around, he was gone."

"Hard to look at—like he was deformed or something?"

"Who knows—she started crying every time I asked her to describe it."

For a moment, Joycie feels an urge to press on with her questions, but some deeper part inside of her already understands. There was something about reading the man's letter that she can't describe herself—even just holding it, knowing that he held it too. Terry can't deny it either, but he offers no sympathy.

"We'll be back at the station in a few minutes. Send Wertman over to the Roddy's address. School will be out soon and the Chief will want a sketch made, even if this guy is fucking faceless."

"Copy."

T E R R Y ' S   L E G   V I B R A T E S as he turns into the small lot out front of the precinct and parks in front of the blue sign marked "T. Volker."

"Go inside and get cleaned up and then head over to Good Time Charlie's," Terry tells Eddie as he presses the lock button on his phone to end the buzzing. "I would've stopped on the way back but you still reek, and I figure if any of them over there are going to talk to us, it'll be to you."

"Where are you going?"
"Apparently, Liam found something."

CHAPTER XX:
Redeloos—Radeloos—Reddeloos

"WHAT'S THIS?" Terry asks, taking hold of the papers that Liam hands him.

"It's the transcript from a podcast interview that Émile Lepus gave a few years back for some art magazine," Liam says. "I figured you'd want to just scan it over and get to the good parts, rather than sit through that damn grating voice of his." Terry looks down to a strange block of words printed at the top of the first page and raises an eyebrow.

"M O T O R
O C U L I
T U L I P
O L I V E
R I P E N"

"Good parts?"

"It's some type of 'magic square', from what I gather. Sometimes they're assembled in other shapes, but squares appear to be the most prevalent. As you can see, the same words can be read both vertically and horizontally." Terry looks back up to the block and nods. "They're more frequently made with numbers and involve complex mathematics to solve—one of Émile's

180

fortes—but these ones created with words are the real anomalies. They go far back, as early as the Zhou Dynasty, at least—probably even further. The Romans were particularly fascinated with them—they appear all over in their architec—"

"Liam," Terry says, knowing that the federal wordsmith will fully nerd out on him if he doesn't interject.

"Originally, they were used for divination—like rain dances or favor in war, even aiding in childbirth—don't ask. This one that Lepus uses though, the kind constructed with words, comes from some ancient belief that words have an innate power which can be accessed when written in special arrangements."

"So, you're telling me this block of words is some kind of *spell*?" Terry asks.

—all words are spells—

"Whether it is or isn't hardly matters," Liam says. "Lepus, as I'm sure you know, isn't a spiritual buff and certainly doesn't ascribe to magic and voodoo. The computation behind them is the only thing that interests him. He's too pragmatic for witchcraft. What Lepus likes is magic *tricks*; the sleight of hand; the secret passage; constructing puzzles." Liam pauses as Terry reflects.

Motor.
Oculi.
Tulip.
Olive.
Rip—

"The only thing that matters," Liam continues firmly, "is what the old bastard said during the interview: '*Only death and death alone.*' Do you remember that one?" It's not as clear in Terry's mind as the bestial allusions that led him to the Thompsons, but it's there.

"I think so, yeah."

"I highlighted it for ya—along with all of the other incriminating parts. I don't think that letter was written by just some psychopath anymore. I think it's more likely misdirection, y'know? 'The river this, the river that'—he's trying to send us off course by looking for nuts like The Thompsons—or someone who'd believe that 'all words are spells.' Only, the artist in him couldn't resist putting in a bit of his own aesthetic. They can't help themselves, that's how they are—prodigal narcissists."

"Artists or psychopaths?" Terry asks.

"Both."

Terry swings a swivel chair over to sit in as he reads and Liam's voice fades into the background:

"And not to mention, but the interview itself bears quite a resemblance to the tone of the letter—without referencing the river, that is. He does quote some known phrases, mostly anarchist slogans: 'Deface the currency', 'Eat the rich', and a few others. But that one about death, it's inimitable..."

> **Interviewer:** Joining us here today at *Rampjaar Magazine* is French Canadian artist Émile Lepus. Émile first came onto the art circuit in the 1960s with his controversial kinetic sculptures and has since made quite a stir in the world of contemporary art with his even more notorious philosophical writings and critiques on the scene that he helped shape. Presently, he has returned to the role of creator with his highly anticipated piece, "Card House." Émile, it's an absolute pleasure to have you here. On behalf of Rampjaar, let me just say how thrilled we are that you finally agreed to sit down with us after so long. I've been a fan of everything you've done ever since the debut of your "Nude Energy" series, so it's a personal delight that I get to be the one to interview you.
>
> **Lepus:** Oh, I think those are quite before your time.
>
> **Interviewer:** [laughing] Well, nevertheless. Now, aside from all the writing that you've done, such as the highly criticized article, "Art is Dead," and the actual sculptures that you make—
>
> **Lepus:** *Installations.*

Interviewer: Yes, excuse me, aside from those, you have somewhat of a reputation for keeping yourself out of the public eye so, we're all wondering: is there any reason why you've chosen now, after such a long and interesting career, to finally make an appearance?

Lepus: Well, for one thing, let me preface by saying that my work is not complete. It's not 'after', as you say, but rather, amidst it—at its pinnacle, really.

Interviewer: Of course, of course. But the fact remains; you've never gone into much detail regarding your own work before. The essays you've written are pretty much just "commentary" on other artists. So, what changed and why haven't we heard from you until now?

Lepus: I thought that was obvious; I didn't want to become the thing that I critiqued—or use my reputation to soapbox my own work. Unfortunately, we have no shortage of artists today who will jump at any opportunity they can to glorify what they do. In fact, I believe it's become a requirement. It's the only way that most of this so called "art" can be differentiated from putrefied s***.

Interviewer: Wow, they did warn me—

Lepus: Art schools are the ones to blame for it. They prioritize teaching their students how to *talk* about what they paint rather than teaching them how to use a paintbrush. It's no wonder that so many of them amass such astonishing amounts of debt after graduating that they're forced to take jobs waiting tables and cleaning toilets instead of creating masterpieces. My conviction holds that a successful student can graduate from Tyler or UCLA without ever learning a single thing but rhetoric. A successful artist on the other hand,

should promptly drop out and seek only to live an interesting life.
Interviewer: Well, we can't have Vienna Fine Arts create another Führer, can we?
Lepus: Hilarious—side-splitting.
Interviewer: No, I think I agree with a bit of what you're saying there, and I'd like to come back to the subject of school in a moment, but speaking of toilets—do you find it difficult reconciling these views as someone who has often cited himself as a 'disciple of Duchamp'? I'm not trying to insinuate that Duchamp is crap of course, I'm just referring—
Lepus: to Mr. Mutt's *Fountain*, yes, I've heard that criticism before. All I have to say to that is that you're confusing the brilliancy of Marcel Duchamp placing an overturned urinal in The Grand Central Palace with all the *crap* and imposters that followed him.
Interviewer: So, you think he did that as a sort of parody or protest? Or maybe to bring attention to what he believed was nothing more than, well, *pissotières* and mass-produced kitsch that most galleries were exhibiting at that time?
Lepus: Duchamp simply challenged us to ask the question presented by Tolstoy and other great minds which is; wherein lies the characteristic sign of a work of art? He paved the way for us to understand that once we recognize art as more than an agent for Botticelli to convey beauty or for Vermeer to render light, we discover the transformative and revolutionary power that it has to change society.

Terry pauses, takes a deep breath and looks up to Liam, who seems to be watching him read with some enjoyment.

"You're at the part about *pissotières*, huh?" he asks. "I told you, I highlighted all the parts that you need to see to spare you from all that highfalutin gobbledygook." Terry exhales irritably and looks back down to the transcript.

> **Interviewer:** Interesting. I suppose I can accept that, and this may be a good segue into talking about what you really came here for, your latest *installation*, "Card House,"—which I'm totally stoked for. But, before we get into that, I was hoping you could give us a little background information for our listeners who may not be familiar with your work. You've led a fascinating life, my man. How did you begin such a multifaceted career—which didn't even begin in art—is that correct?
> **Lepus:** Not exactly, no. Originally, I went to school at MIT for Robotic Engineering.
> **Interviewer:** Wait a minute, you're advising kids to drop out of school, but you yourself are a college graduate?
> **Lepus:** I said that an *artist* should drop out; not someone who plans to work innovating sea barometers and hydraulic presses—or delve in any other heavy mechanical instrumentation with analytical vigor, as I did. I also contributed greatly to modern prosthetic technologies—even designed my own wheelchair—and briefly served as a building code inspector—which some credit to my love of architecture and eventual construction of Card House.
> **Interviewer:** Ah, I see. I bet the carpenters loved you.
> **Lepus:** So long as they worked within the margins of their codes.

Interviewer: Wow, that's pretty extraordinary, but it's quite a jump to Dadaism and the Situationist International.
Lepus: I was never a part of the SI.
Interviewer: No, but your work does often have the air of a *spectacle* to it, wouldn't you say?
Lepus: *Everything* is a spectacle today. Society has become a caricature of itself.
Interviewer: Still.
Lepus: I've never associated the things I create with the spineless endeavors of those Marxist libertarians in Paris. That was merely the tabloids—probably no better than this one—who grouped my artwork alongside theirs.
Interviewer: Perhaps it's the French accent.

"What's the Situationist International?" Terry asks, looking up from the papers.

"You're persistent, aren't you?" Liam asks. "I respect that, but I'm telling ya, I didn't miss anything." Terry blinks calmly without moving. "It's some countercultural art movement from the 60's, if you really want to know. They—"

As Liam continues explaining, Terry skips around the interview more freely—only half-listening—hoping that he won't hear the word "avant-garde."

"—were more activists than 'artists'—"

Lepus: If I truly wanted to make a disturbance to the corporate capitalist reign, I needn't do anything more than deface the currency. There's no need to exert oneself into the strenuous task of making art to do that.
Interviewer: Ah, a Diogian he. I guess you're not a crypto guy then.
Lepus: [grunting] Cryptocurrency is a dream of fools, or if were speaking in terms of finance, the epitome of greater fool theory; if not an

altogether worse scheme than the Federal Reserve itself.
Interviewer: Sounds like SI to me, Émile.
Lepus: [sighs]
Interviewer: I suppose it's since capitalism has been good to you—that's why you're hesitant for change. How about NFTs?
Lepus: Please, stop.
Interviewer: NFTs are the future—it's a digital world out there now, Émile. And as an artist—
Lepus: They're a *fad*. This week Shitcoin, next week Pissereum. Tamagotchis and pokey-men for grown adults—it's pitiable. Just like everything else that's produced these days; Facebook, TikTok, The Kardashians. It's all a trap for our attention and a rug pull from under our material wealth. If this *future* you speak of is ever realized, rulebooks will be overwritten by losers, laws by fascists, feats by sissies, and art by robots. The only artists getting involved with Non-fungible Tokens are students of Charlies Ponzi; *con* artists. You'll not see them produced by anyone with self-respect or integrity. We must stop bulls***, not invent more.

"—who devaluated the politics of the time, which they believed had become a performance—"

> **Interviewer:** For someone who reveres artists who make use of the *readymade*, you yourself are quite a hands-on "maker." Don't you find it difficult juggling modern art with your fundamentalist nature?
> **Lepus:** Next question.
> **Interviewer:** I'm sorry—what's wrong?
> **Lepus:** I'm an old man and don't have time to be asked the same question over and over. If you

don't like my answer, then don't ask. I don't believe someone should be allowed to drive a car if they can't put one together—if that's what you mean by fundamentalist. What we create with our hands makes who we are.

Interviewer: That's exactly what I mean! On one hand you're denouncing art schools and essentially condemning their students for hijacking the word "artist" but then you idolize Daddy Dada.

Lepus: The difference between Marcel Duchamp and the multitude of pompous teenagers that are being churned out by universities—under the tutelage of professors with no more artistic merit than Yoko Ono—is that Duchamp could make us *think* and *react* without necessitating self-indulgent ramblings that don't ever prove to be anything more than, "It's art because I say so." Duchamp intended to de-deify the role of the artist, whereas kids these days are only interested in becoming deities by any means necessary— even explicitly ripping off the work of a dead and noble man.

Interviewer: Haven't you ever heard that great art isn't made, it's stolen?

"—they produced pamphlets, films, graffiti, and most commonly, repurposed everyday items into mediums that would ideally incite the viewer to scrutinize their environment... in some cases, even riot—"

Interviewer: I just don't understand why you're wasting time with Duchamp. Is it because of the handicap?

Lepus: Leave it alone.

Interviewer: Surely people understand that you're the mastermind behind your work. No one cares who physically puts it all together—they're your designs.

Lepus: I said, "Leave it alone."

Interviewer: [sighing] On paper, you seem like such a humanitarian, but now I can't shake the thought that you must just hate kids.

"—with a lot of clever aphorisms, 'work is the blackmail of survival', 'protect me from what I want'—"

Interviewer: Let's talk briefly about Motor-Oculi-Tulip-Olive-Ripen. This block of text has become an image on its own for many of your fans and critics alike. Many of them believe it alludes to doomsday or while others condemn it as some sort of occult device on par with the Key of Solomon, but most of us simply take it as a symbol for your work—like a signature. Can you perhaps tell us about its true significance?

Lepus: [grunting] Criss, tire-toi une bû... Religious zealots can't even help themselves from the innocuous wordplay of magic squares now? Mine of which doesn't even possess the full palindromic properties that are supposedly needed for evoking evil spirits like the legendary Sator Square. To be honest, I originally created it out of boredom. It was one of the ways I entertained myself amidst the incessant chatter of my colleagues at some part-time job I had while in school.

Interviewer: I must admit; I'm finding it difficult seeing you working with others.

Lepus: At the time, it was merely an exercise in free association—getting the words to fit—much like the exalted Surrealist game of automatic writing. Therein lies the only "magic" to it; allowing the subconscious to speak without interference. It wasn't until years later when I rediscovered it that I knew its true meaning. Similarly to how we interpret our dreams, I cannot definitively say whether I ascribed this meaning or obtained it—only that it's been a common theme in my work ever since. I wouldn't necessarily say it's an "end of days" allusion as you suggested, but it does convey impermanence—which actually implies renewal. Each word represents a stage of humanity, and the palindrome effect itself represents the cyclic nature of these stages; the rise of our pretty inventions—Motor—which, inevitably get reclaimed by the earth—Olive. In between, we are confused by science and beauty—Oculi and Tulip—until we ripen and rot and start again.

"—to wander the city like tramps, to intentionally get lost for the purpose of provoking spontaneous experiences—"

Interviewer: You mentioned Surrealism a moment ago and since your work is often considered Dada and the two are closely related, I was wondering if you had any inclination to create anything Dalí-inspired in the future.
Lepus: Well, Dalí and Surrealism have influenced me all along, however, it's probably not that evident in my work until the construction of Card House. It's more so been an influence on my lifestyle as a human rather than as an artist.
Interviewer: In what way?
Lepus: As I'm sure you know, the Surrealists placed an immense importance on the subconscious and how dreams conversely inform us about the fantasy that we live in day to day. Developing perfect dream recall is the easiest

way to face your own psyche and pull yourself out from this illusion.
Interviewer: And how exactly does one do that?
Lepus: Simple—by logging your dreams immediately every time you wake up. They require no tarot cards or traveling gypsy's elaborate crackpot construal either. The simple act of writing creates a sort of... personal blueprint. Most of the books on my shelves are marble composition pads I've filled from years of recording.
Interviewer: What a library that must be.

"—disorientation, cutting up and reassembling maps, *psychogeography*—or some horseshit," Liam continues.

Lepus: I don't hate kids. In fact, Card House got its inception while I was teaching a welding course at a juvenile detention center. Art has two aspects: the purely visual and its utility. Contemporary art hardly ever has both—or either—but it's least likely to have the latter. Working with architecture now as my main medium facilitates more than a decorative way to house my installations. Yes, it allows me to arrange the structure in a visually appealing dreamscape; a constantly transforming meditation on the ephemeral world—but the utility that Card House generates is far more transformative. By providing a home for the homeless—who are mostly *kids*—they not only become a piece of the art, but through living and working with me, each of them become the artist themselves. I don't simply give them lodging; I give each member of Card House *use*. I'll go so far as to say that when it's completed and open to the public, it'll be impossible for anyone to enter Card House and not become an active participant who must interact with all its mechanisms. Motor-Oculi-Tulip-Olive-Ripen is no longer just an emblem, but *equipment* that demands the viewer to operate.

"—sought to create 'situations' that revealed the 'spectacle'; that we are all slaves to our desires—"

> **Interviewer:** Do you feel that Card House is more your retreat or your exile?
> **Lepus:** Neither. Card House is designed to reflect the world outside, so there's nowhere to retreat to or be exiled from. I want it all daily before my eyes—like the nearly 3,000 homeless men and women across Alaska. I know who I am and how people look at me. I too have been shunned by society, but I'm still a part of it—whether they like it or not. Give me all your scorn and still I'll have no desire for refuge or surrender. I'm there with them on the corner—holding my sign for the world to see—and I won't *retreat* or be *exiled*, or succumb to sickness and old age or—
> **Interviewer:** Freezing to death on a park bench?
> **Lepus:** There is *only* death… and death *alone*—

"Have you sent a copy of this to Judge Raynor yet?" Terry asks, finally having read enough and flips back to the block of text on the front.

"Waiting on your word. Agent Bressi is talking with the field office right now, but he thinks we have enough already from this interview. We should have a warrant to raid the place before tomorrow morning."

"Alright. Let's round up everyone at the station by 4 o'clock so we can plan out how we're going to go about this."

"You got it," Liam says, but appears to have more to say.

"What?" Terry asks, tossing the transcript down.

"There's something else," Liam says, "in the letter."

"What is it?"

"I was checking each line for acrostics when I happened to notice the word count. It doesn't necessarily connect the letter to Lepus," Liam says as he rifles through some papers, "but it's *something*. Remember how we were talking about the letter having a poetic meter to it?"

"12-7-7 something?" Terry asks.

"12-7-7 and 9-7-7. Well, it turns out those aren't the only hidden numbers here." Terry narrows his eyes a bit skeptically as Liam hands him a copy of the letter with his scribbles all over it. "There's exactly six hundred and sixty-six words. It's the key to the cipher. The 666 tells us that he's familiar with bible verse. So, when you apply these two meters to the books of the bible—" Terry looks up at Liam like he has six heads. "You're not a Christian—okay. So, the bible is comprised of 39 books. Y'know; *Genesis, Exodus, Revelation*—"

"Alright," Terry says.

"You've heard of famous passages like John 3:16, right?"

"I can't recite it but yeah, I've heard it before."

"So, it can also be written as 4:3:16—*John* being the *fourth* book of the New Testament. Book: four, chapter: three, verse: sixteen. Now, our 12:7:7, if applied in the same way, points us to *Kings*—the 12th book—and then we go to the 7th verse of its 7th chapter, giving us the passage Kings 7:7."

Seven & Seven, Terry says to himself, unable to avoid thinking about his acid ordeal with Steve "Fullsend" Albot.

"Make sense?"

"I think so," Terry says. "That'd make the other one from the 9th book then?"

"Right, *Samuel 7:7*."

"So, what do they say?"

Liam hands him a dusty bible that he found on a shelf in the back of the station and Terry opens it to the first of two yellow sticky tabs.

"When the devil heard that the

>people had gathered around
>the tower, he went up to chop
>them down."

Terry frowns as he flips a chunk of pages over onto his thumb and then reads the second passage.

>"So they tried to escape in the
>twilight and abandoned their
>tents and horses, leaving the
>camp just as it was, and fled
>for their lives."

ACT III:
SOMETHING IN THE BLOOD

CHAPTER I:
Pins

"WE HAVE A CLEAR connection now to Émile Lepus—and as far as I'm concerned, this other finding of Liam's just further puts the pin on him," Agent Bressi says conclusively. "Émile's obsession with numerology and puzzles—"

"But it's *scripture*," Terry says. "Lepus is hardly religious."

"We're not expecting that the killer is either, Ter," Liam says. "The point of those verses is only to incite fear and panic. '*666*'—'*the devil will chop them up.*' Whoever it is just wants everyone in Bloodrun gone—'*fleeing for their lives.*'"

"Now," Bressi cuts back in, "is there anyone in this town more misanthropic than Émile Lepus? The woman we got coffee from earlier was no treat, but she doesn't exactly have the same resources available to her that Lepus does. Plus," he stresses, "we have statements from your town librarian and the delivery boy that both point to Émile. He probably even put all that '*sabre-tooth-reptile-claw*' bullshit in there on purpose to get us on the Thompsons—he probably has a grudge against them for drawing in tourists. It should be clear to your judge that we need to obtain a warrant immediately."

"Let's hope so," Chief Eddowes says. "I know Raynor; he'll understand the severity of the situation, but he's not going to rush looking through anything and risk blemishing his reputation—especially with a public figure like Émile Lepus."

197

"The kid who dropped off the letter said that the man driving the van looked like Eddie," Terry says, causing Bressi to look Eddie up and down unsurely. "Lepus is white," Terry adds.

"You're not white?" Bressi asks.

"Half," Eddie says indifferently.

"Not to mention," Terry says, "Émile's a senior citizen."

"Tashira Roddy's description of whoever she saw is hardly useable," Bressi responds and holds up the unremarkable sketch that Officer Wertman returned with. Terry can't help but agree, thinking that it could even pass for the indistinct sketch of the naked boy who killed Bill Sullivan. "We're not supposing that Émile Lepus was the one driving the van anyway. He must've had one of his cronies doing it. I mean, we know that Lepus couldn't have done any of this alone. If the black car that Tina Sullivan saw *was* Émile's Charger, it'd make sense that someone else was driving the van. Perhaps it was," Bressi lifts up one of the files that they collected on the known residents of Card House and reads off one of the names: "'Thomas O'Toole' or what was that boy's name—Talon?"

"Son of a bitch probably has his own Manson Family up there," Rudd Hasson mutters as he adjusts his hip in one of the stiff interrogation room chairs. "Filling those kids' heads with all kinds of helter-skelter bullshit."

"Do we have any reason to believe that the kids didn't do it alone?" Eddowes asks. "Maybe Lepus has no idea what's going on. Maybe they've read too much of his artsy-fartsy anarcho-nonsense and just accidentally let out too much."

"At this point, we don't," Agent Bressi says. "But based on everything we've gathered about this bastard, it *is* possible that they've finally had enough of the old man and who knows—maybe they want to frame him."

"Killing two innocent girls with a chainsaw strikes me as an elaborate scheme just to frame someone," Terry says.

"Our position right now is that Émile is just the mastermind behind this, like Detective Hasson said; a cult leader—pushing radical ideas on them about anarchy and nihilism and *art*—warping their minds until they've been coerced enough into murdering for him," Bressi says. "Until we make an arrest, we can't say for sure, but *something* is going on in Card House. All that matters right now is that we found a link."

"No one living in that house gives a damn about him," Terry says. "They're all there because they got no place else to go. None of them would be caught dead helping him with anything other than his sculptures. We should wait, Chief."

"We can't wait any longer, Terry," Eddowes says. "I'm not having another dismembered body from this town turn up in the snow again tomorrow."

"What about the kid—Talon?" Bressi asks. "You said yourself that Émile was laying into him the other day when you and Eddie went to question him. Maybe he's caved in."

"Talon couldn't do this; he's just a boy. Plus, he probably hates Émile most of all of them."

"Boys are capable of terrible things, detective," Bressi says. "You ought'a know that."

Terry recognizes that the fed is referring to the two boys from his past—the one with no shoes who shot up the Rod & Reel, and the other who stabbed Bill Sullivan before running off naked into the woods. But still, in his mind's eye, Terry has a flash of the closed door at the end of his hallway.

...open up the gates...

"If their Kevlars aren't in their trunks already, order everyone to go home and dust them off. We're going to do this as smoothly as possible, but let's be prepared to go in as SWAT, if need be," Eddowes says. "Tomorrow morning, you and Eddie will knock on the front door and try to enter peacefully. Read the warrant, but don't make any arrests until Lepus is in custody. They'll be more likely to cooperate if they think were just there to talk to him. I don't want any of them freaking out or shutting down on his whereabouts before we get him. Hasson and Peery will be your backup and the rest of us will standby outside."

CHAPTER II:
Last Call

"NO, DON'T WAKE HIM," Terry says softly as Joycie goes to pick Spartacus up from his little bed under her desk. "Not yet; I need to make a call first," he says, retrieving his phone from his pocket and slipping outside. He knew he was going to call her from the moment that the meeting with the suits was over, but yet, he hesitates—as if in control—and stares at the black rectangle highlighting her name.

"This is Hannah—" Terry chokes for a second when he hears her voice, but he quickly realizes that it's only her voicemail "—your name and number and I'll get back to you when I can."

"Hey-ey," he stammers after the beep as he clears his throat. The voice of reason—which should be urging him to hang up the fucking phone—has abandoned him, leaving behind a broken utterance he can't recognize.

"It's me. Um, this isn't, uh... I—" Terry laughs awkwardly, not remotely amused. "I don't mean to bother you, but I'd like to talk to you about something." He searches unconsciously through his coat pocket for his badge—grabbing at nothing until he scratches crumbs of dog food—

Don't say, "Spartacus misses you."
Don't say, "I miss you."
Don't say—

"I—I'm sure you've heard about the recent murders. They were both women, and—"

—well, you're a woman, haha—

"I just wanted to check in and make sure you're okay."

That's it, scare her into talking to you.

"I mean—that's not why I'm calling. I'm not *worried* about you—I mean, I *am* worried about you, but…"

Smoothe.

"It's just—it's been a while since we last spoke and I was hoping—"

That we were over this?

That you could talk to me like an adult?

"I hope—I hope you're doing alright, that's all."

Terry lowers the phone to his side and exhales deeply as he considers smashing it on the pavement.

"D o   y o u   r e m e m b e r that drawing class we had?" The words contort his face as soon as they leave his lips.

Do you really think she's forgotten about how you met?

"Someone in the class did a project on that artist Émile Lepus. Remember, I even got called up to Card House once to—"

Yeah, real smart; ask her to remember that *night.*

Terry recalls the selfish thought that had crossed his mind afterwards: that a stray drop or smear of blood from Émile's girlfriend could've helped him avoid another argument when he got home. Hannah would've been too concerned to be angry if he walked in with blood on him. All it would've taken was dipping his fingers in that red puddle from the broken glass in Émile's kitchen and wiping it—

"Well, there's a good chance—I mean, the FBI's working with us on this one—"

A little boasting now too, why not?

"They think Émile had something to do with the deaths of these girls…"

Get to the point, Terry—quick, he imagines her saying.

"You always did better than me with the art stuff—I mean, you *are* an artist—so, I just thought we could talk about anything you might remember about him. There's a chance you could save some lives," he immediately regrets saying. Not only did he not intend on guilting her into talking to him, but he's also quite certain that his inability to balance work and private life attributed to most of their fights.

Why the fuck would she want to help you now?

"I'm sorry about this—about *everything*. I'm gonna hang up now. If you think of anything just—"

But Terry finally forces himself to end the call. He drops his head back and releases a huge plume of steam, as if he hadn't taken a single breath during the entire call. He stands there for a long a time watching the cloud dissipate into the cold air and then reenters the lobby.

"Ter?" Eddie asks, but Terry walks past him without meeting his eyes. He doesn't acknowledge Joycie's concerned face either as she rolls her chair back from her desk to give him access to his sleeping dog.

Spartacus wakes as Terry picks him up and he yawns widely in his face. His whiskers tickle Terry's cheek, but Terry's mind is too jostled—hijacked from his foolish voyage into the past to put forth any smile. Flashes of memories—like a grim slideshow of every misstep in the Volker marriage—spit onto a projector screen in his mind—

"I can fix this—"

—Click-click.

"Terry, would you please just listen—"

—Click-click.

"Get off of me!"

—until finally stopping on the day of Hannah's father's funeral.

"Terry?" Eddie asks again.

"I gave you an order, Eddie—what are you still doing here?" Terry asks and walks out of the building before Eddie can respond. He crosses the parking lot holding Spart, all the while trying to push the image of Roy Lindskog's open casket out of his head.

"W H A T   T H E   H E L L was that?" Joycie asks as she watches Terry peel out of the lot.

"Looked like a Charlie burger with everything on it. But I think I saw some spaghetti in there too."

"What?" Joycie asks, turning from the window. Eddie is standing in his socks and looks up to her with his wet boots hanging in his fingertips. "Not the smell, Eddie. *Terry*. What was *that*?"

"I guess you don't notice that much from behind the desk, but he hasn't been well for a long time."

"His ex?"

"Yeah, I'd say that's part of it."

"I thought he was over her," she says sympathetically. Eddie suddenly wonders if Joycie is the type of woman that you never get over. "Maybe it's just these murders—"

"Trust me, it's not. We already know who did it."

"You do?"

"Well, Terry was supposed to go over some new evidence with me just now, but…"

"Is it the Thompsons?"

"Nah," Eddie says, brushing her question off condescendingly, "there was nothing there."

"Nothing? What do you mean? What was it like in there?"

"Well, we didn't actually go in. I mean we went *in*, but Terry kind of blew up and we had to leave."

"Aren't you curious though?" Joycie asks. "What if they have an exhibit in there about people getting cut up or something? I heard they have all kinds of nasty shit inside but no one from town is going to tell us because the only people who have the nerve to go in there are—"

"Freaks?" Eddie asks, trying to recall how Terry put it. He pictures Greg Thompson's face turning red and then remembers the word: "Dipshits."

"I was going to say 'tourists', but yeah."

"Well, why don't you do a little more detective work?" Eddie asks playfully. "Go check it out yourself again—*undercover*," he suggests. He intended for this to come off as flirting and not a serious proposition, but all Joycie can think of is how easy it would be to pull off—she wouldn't even need a disguise. "Stop in one of the gift shops," Eddie continues casually, "pick out some goulashes—"

"It's 'galosh'—"

"—and come back to me with whatever you find. Maybe it'll be worth more than whatever this new evidence is. You know that's how Terry did it, right?" he asks. "He's like a secret agent," Eddie says amorously and Joycie laughs.

"What?" he demands.

"Sounds like you have a man-crush."

"Oh please, like you're any better," Eddie says and then poorly mimics her voice. "Hey Spart! Oh Spart, I love you! Come lay in my lap, Spart—Eddowes doesn't even want that thing in here."

"*Thing?*"

"And hey, afterwards, maybe we'll see your picture up on the wall."

Joycie doesn't bother telling him that her picture *is* up on the wall—with Eddie's. In fact, there were only two officers standing between them on the day that the current group photo of the precinct was taken. Still, she feels that there are far too many men in all those nicely framed pictures around the station and not nearly enough women.

"I'm going to head over to Charlie's," Eddie says, pulling the gym shoes on that he retrieved from his locker.

"You're a glutton for punishment."

"Not that Charlie's."

CHAPTER III:
Johnny Cocheroo

E D D I E P A R K S I N T H E L O T outside of Good Time Charlie's. It feels strange for him to be here at this time, but even stranger knowing that Mel Nestor won't be inside waiting. He grabs a small flat tin from his cup holder, removes a toothpick and stares at it for a long time before sliding it between his lips…

* * *

T H E F I R S T T I M E that Eddie had ever been to Good Time Charlie's strip club occurred one night after having dinner at the Volker's. Terry had been raving about some sandwich place back home and gradually convinced Eddie that all the places that he's ever dined in—and up until now had no problem with—were trash. Eventually, Terry took it upon himself to experiment with making his own roast beef sandwiches to prove his point. That night was the first trial, and none of them enjoyed it. The meat tasted tough and dry and according to Terry, lacked any flavor resembling Nick's Original. They managed to finish their plates, but it was Spartacus who'd be eating like a king later.

"Where salt?" Eddie heard Terry ask as he and Hannah argued playfully in the kitchen. "Man need salt. Girl burn food."

"I didn't burn it you jerk off," Hannah said laughing. Eddie smiled and sipped his beer as she pivoted, showcasing her round pregnant belly.

Uncle Eddie, he thought.

Hannah presumed to make stabbing motions behind Terry's back, causing Eddie to chuckle some. He envied the humorous sexual chemistry that they had. They were always touching each other in some way; a gentle stroke on one's back as the other passed, a pinch on one's arm from a smart remark, and of course, the kissing. And what was odd, he didn't find it rude—the way he had when couples kissed in bars. Even Spartacus was lifted up and got his fair share of it. Eddie found that they were just genuinely affectionate people, which surprised him, given Terry's general impassive demeanor at work. It never occurred to him that it might all just be for show.

"So, let me get this straight," Eddie said as he made a sucking noise between his teeth. "The two of you have the exact same tattoo, and neither of you know what it means?"

"Eddie," Terry said, "shut up and eat the sandwich."

"I'm trying," he mumbled and sat there with his mouth open trying to pry a piece of meat out of his upper molars with his tongue.

"You're a real prince," Terry said, taking a sip of his beer.

"Here let me get you a toothpick," Hannah said apologetically as she stood up and swatted the back of Terry's head going into the kitchen.

AT THE END OF THE NIGHT, Eddie left with a strong desire for someone like Hannah. He wasn't about to change his opinions on the ludicrous tradition of marriage, or even relationships in general, but he felt a hunger for more than what Terry's charred roast beef sandwich had left him with. Not knowing where else to turn to satiate this appetite, Eddie headed towards the neon lights at Good Time Charlie's.

He sat down in one of the seats that encircle the low stage and watched girls dance and undress for an hour before deciding to pack it in. His spirits were no doubt lifted from seeing all the naked women, but there was something missing—someone else that he wanted to see. Someone that he could pinch and kiss and talk to jokingly like a caveman.

"And now, making her way to the stage," the DJ said as he changed the music to an upbeat rendition of Muddy Waters' "Hoochie Coochie Man." "Everyone make some noise for Miss Meliss!"

Eddie stopped digging at the tough piece of gristle that was still stuck in his teeth and left the toothpick hanging from the corner of his mouth as Mel Nestor ascended onto the stage. Even amidst all the catcalls and whistles and dozens of other eyes on her, she felt one set in particular above the rest. They were unlike any of the ones belonging to the men who were crumpling up dollar bills and throwing them at her feet. She spun around the chrome pole to pinpoint where the look was coming from and then she found him, sitting all alone—like a shy little boy in a police officer costume.

She stepped off the stage directly onto Eddie's seat—taking care not to stab him with her heels—and removed her corset as she knelt into his lap in one fluid motion. Grabbing the back of his head, she bit down onto the opposite end of his toothpick and gently pulled it from his lips. After flashing him a mischievous smile, she got back up on stage with equivalent grace and continued dancing as the toothpick poked out from between her teeth…

* * *

THE HALF NAKED girls all welcome Eddie inside warmly with tears in their eyes. They loved Mel Nestor like a sister and know how much she adored Eddie.

"Any out-of-towners come in lately?" Eddie asks. "Or anyone remember seeing her with someone who didn't fit in?" They all shake their heads and wipe wet mascara from their cheeks. Eddie sighs and looks over to the small stage where he first saw Mel dance and rolls the toothpick between his teeth with his tongue. "How about a van—anyone see a white van in the lot?"

"What's with the kicks, Ed?" one of them asks sniffling and Eddie looks down to his sneakers and blushes. He opens his mouth to say something, but nothing comes out.

WHILE EDDIE TALKS with the girls at Charlie's, Terry is driving aimlessly in circles as he tries to clear his head. The memory of Roy Lindskog's funeral relentlessly attacks him and he keeps turning the wheel in an effort to regain his focus. After driving past the same gas station three times, he finally pulls in and parks beside the outdoor freezers. The cashier watches him curiously through the window as Terry loads up the back of his Bronco with bags of ice and then stomps through the slush to pay.

IN ADDITION to Spartacus, Hannah left some other things of hers behind when she left and Terry takes inventory of them as he dries his hands: a couple of picture frames with the three of them together, some candles, a jar of shells, a piece of driftwood—trophies from their hikes around Point Woronzof—and her books. He rests one of his cold fingers on the Bhagavad Gita, but then reconsiders and pulls out The Tibetan Book of the Dead. He walks through the kitchen, back out into the garage and stands in front of his freezer as he flips through the book until finding the passage he saw Hannah highlighting after her father died:

> "O child, that which is called
> death has arrived. Visualize
> him without substance—like
> the moon on water.
> Do not picture him with a face.
> The countless wrathful gods
> will now appear, dancing with
> crescent knives and drinking
> from skulls full of blood,
> stretching banners made from
> ribbons of human skin,
> garlanded with black serpents
> and wolf headed.
> There'll be voices from the
> mountains, of rivers flooding,
> of fires spreading. They'll teach
> with words that will sever the
> two pulsating arteries which
> induce everlasting sleep—"

"—*where the aorta bifurcates into the lower extremities*—"? Terry asks and then snaps the book closed and tosses it as he shakes the coroner's voice out of his head. He climbs the stairs to the bathroom, but at the top of the steps, he turns instead and walks towards the room at the end of the hallway—passing old holes that he punched in the wall…

* * *

"YOU NEVER TOLD ME," Hannah began as she stood in front of the mirror trying to zip up the back of her black dress on her own. "When did you start loving wolves?" Terry sat behind her on the edge of their bed putting on his only pair of dress shoes.

"What?" he asked. It wasn't her question that confused him, but the fact that she wanted to ask it an hour before her father's viewing.

"I'm just curious, that's all," she said. "I couldn't even discuss getting a dog with you—had to just bring Spartacus home with me one day—but here you are a wolf lover. My city-boy husband is regular nature-boy."

"Look," Terry sad, "just because I didn't want a dog doesn't mean I'd kill one."

"What the hell is that supposed to mean? You've had an affinity for animals all along and never expressed it?"

"I didn't have to 'start loving wolves' to not want to kill an innoce—"

"*Innocent!*" Hannah shouted.

"The wolf—"

"That wolf was standing over my father—who was having a heart attack—contemplating an easy meal."

"What would we have done, huh?" Terry asked. "Killed the wolf and then what? Ran inside and grabbed our handy-dandy defibrillator?"

"You're a coward," she said turning around to face him, her dress only half zipped.

"And what about you—coming downstairs wearing my shirt with your ass out?"

"Oh, so, I'm a whore now, is that it?"

"I didn't mean that."

"No, no, no, I'm a whore, and *that's* what killed him," she said and began crying inconsolably. He pulled her in close and pressed her against his chest while she swatted at his back with closed fists. "Get off of me!"

"I didn't mean that," he said again.
"Get off of me!"
"Let me make it right—"
But words can't be taken back.
..spells cannot be unsung...

* * *

CHAPTER IV:
Split a Piece of Rotting Wood

TERRY TOSSES AND TURNS for the first few hours after lying down with confusing dreams that bleed into reality until he just lies in bed staring at the ceiling. He tries not to think about Hannah, or the ice—or wolves—but every time he manages to do so, he realizes he's dreaming and wakes up again.

The raid on the Lepus Estate isn't scheduled until 6:00am, but by 2:30, Terry is already awake—partially, at least. He half dreams—half hallucinates—in a puzzling hypnagogic state right on the border of consciousness. He watches himself get dressed and is quite surprised when he turns the light on in the bathroom around 3:15 that he's still in his underwear. Come 4:00am, Terry is fully over trying to go back to sleep for the last half-hour before his alarm clock is scheduled to go off with the shrill sounds of seagulls fighting over beach trash.

He's not exactly sure why he chose that sound, but it's infinitely better to wake up to than the severe ringing of bells and chimes or other obnoxious preprogrammed alarms which only raid his dream state, rather than coax him out of it. It was Hannah's idea. She herself opted for the sound of someone splitting wood; the *whoosh* of the ax as it falls through the air— the swift *crack* as the log divides—and the two *thuds* of the pieces falling into piles.

Whoosh—crack—thud, thud.

211

"No dream is fit to end until the making of a fire," she told him.

Whoosh—crack—

At one point, it actually worked. Terry would wake up feeling refreshed after the squawks gradually grew louder and more numerous until finally, he was nudged over that thin line between sleeping and waking. Unlike being jerked out of sleep from a car alarm blaring in the middle of the night or the screaming of a fox killing an alley cat, the strange appearance of a flock of beach birds flying into his dream would cause him to question reality until his eyes opened naturally.

But not anymore.

Terry is awake when the gulls begin their ranting and raving this morning, but he hardly hears them. He's groggy and listless and not at all prepared to go kick down any of Émile's trap doors.

"Oh, so, I'm a whore—"

He has to clear his mind.

"Get off of me!"

He needs to be sharp as a tack.

TERRY ROLLS OUT OF BED and goes to the garage in the dark. He stares down at the freezer he bought to impress Roy Lindskog. The cold air assures him that he's awake now and he knows that the fresh bags of ice within the freezer are the only things that can help silence his troubled mind, but there's no time. He has to go hunt a man madder than he.

He exhales forcefully, flips open the lid to the freezer and stares inside. For a moment, the bags of ice look like hills—the rising flow of fog like clouds—as if he were up in the mountains looking down.

THE SOUND of a Cessna's propeller tears through the air as it flies low in the dark morning sky above the Lepus Estate. Two BBPD cruisers are patrolling a half mile radius around the property when Terry and Eddie arrive. They pull up beside the winding driveway and park in front of a tan Mustang that the two Special Agents are sitting in with the heat blasting.

"Ter?" Eddie asks, reaching over and lowering the volume knob on the radio. "Are you ready?" he asks, looking at the dark circles under Terry's eyes.

Whoosh—crack—thud, thud.

Whoosh—crack—

"Come on," Terry says, unbuckling his seatbelt, "let's go."

♪ ...I gave up everything I had
I moved away to a new foreign land, you know that
Family's so important to the dream, hey
If you wanna change the world
You first got to change your scene
You come to see just how we do
Well, Mr. Ryan I sure can assure you that everybody here is happy as can be
We gonna stick around and
Ain't never gonna leave

Father knows what's best for us
Father knows what's best for me
In all the days since I've been born never heard a man talk like this before
We're all gonna go,
don't you know?
You can come too... ♪

CHAPTER V:
INCLUSIVE CASE REPORT

Bloodrun Borough Police Department
1541 Brigantine Boulevard
Bloodrun, Alaska 99287
(907) 317 3349

Case Number
BBPD129127-824

Type of Incident: Homicide
Location of Incident: 456 Hilldrum Road
Bloodrun, AK 99287
Supervisor Review: BBPD Chief of Police Derrick Eddowes

Narrative Supplemental 1):
Officer Edward Koyukuk

At 6:02am on Friday January 14th, BBPD arrived at the Lepus Estate for the arrest of Émile Lepus. After a few moments of knocking, Detective Terrance Volker and I gained entry through the "front door" of the residence by the suspect's girlfriend, Holly Lo (age 24).

Before continuing, I think it's worth noting here how disorienting this house was upon our arrival. The inside is even more oddly constructed than its exterior. The first room that we entered had a circular dropdown floor with a spiral staircase in the middle which hung from steel grated rafters above us. Encircling the floor were many strange sculptures, most of which resembled medieval torture devices. Once we began the search, we found many doors that led nowhere, dark hallways that went in circles and mirrored walls that further mislead us.

While Detective Volker and I were taking in our surroundings, Holly informed us that she had just woken up when she heard us knocking and was unsure of Émile's exact whereabouts. She went on to say that he was ordinarily sleeping at this time, but since he wasn't in bed, then he was most likely just getting something from his storage unit and would be back soon.

Chief Eddowes then directed Officer Eric Wertman to head over to the storage center, in case it was possible to intercept Lepus at his unit and avoid a vehicular pursuit. It was right around this time that Holly realized that Émile's van and Charger were still parked in the garage.

At this point, it was vital that the entire property be searched immediately to detain the suspect as we assumed that he must still be nearby. Detective Rudd Hasson and Officer Paul Peery flanked both sides of the house from the outside to block off any possible points of escape while Detective Volker and I began to sweep the interior.

Detective Volker was announcing that we had obtained a warrant for Émile's arrest and for him and anyone else to come out unarmed when we heard screaming from the other side of the house. We located the source of the cries to be coming from another one of the residents, Audrey Wiland, (age 19). The girl apparently woke up and discovered an enormous puddle of blood smeared across the floor towards a storm door, as if a body had been dragged outside. We waited for Hasson and Peery to reach the back of the house and confirm via their radios that the blood trail continued outside and that the yard was clear before exiting.

By then, Audrey's scream had woken up more of the residents, which caused Officer Peery and I to fall behind and ensure that they were safely detained while Detectives Volker and Hasson pursued the blood trail which led into the woods behind the house.

Narrative Supplemental 2):
Detective Terrance Volker

Upon the discovery of the blood and the hysterics of the emerging residents, I made the order for both Officers Koyukuk and Peery to standby and maintain control. Detective Hasson and I then followed the blood into the woods with our flashlights after radioing for a block-off of Hilldrum Road and the numerous trails that went beyond the property line. It wasn't long after that when we heard dogs up ahead through the trees.

At first, it was just whimpering, but as we came nearer it turned to growls. Once we were close enough to shine our lights on them, the two dogs began barking wildly at us. Behind them, we could see the end of the blood trail where a body was lying in the snow. The dogs appeared to be guarding it as our approach coincided with their increasing hostility towards us.

Hasson then released one of his hands from his pistol to check in on Eddie and Paul with his radio and get someone out there with tranquilizers. After waiting a moment with no reply, he tried again. It was on this second attempt when an incoming signal interfered with static and he quickly released the call button to catch as much of it as possible but,

"—the girl," was all we were able to hear Officer Koyukuk say. Hasson then stayed off the short waves in case Eddie tried again and a moment later, his voice came back through, but far more frantic:

"Ter, the girlfriend is going nuts—" but he was cut short by the sound of another scream and then the radio abruptly went silent. This caused one of the dogs to lunge for Detective Hasson and he quickly fired a shot off at it but missed and unintentionally hit the one behind it. I was then able to take my aim away from the dead dog and shoot down the one attacking Hasson.

Narrative Supplemental 3):
Officer Paul Peery

Everything was going fine at first. After we found out that the cars were still there, Officer Wertman waited with Émile's girlfriend on the other side of the house while Eddie and I watched over the girl who found the blood. As he tried to console her,

I was able to keep an eye out for the other tenants who were now rising to all the commotion. Talon Warth (age 19) entered the room next, and he rushed over to join Eddie in calming the crying girl.

The strange layout of the room was making me feel vulnerable. There were doors all around us that could open at any minute to an assailant. After Talon took over calming Audrey, Eddie suggested that I move the two of them into the room with the others while Eddie secured the blood room.

Of course, as soon as Eddie said this, one of the doors swung open and an irritated hung-over man, Thomas O'Toole (age 53), burst into the room and shouted, "What's going on you f****** wankers?" and then vomited at the sight of the blood. It wasn't until we were trying to usher everyone out that we began to lose control.

With our attentions focused on O'Toole, Émile's girlfriend Holly rushed in behind us and began going crazy. She kept yelling, "Whose blood is that?" and "Where's Émile?" over and over as we tried to escort her and the others out of the room. That was when we heard Rudd over the radio. Eddie attempted to copy back that we were having a problem when Holly spotted Émile's empty wheelchair in the corner and went berserk. "If Émile's not in his chair then where the f*** is he!?" she started shouting hysterically. I remember trying to get her back into the main room with the giant chessboard floor when we heard the two gunshots go off outside.

Eddie was able to restrain Holly in a bear-hug and was trying to get cuffs on her while I tried to subdue Audrey. Talon then became enraged, and a struggle broke out between us when I heard the third gunshot. I didn't realize anyone was dead until the feds ran in and pulled Talon off from choking me.

Narrative Supplemental 4):
Officer Eric Wertman

I knew something wasn't right from the moment Holly realized that both of Émile's cars were still in the garage. I instructed her to sit down while Detective Volker and Officer Koyukuk went to investigate the source of the scream and she complied without protest. Admittedly, my attention was pulled in other directions once I felt that the girl didn't pose a threat.

There were boxes of junk everywhere, random tents set up in the few clear spaces and all sorts of streetlights and things hanging from the ceiling to bump your head on. My eyes diverted up the spiral staircase and I was right about to ask her how Émile could get up there when I heard a door slam behind me. Luckily, she didn't lock it and I was able to pursue her into the blood room. By the time I caught up with her, Eddie was already attempting to cuff her. Talon and Peery were in a wrestling match while Audrey and the drunk carpenter were staggering around getting in the way of everyone in the narrow hallway.

Once Holly was handcuffed, I went to grab the intoxicated man while Eddie assisted Peery with Talon. The three of them were tangled up in the foyer fighting over Peery's gun when Peery regained control. He raised his gun to Talon right as Koyukuk got knocked to the ground in the scuffle. As Officer Koyukuk fell, he reached out to brace his fall and inadvertently grabbed onto the lever of one of Émile's sculptures. This released the blade of a large guillotine-looking device that Peery was standing too close to and it hit the tip of his pistol as it made its way down towards a log. The gun fired as it was knocked out of trajectory and struck Audrey Wiland in the forehead. She was killed instantly as two halves of wood dropped perfectly through the holes made in the floor leading into the furnace room below.

Narrative Supplemental 5):
Detective Rudd Hasson

Once the two dogs (later identified as B.K. "Billy the Kid" and J.J. "Jesse James") were subdued, Volker and I were able to examine the dead body. We quickly determined the identity of the victim to be the suspect that we were there to arrest; Émile Lepus (age 72). We believe that Lepus was attacked in the house with one of his tools, probably a wrench or a pipe, dragged out of his chair through the snow and then cut in half outside.

"Look at all of this blood," I remember saying out of shock from seeing so much of it this time when the others had none.

"This isn't right," Terry added. "His head's bashed in, his clothes are still on… And that wound—"

As we stood there taking all of this in, I was about to radio back to the house and check in with Eddie and Paul when a gunshot rang out from the direction of the house. Volker and I then navigated our way back through the trees with the trail of blood that guided us out. I couldn't get a response on the radio and by the time we returned, the FBI was already escorting Talon away in handcuffs. It was too late.

CHAPTER VI:
3

"NOT ONLY THAT," Francis Helduser says after Terry handed him one of Sheri's photographs of the red stained snow where Émile's body was found. "This bisection was done savagely. The previous two had identical uniform cuts all the way through them that were made in single attempts, whereas this one didn't... *take* on the first try," Helduser says and squints as he looks at all the saw marks across Émile's stomach. "He must've used something manual this time."

"Like a hacksaw?" Terry asks.

"No, not quite," Helduser says looking up from the jagged wound. "These look more like the marks that are made by some type of backpacking saw—hikers carry them in case a tree blocks their path—handy for firewood too. They're lightweight and can be coiled up to fit in a pocket. Essentially, they're just bladed chains with handles on either end."

For the first time, Terry can see a hint of empathy in the stoic pathologist's eyes as he points to the streaks of torn flesh across Émile's torso—failed attempts at keeping the serrated edge straight. Terry already saw them when the body was zipped up in black plastic and he looks away.

"We were able to pull a partial footprint off the back of Émile's sweater, it appears to be a boot—somewhere around a size 10 or 11—but the melted snow and blood have obscured any of the patterns we'd need to track the brand. If I'm right about the backpacker chain, I suspect the killer pinned Émile down with their foot while pulling the chain upwards—back and forth—the same way you'd cut a branch."

"We also found a hair," the assistant speaks up as Terry shakes his head in disgust. "Blonde—looks bleached—you can see the root is darker than the tip," she says holding up a plastic bag with a shimmering wire in it. "It'll take a few days for us to get the results back on it though."

"It's all too different, right?" Terry asks. "No stripping, no gasoline. Leaving hairs and prints behind. I mean… do you think it's the same guy?"

"I don't know, Ter, that's not really for us to say. The variations here could certainly indicate that this was done by someone else, but… it's hard to imagine more than one person being this evil."

"Maybe Émile's wheelchair just complicated the abduction part," the assistant chirps again and Terry considers it for a moment.

"Plus, if the same killer *is* doing house calls now," Helduser says, "he'd need to be quiet. And spry."

The three of them stand there silently in the cold sterile autopsy room wondering which scenario is worse until Helduser speaks again.

"Also, the girl had a cut across one of her cheeks—I'd say about two or three days old," he says as he guides Terry away from Émile's dead body. "It's extremely clean, must've been from a razorblade or a piece of glass."

S P E C I A L A G E N T S Bressi and Liam are collecting formal statements from the remaining Card House residents in the interrogation room while Terry, Eddowes and Hasson stand watching on the other side of the one-way mirror. Of the seven still alive, only two are willing to talk: Cameron Heckert and the Irish carpenter, Thomas O'Toole—who appears to still be quite intoxicated.

"It's a fockin' werewolf—I know it!" Thomas exclaims in thick Munster brogue. "I knew it when I read about it in d'papers.

I thought it may've even been Jesse at first, that's why I was always good to 'at one. But I suppose if he was, he would'a turned back into a man after you shot him."

"Thomas, maybe it would be a good idea to postpone this discussion until later, when you're feeling—"

"'At's how it goes in d'stories, y'know? Cursed rivers and upright wolves. The Nile. The Ganges. Ol' Black Shuck's back."

"Is the Ganges cursed?" Bressi asks and Liam glares at him for entertaining the man.

"Jus' like d'Bloodrun. It happens all over—Ireland too. That's how the Cuyahoga caught on fire—how else could that be without the hand of the devil?"

"The Cuyahoga River caught on fire because of pollution," Liam says, attempting to avoid going down this road any further.

"Words," O'Toole contends, as though presenting an unassailable argument. "You don't know about The People *Wit'out* Words, do ya? I don't know how the story goes here, but in Leinster it goes like this—"

"Thomas—"

"Cormac mac Airt, of the first people—The People Wit'out Words—learned to *speak* from the wolves. Their river was The Shannon. But now—with words—damned if they all didn't go about cursin' the land into famine. The Shannon dried up and not'in but the wolves remained. Bloody bastard of a mess our words make, don't they?" The man's accent and drunk slurring irritates Bressi, but it's the blaming of Ireland's famines on talking wolves that does it for Liam.

"So, what happened—did the people eat the wolves?" Liam asks, already guessing the ending to the drunk man's tale.

"That's right—oh, man! But when the spirit of the wolves returned, *they* ate the men. Émile seen'em too. We call'em '*Barghests*.' They loved hanging 'round his bullshit—all those gallows and gibbets, y'know? The magpies too."

"So, you and Émile saw *Barghests* in the Lepus Estate?" Bressi asks.

"What?" the hungover man asks. "You can't *see* a Barghest, it could be anyone—could be him," Thomas says and looks to Liam and flashes his eyebrows. "After the wolf kills ya, it uses your body as it sees fit—*that's* a Barghest. We only saw the wolves."

"*Spirt* wolves," Liam jumps in, hoping that the man will see the absurdity.

"Aye. They loved Émile's sculptures—must remind'em of all the vengeance they're here to take on us. That's why the people were without words—'at's why your man there said a wise man would bite his tongue or what 'ad he?" Thomas asks, pointing to their stack of papers after spotting a copy of The Crests' *Bloodrun Butcher* article. He then sits back in his chair looking particularly satisfied.

"Émile wasn't eaten by a wolf, Thomas," Liam says. "He was cut in half with a chainsaw."

"More words," he replies. "A wolf in a man's hide—with a man's *words*—can figure out many things. They're a crafty lot—wolves. You boys must've never raised chickens. More cunning than a fox, more vicious than a—"

"Do you really get wolves up here?" Bressi asks as he throws Thomas O'Toole's file down on the desk in the other room. "Most we ever get down in Anchorage are a few moose."

"From time to time," Terry says.

"Just shoot it!"
"—coward—"
"Get off of me!"
"Get off—"

"CAMERON, I'm Special Agent Zach Bressi and this is my partner, Special Agent Liam Hollingsworth, we're with the FBI. We'd like to ask you a little about your relationship with the deceased. We understand that you're close friends with Holly Lo, Émile's girlfriend, is that correct?"

"Yes," she says, but then hesitates, "I mean, we live together."

"Can you tell us a little about their relationship?"

"I don't know what to say, I mean, they fought sometimes—but doesn't everybody?"

"Did he ever—" Bressi pauses and reconsiders his words, "was he ever violent with her?"

"He was *paralyzed*," she answers, not picking up on the nuance of Bressi's phrasing.

"Yes," he agrees, "but yet, somewhere in these files we have a police report that says he was responsible for an incident that ended with her needing stitches."

"That was an accident," she says, trying not to betray her friend.

"Were you there when it happened?"

"I mean… I was *there*."

"Did you *see* it happen?" Liam asks.

"No, but—"

"Cameron, we're only trying to help," Liam says. "Émile is dead now; you don't have to protect her anymore." Cameron's eyes jump back and forth between the two agents nervously. "Was he ever violent with you or anyone else?"

"Why are you asking me about *Émile*?—he didn't saw himself in half! That psycho *butcher* killed him—you should be out there trying to find him!"

"That's exactly why we need to ask you about Émile," Bressi says calmly. "We have to know why the killer chose him so we can stop him from doing it again."

"Is he going to come back for the rest of us?" the girl asks, her anger quickly turning to terror and then tears.

"You're safe, Cameron," Liam says. "There's no reason to suspect that you're in any danger. He's never returned for any of his victims' relatives or acquaintances before. These two other murders were completely isolated incidences, but they're not random. If Émile's killer wanted anyone else from Card House dead, he would've done it already. Trust me, Cam, the whole Lepus Estate is going to be under surveillance until we catch him—it'll be impossible for anyone to harm you now. Agent Bressi and I study this type of thing and we've caught men like him before, but in order for us to do that, we had to kno—"

"One time," she stops abruptly and wipes her face. "I mean, I don't think he would've actually tried to hit me," she feels silly explaining how easy it would be to simply back away from his chair. "He just wanted me to shut up—like a threat."

"I see. And what were the circumstances that lead to this threat?"

"He," she pauses to collect herself. "He was telling Talon to hit the dogs."

"To *hit* the dogs?" Bressi asks.

"Yeah—Jesse and BK—they were wild. He would've hit them himself if he could. I mean, he threw stuff at them and yelled at them all the time. I tried to tell him how to train them—it's what I did for work before I moved into that hell house. Dogs learn more from positive reinforcement than a club. They lived in constant fear of him and as a result, he was the only one that could control them. It's ironic," she says with a sad smile. "After enough abuse, they actually started to guard him and were hostile to the rest of us. It was impossible for us to work like that. They were always snarling at our necks. So, I told him to stop, and he raised his hand to me and said, 'Shut up, dog killer, or you're next.'"

"Why would he call you a 'dog killer'?" Liam asks.

The girl sighs deeply and shakes the term "operant conditioning" out of her mind, unaware that these two men have studied behavioral science at Quantico.

"To make himself feel better," she says and wipes her eyes again before explaining. "Positive reinforcement training was failing certain dogs, which is why I eventually quit—but I'd never hit one! The only valid criticism against all the force-free dog trainers is that dogs with certain behavioral issues—aggression, mostly—can get left behind. All we can do in those cases is remove the stimulus, but that's no excuse to beat them… Émile loved to point out the recent correlation between force-free dog training and the increase of unwanted dogs in shelters—which, he assumed meant more euthanasia."

"I see," Liam says. "So, what did Talon do?"

Cameron swallows hard and blinks her welling eyes before answering, causing more tears to roll down her cheeks.

"...He hit them."

B R E S S I A N D L I A M deliberately wait an hour before reentering the interrogation room. They believe that forcing Talon to sit there all alone with nothing but his own thoughts will help stress the boy out and make him more likely to confess. Meanwhile, it gives Sheri and the others some more time to find a bloody wrench or saw in the woods.

Liam closes the door behind Bressi and slides a photograph of the maroon boot print that was left on Émile's sweater across the table. It enters Talon's line of sight, which remains fixed on one spot, but he shows no sign of seeing it. Beside it, Agent Bressi places a plastic baggie containing the strand of blonde hair.

"Sorry about the wait," Liam says as he makes his way around the table with his partner. "That O'Toole fellow is a real character, isn't he? What a chatterbox—but I'm sure you've heard all about his wolf stories, huh?" Talon blinks but makes no acknowledgment.

"Say, would you mind just telling us what size shoe you wear?" Bressi asks. "And we can send you on your way."

"W E L L, he's smart enough not to say anything, but not smart enough to ask for a lawyer. We can keep pressing him until he realizes that or start processing him," Liam says.

"I say we charge him right now. No more bullshit," Bressi says.

"For Lepus or for everything?" Eddowes asks.

"For everything," Bressi says. "Let's put a fire under his ass. It'll get him to at least confess to Émile."

"And what if the conviction goes through and the real killer skips town?" Terry asks. "You think he's going to stop just because we do?"

"Terry," Liam says before Eddowes can interject. "We don't know that Talon *isn't* the real killer yet. If we threaten him with this type of sentence, he could spill on the whole thing. We have the footprint, we have a motive—and that hair *must* be his—I haven't seen anyone rock a Slim Shady peroxide bleaching in twenty years."

"Chief, we're wasting our time here," Terry says disregarding the agents. "He probably killed Lepus—I don't doubt that—but not the girls. He heard about the murders from the paper and thought he could replicate it, but we didn't release enough information for anyone to do that."

"What do you propose then, *Acid Cop*?" Bressi asks.

"Let me talk to him," Terry says, and Eddowes rolls his eyes.

"I don't think so—I don't need you going in there and getting into a fight with this kid over whatever happened. We have *something* here and this town needs a win right now. If that kid walks because you forced him into a confess—"

"I'm not going to force him to do anything; I just want to talk to him—for myself. If I get out of line, you're right here on the side of the glass. Please, sir, let me try."

"*If* I let you go in there and you come out with nothing, I don't want to hear a word. You put your badge on my desk and stay home until this is over. Do you understand me?"

"T H O S E T W O S U I T S," Terry says nodding to the window, "they want to pin this whole thing on you—and they're gonna." Talon continues his silence and stares down at his handcuffs. "I can help you if you talk to me, Talon, but the longer you wait, the worse it's going to be. We know that you did Émile, just tell me why."

No response.

"Do you know what the difference is between first and second-degree murder? Maybe ten or fifteen years and life in prison. You're still young, Talon. Do you really want to spend the rest of your life behind bars? I'm talking about the Anvil here; maximum security prison—no more juvenile delinquent halls."

Talon takes a deep breath but continues staring down without saying a word.

"What did he do to you? I know that Émile was a bastard, believe me—I wanted to bash his head in myself the other day. A jury will see that he could inflict more than just verbal abuse on you guys from that incident with his girlfriend. You could even make a case that you bludgeoned him out of self-defense and then panicked and tried to make it look like it was this psycho were after. That's what happened, isn't it?"

Don't force him, Terry catches himself and quickly glances over to the one-way mirror.

"Whoever this guy is has an opportunity now to disappear and have you take the fall for killing those girls. I'm not trying to scare you, Talon, I want to help you. I want to catch the son of a bitch who *really* did this. I want justice for what he did to them, but if he leaves and they lock you up instead… you're never going to get out."

When Terry mentions the other victims, he notices Talon start to become uncomfortable. His hands tighten into fists—his knee starts bouncing.

Audrey and Cameron, Terry says to himself and thinks back to when he and Eddie were walking up Émile's driveway and encountered two pot smoking teenagers.

Young and pretty.

Just like Paige and Mellisa.

"It wasn't anything he did to you, was it?" Terry asks. "You're a tough kid—you could handle the old man's cruelty. It was the girls. You were their protector." Talon finally looks up into Terry's eyes and his eerily familiar face reminds Terry again of the boy with no shoes.

"But it was more than that," Terry goes on as the pool of blood in the Card House kitchen quickly materializes in his mind. As he focuses, Talon's eyes begin to resemble more than just the war painted eyes of the boy that he shot long ago—they're the same eyes that Terry sees in the mirror everyday—brokenhearted.

"What did he do to her, Talon?" Terry asks, but the boy only stares back at him angrily, continuing to not speak. Terry looks back to the window again, this time where he imagines

Chief Eddowes is standing and wonders how much longer he has before they pull him out.

"Which one was it?" Terry asks, shifting back to Talon. "It was Émile's girlfriend, wasn't it? That must've really bothered you—seeing that old toad with such a pretty, young girl. What's her name—Holly, right? You fell in love with her and he hurt her again, didn't he? I can see it—*that's* why you killed him; so the two of you could be togeth—"

"She wasn't his fucking girlfriend!" Talon roars. For one short-lived moment, Terry feels triumphant until he sees Talon choking back tears.

"It's extremely clean, must've been from a razorblade or—"

A piece of glass.

"It was Audrey," Terry whispers as he closes his eyes in anguish over the BBPD-issued .38 caliber pistol that fired through her forehead. Talon lifts his cuffed hands up to his face to wipe away the tears, snorts and then lowers his wrists to his lap.

CHAPTER VII:
Descenntial

S T E P H E N J A M E S A L B O T takes his first sober step onto the frozen ground of Bloodrun, Alaska in ten years. He exits off a small blue Cessna that glided its way down from Nome.

"You're a free man now," the pilot says and considers giving Albot an encouraging pat on the back, but instead just says, "good luck."

Albot's jacket is still as grimy as it was on the day that he was arrested, but his breath fogs without its customary mordant stench of Old Crow and Rich & Rare. The ten years of imprisonment at Anvil Mountain Correctional Center had forced him into sobriety, but now he's unbound.

T H E F U L L S E N D S T E V E of so long ago was a resolutely self-affirmed alcoholic, but this man, Stephen James Albot, returns a corrected felon. As one would expect, it was no small task getting the fermented old beast on board though. It's the only thing in Albot's entire life that he ever fought against, so, it was fierce—but untrained. All of his petty defiance was utterly useless in the end—when the steel cell doors were shut. The only two options he had were to surrender or thrash. So, Albot thrashed.

He got through the mentally distressing stage fairly quickly; only a few nights of screaming and pacing—with the aid of nightsticks and boots, of course. It was hopeless to do otherwise. The tricky part with Albot was that his reckless abuse of alcohol required his body to be rehabilitated from its physical dependence first.

At the time of his arrest, the withdrawal in store for him was so severe that it would've killed him if medical intervention wasn't made. Before being transferred to his tiny prison cell in the Anvil, Albot spent two weeks handcuffed to a hospital bed in Bloodrun's Fitz-Mercy hospital detoxing.

N O O N E I S W A I T I N G for Albot at the lonely airstrip, and he reckons he deserves that. No one is there to help support the addict stay sober. Nobody cares.

The high school kids that Albot used to buy beer for have all grown up and moved on. Many of them are busy pursuing careers and starting families. The only time that Albot ever crosses any of their minds now is when they meet up for a few drinks at the Rod & Reel and occasionally reminisce about their youthful misadventures in the woods with that *Canadian in a red hat* whom they dubbed "Fullsend Steve."

Albot has no identification, no money, no one to call and nowhere to go. He does, however, know the layout of the town better than anyone; he's had to walk across it more times than he can count. He assumes that it must've changed a bit, perhaps some new condos or a restaurant—even a bar. But things couldn't have changed that much. They never do. At least, not for long. This is his home, and he is their fool.

So, he begins to walk.

A L B O T ' S C O U S I N J A C K isn't home when he finally reaches Penland Trailer Park. It's a long hike from the airstrip, but he made it in record time. Without alcohol swirling in his blood, Albot feels what it's like to be cold again and hustled ass. No more pit stops. No more pissing in the woods or napping in the snow or yelling at people across the street.

He knows how unlikely it is that Jack will be happy to see him, but his fingers have gone numb and his socks are wet. He foolishly envisions a long-awaited reunion between them as he climbs the first step up to Jack's trailer. He tells himself that they'll embrace, reconcile their differences and exchange stories about how prison saved their lives. He pictures all of this as he ascends the top step to Jack's front door and tests the knob with his shivering hand.

Unlocked.

CHAPTER VIII:
The Word Becomes Flesh

T H E   I N T E R I O R is much the same as Albot remembers, granted, he only has a few hazy memories of it—mostly from the night that Jack quite literally kicked his ass out. The musty smell particularly helps bring back some lost splices and he recalls the crunch of his tailbone.

He walks into the kitchen puffing hot air into his cupped hands and sees a polaroid of Jack's old pit bull taped to the refrigerator.

"Mm... Momo," he says, trying to remember the dog's name. Scribbled on the back in Jack's handwriting reads: "Mumbler, 1997."

I N S I D E   J A C K ' S   B E D R O O M, Albot notices a familiar looking book on the dresser. He rubs his cold hands together as he stares at it and when the feeling returns to his fingertips, he picks it up to confirm his suspicion.

Under the cover, he finds a long list of crossed out dates and is certain now which book it is. It's the bible that he once used to mark and swear his sobriety in to his loved ones. He's not sure how Jack ended up with it, but he assumes that he must've brought it over once—pleading for something—his trademark move, besides pissing on the rug. Every date marks a different manipulation for something and never an honest attempt to get clean:

Forgiveness.
Another chance.
Money.
A ride.
A place to crash.
More money.
One more chance.
Always a lie.
Always deceit.

Always to get something from someone so he could sneak a drink when they weren't looking.

But all that's to end, starting today. Albot finds a pen in Jack's squalid trailer and writes today's date at the bottom of the list of broken promises; the first one that he intends to keep. He smiles, but before returning the bible to its place, Albot notices handwriting bleeding through from the other side of the first page. He peels the onionskin-like paper over and reads:

> *"In the beginning there was only the Word, and the Word was God. Place this word in your soul and use no other words. It is sharper than any blade, slicing to the division of your marrow. He who knows the secret of words will receive that which he desires, for by your words I will justify thee—by your words you are condemned."*

Don't remember writing that, Albot thinks, although this doesn't surprise him. The only thing strange about it to him is that it isn't one of the bible verses that he picked up in group. Without giving it anymore thought, Albot snaps the leather shut and slides it back on top of Jack's dresser.

T A L O N W A R T H is being moved into a holding cell for the murder of Émile Lepus when Jack Albot turns his car into the gravel parking spot beside his trailer. Inside, Albot is lounging on

Jack's couch—aimlessly flipping through channels on the TV that Jack bought to replace the one that his cousin infamously destroyed and consequently, received a steel toe boot in the coccyx for. Albot first resolved to not even look at it—fearing that he'd end up breaking this one too—but the boredom that he faced alone was too much to bear.

He did try tidying up Jack's trailer, even took out the trash and boiled some hotdogs and mac n' cheese for them, but eventually, there was nothing left to do but wait. Somehow it was easier in the pen—he could always find another inmate to assault with his ramblings about famous actors and professional athletes who were incarcerated for crimes similar as theirs.

J A C K slams his car door shut and makes it halfway up the driveway when Albot flings open the front door.

"Jacky!" he shouts.

"Steve? What the fuck are you doing here?"

"I—I got out," Albot stammers.

"You're supposed to be at the airstrip," Jack says irritably. This stuns Albot for a second and he doesn't know what to say.

"You—?"

"I took off work to pick your deadbeat ass up and sat there all-fucking-day waiting for you like an asshole."

"Jacky," Albot blubbers as he descends the steps, raising his arms up for a hug.

"Ah, come the fuck on," Jack begrudges as Albot closes his arms around him. "You may be a no-good lying drunk and I hate your fucking guts, but I know you only got mixed up in that acid murder bullshit because you're an idiot." Albot laughs through his tears as he lets go, but Jack pulls him back. "Plus," he says, "you're still blood."

"Y O U ' R E G O I N G T O R E I M B U R S E M E now for that TV too," Jack says when he's finally able to get a word in between Albot's nonsense and spoonfuls of macaroni.

"You don't have to worry about that, Jacky," Albot says from across the card table that the two cousins are dining on. "Tomorrow, I'm going to go out and find a job and start paying you back every cent I owe you," he proclaims.

"Is that right?" Jack asks, pushing his empty plate away. "Well, you can take this when you go then," he says as he gets up and walks into his bedroom. When he returns, he's holding up one of his old jackets. "I never wear it anymore, but it's still good—doesn't smell like piss and vomit at least."

Albot smiles widely and immediately puts it on, concealing the discolored raglan that Jack also gave him with the words, "GO BACK TO CALIFORNIA" printed in big black letters across the chest.

"I gotta' be in early tomorrow for taking off today, Steve," Jack says and Albot's smile vanishes, knowing that he's about to be left alone again. "If you so much as drink a fucking drop while I'm gone, you're dead to me, y'hear me? Deader than you already are."

"Jacky, I'm telling ya—"

"Not. A fucking. Drop."

"Alright, alright," Albot moans as Jack grips his shoulder tightly before heading to his room.

CHAPTER IX:
Dry

I can sleep all day while the other boys play
I can sleep at the wheel though it's not ideal

THE TRAILER IS QUIET AND DARK except for the glow of the television, which Albot flicks through anxiously as he lies on Jack's futon. He turns the volume down low so that it doesn't wake his charitable cousin, but the faint murmur makes the returning ennui even worse. He stares up at the dancing shadows and reflections on the ceiling—unconsciously pressing the CHANNEL UP button—and prays for sleep.

Eventually, a great idea comes to him—go to the Buckaroo. Not to drink, Albot tells himself—just to check it out. To unwind. He has no money anyway and he isn't about to steal Jack's wallet again, but more importantly, he doesn't *want* to drink. He just needs to get out of the trailer. He feels like he did on his first night behind bars; restless and afraid. Caged—thrashing.

Albot knows that he can hoof it if he has to, but the thought of how quickly his fingers went numb from his previous excursion makes him wince. He's also aware that Jack's trailer is in a part of town which is notorious for being frequented by moose. Albot was never cautious about any of the various wildlife that came in to explore Bloodrun before—back when he trudged insensibly through its streets—but after drying out for ten years, the thought of getting crushed and broken beneath a 7' bull disturbs him greatly.

So, there's only one other way.

ALBOT CLOSES HIS HAND around the keys dangling on a hook by the front door and then turns back to Jack's bedroom one last time as he fully resolves to steal his cousin's car—no, borrow. He slips out into the cold and pulls the door closed as quietly as he can—looking like one of the teenagers who used to sneak out to attend his parties in the woods. He pauses for a moment before descending the steps to listen for any stirring of Jack, but there's only the soft hum of the television.

Sitting down inside of Jack's busted Plymouth, Albot closes his eyes and turns the key in the ignition.

THE SAME SMALL STAGE for open mic night sits vacant in the corner of The Buckaroo Club. New dartboards hang on the wall by the old jukeboxes where Albot often slept standing up, along with a few updated beer posters, but not much else has changed. Even the same two bartenders are working from the night when he and Terry were tripping on acid and they both look up wide-eyed as Albot steps inside.

"Holy shit!" someone yells in drunken amazement, "It's Full-throttle—back from the dead!"

"More like back from the Anvil," someone else adds and laughs.

"Okay, okay," Albot says, nodding his head acceptingly as he walks up to an empty stool.

"What'll it be, Steve?" one of the bartenders asks.

"Hey, let me buy his first drink back," a fat man who Albot had vomited on before demands in jest. "What's that shit you used to like—gasoline, right?"

"I think it was turpentine with a twist of lime," a woman across the bar cackles.

"This one's on the house," the bartender says and winks at Albot. "R&R neat, right?"

"No," Albot answers.

"Oh," the bartender says and then tries to think of another one of Albot's customary drinks. "Tall boy? Black Tooth Grin?"

"Nope. I'll just have a ginger ale, please," Albot says, inadvertently causing more laughter to burst out around him.

"I never knew you were funny," the fat man says shaking his head.

"I'm not joking," Albot asserts.

"What kind of gin do you want in it?" the bartender asks rolling her eyes.

"No gin—just the soda."

"Just soda?" she asks, this time raising a skeptical brow, almost concerned. "I said it's on the house, Steve, you don't have to go spike it with your flask."

"Yeah, or any acid—please," the woman across from him says with another cackle.

"I just want a damn soda!" Albot shouts.

"Alright, Steve, settle down—we're just messin' with ya," the bartender says and steps away to grab a glass.

CHAPTER X:
Acts 20:29

*♩ Everywhere the child went,
The little lamb was sure to go, yeah ♩*

THE PLYMOUTH'S orange tire pressure light turns on with the accompanying *bing* and Albot groans as he looks down to the dashboard. He's not even halfway through the pines back to the trailer park yet and it's begun to snow. He remembers driving past this warning light before until he tore up the rubber and destroyed the wheel.

"Fuck!" Albot yells as he surrenders to the alarm and slowly pulls over before the tire begins flapping. "Fuck—fuck—fuck—fuck—FUCK!"

The trunk pops open and a dim light shines enough for Albot to see that the donut is missing. His fingers stick to the painfully cold steel as he slams the trunk shut and shuffles around the side to search the backseat for a road flare or some tire plugs. He's too tired from this morning's venture to attempt it again and the snow is falling heavier with every passing minute—even a younger, lit up Fullsend Steve would have difficulty traversing through the buckets of snow that'll be dumping down soon.

As he rummages through all the trash in the backseat, Albot's bony fingertips make a familiar *clink* on something. His heart skips a beat as he reaches further into the balled-up napkins and soda cans and pulls out a brown paper bag containing a glass bottle—Jack's "emergency" stash.

A L B O T   S I T S   B A C K   D O W N behind the wheel and unsheathes the clear bottle from the bag like it's the blade that he'll perform *hara-kiri* on himself with. He looks at the label; Русский Стандарт—the good shit. Albot has no idea how good, but anything in a glass bottle is better than what he's used to drinking. Never in his life has he had the good shit, at least, not in a capacity that would allow him to appreciate it. He's stolen bottles of Grey Goose and Absolut from friends and family of course, but he was always too sluiced by that point to ever taste any difference from the swill that evidently put hair on his chest. Not to mention, he'd chug them like a fiend and never even attempt to savor their flavor.

Albot's mouth waters, but he slides the bottle back into the bag and rolls it between his palms.

"No," he begs out loud.

"Only a sip," the addict in him argues. *"Just to keep you warm until someone drives by."*

"I don't do that anymore."

"What's one sip?"

"One is not enough—" Albot attempts reciting what he learned from the prison AA meetings.

"You'll freeze to death out here once you burn through the rest of Jack's gas," the addict warns, and Albot looks down to the fuel gauge for the first time. It's already close to E. *"Two little sips; cold and crisp. Then we'll wait."*

"—two is too many," Albot says. It was nothing behind bars—when he didn't have a choice—but he's out now; *a free man.*

"Jack doesn't actually expect you not to drink."

"He loves me, he—"

"Nobody loves you. If they did, they wouldn't keep tempting you."

"Jacky probably just forgot about it."

243

"Forgot about a bottle of Russian Standard? Come on. He probably wants you to drink. Like you's used to."

A TEAR ROLLS DOWN one of Albot's weather battered cheeks as he dredges up a memory of him and little Jacky raiding his aunt's liquor cabinet. They'd refill her half empty bottles with flat soda and run back upstairs giggling. He remembers throwing up in their hallway. He also remembers the thick leather belt and the beating he received with it at the hands of his father.

"'Lord, train us to renounce impiety and worldly desires and live life in the present, self-controlled, upright, and sober.' Titus 2:12," Albot says aloud.

"What are you doing?" the addict in him asks—testing his sobriety for the first time in his life with nothing more to defend it with than group scripture.

"Discipline yourself, keep alert. Like a roaring lion your adversary the devil prowls around, looking for someone to devour. Resist him. Peter 5:—"

"I'm not your adversary," the addict says. *"Your father was. You and Jack just wanted to have a little fun, remember?"*

"Let us live honorably, not in reveling and drunkenness, not in debauchery and licentiousness—"

"—not in quarreling and resentment," the addict says, *"Romans 13:13."* He knows the verses better than Albot does—he's the one that always twisted them to his liking.

Albot draws the bottle back out of the paper bag and stares at it.

"You don't even believe in any of that," the addict says and tries to take the bottle from him. Albot yanks his hand away and rifles through his jacket for his ten-year chip—

"Don't look at wine when it's red," he says frantically, "when it sparkles in the cup and goes down smoothly, Proverbs 23:3—"

—but this is not his jacket.

"The priest and the prophet both reel with strong drink,"

"They're confused with wine, they stagger and stumble in judgment. Their tables are covered with vomit. They err in their laws."

"All who rely on laws are cursed. They are baptized on behalf of the dead. Galatians 3:—"

"I've gone on with no purse or shoes; I've roamed the road, but now I'm like a lamb in the midst of a wolf!"

"Outside are the wolves. Everyone who is thirsty come here inside. Revelation 22:15."

"When you die, a curse is your lot," Albot says to himself and wipes away the tears from his eyes.

"I die everyday!" the addict cheers. *"Let us drink and be merry, for tomorrow we die again!"*

Albot cracks open the seal and swings the clear bottle up to his lips, but before he can thrill in the old bittersweet sting—headlights flash on behind him.

"Fuck!" he yells, and the bottle slips from his trembling hands in dumbfounded excitement and falls to the floor. He panics as he tries to roll the bottle closer to him with his feet but ends up making it worse.

Glug-glug-glug-glug-glug—

"Shit—hey!" Albot yells as he flips open the door and springs out into the snow. He waves his hands in the air as he runs towards the vehicle and wonders if it was here the whole time just sitting in the dark, or if it just pulled up behind him without its lights on. He slows as he approaches, shielding his eyes from the high beams—and just as quickly as they came on, the bulbs go out—leaving Albot standing alone in the dark.

Glug... glug... glug...

* * *

CHAPTER XI:
The Room at the End of the Hallway

WHEN TERRY AND HANNAH got home from her father's funeral, Hannah undressed right away and took a hot shower. Terry expected to hear her crying in there since she only shed a few silent tears during the service, but there was nothing. Thanks to his tactless remark about the way that she was dressed preceding Roy Lindskog's heart attack, Hannah had most of her sobbing done before they even left the house.

"Hannah," Terry said from the other side of the bathroom door. "I'm sorry about earlier," he tried, but he'd have to dig a lot deeper than that. "What I said—I was so angry and... You know how I am with these things—death and funerals... the *afterlife*—I hate it all." He stopped and listened to the hot water raining from the showerhead and swirl down the drain. "It's important though—because it's important to you. It's just... it makes me think about fucked up shit and then I say things I don't mean." For a second, he thought about mentioning "Hindu shit" again but decided better.

"When I die, just dump me in a hole and be done with it," he said, hoping to get a smile out of her. "That reincarnation stuff—I get why you're drawn to it." The pipes creaked as Hannah turned the water off. "It's kinda like heaven, right? Another chance to see people we lost—to tell them we still love them. I wish I could see my gran again, believe me... but I don't think that's good. If we're always thinking that there's more time—or another life—we don't say the things that we should when we can. Death makes us stronger. It makes us grateful—"

"Is this supposed to be helping?" Hannah asked as she opened the door. "How can you be so cold? *Dump your body in a fucking hole—*"

"Wait a second," Terry said taking a step into the steam. "I don't want to be cold. When death rears its ugly head around like this, it gives us the opportunity to tell people what they mean to us." She looks up to him waiting. "I love you, Hannah, and I can't have you slip away over some stupid bullshit I said when I was mad. I don't believe that we'll be reborn and find each other again—this is it, and I want it all right this time. But if there *is* something on the other side, or Roy gets… born again, he knows you loved him and wouldn't want to see you grieving. I'm so sorry—I'm a fucking idiot—you know that."

She came to him wrapped in her towel and hugged him.

She'd stay now… at least, for a little longer.

"You have to stop getting so angry," she whispered.

"I know."

"The showers leaking," she added and pressed the side of her face into his chest. He smiled and rested his hand on her stomach.

"I know," he said. "I'll fix it. I always fix it…"

* * *

CHAPTER XII:
Ruined

"SLOW NIGHT?" Eddie asks as he swings open the door to the station.

"You're awfully chipper," Joycie says. "Night patrol left this," she says standing up to hand Eddie a report. "One call; stolen car."

"Stolen car, no body—love it," Eddie says grabbing the papers with his free hand.

"I'll take one of those donuts—"

But Eddie turns the corner out of the lobby and sees light shining into the dark hallway from one of the desk lamps in the office.

"Terry?" he asks, not believing his eyes as he enters the room. Terry is sitting at his desk, intent on a mess of files and photographs and doesn't acknowledge Eddie at all.

"What're you doing?" Eddie asks, flipping the switch to the overhead fluorescent bulbs which flicker and buzz before fully illuminating. He makes his way over to the desk in front of Terry's and puts down the unopened box of donuts. Terry turns a page and adjusts his neck, feeling Eddie's eyes fixed on him.

"I'm working," he finally says and flips another page without looking up.

"Yeah, I see that," Eddie says, throwing his jacket on the back of a chair. He stands there for a moment continuing to stare and then bends down and gets a good look at Terry's tired face.

"You look like shit," Eddie says and smirks. Terry just goes on reading silently:

...first two victims drained and wiped clean...
...third body found in a pool of blood...

"Tell me you didn't pull an all-nighter," Eddie says.

...Toss and turn but do not sleep
Because I will eat your drea—

"Do you even know what time it is?" Eddie asks. When he's not met with one of Terry's normal sharp remarks, he decides to approach him with the fresh box of sweets. "Donut?" he asks and holds the box under Terry's lamp, casting a shadow over his papers.

Terry sighs and looks up to the clock and says harshly: "It's 6:30—go make some coffee. The feds will be in soon."

"You don't want one?" Eddie asks and shakes the box a little.

"I want you to get the hell out of my light." Eddie frowns, closes the box and tosses it, but continues to stand there for a moment thinking.

"Oh, I see what's going on," Eddie says, changing his tone with an amusing anecdote—one that always gets Terry going. "The darkness is getting to you—it's messing with your sleep," he says. "Like that time last summer. When I took a nap after work and woke up at ten o'clock at night and thought it was ten in the morning 'cause the sun was still up." Eddie waits, hoping Terry will continue the rest of the story himself as he usually does. "Remember? I called to say I was on my way in and woke you up. Old men go to bed so early—"

"Goddamn it, Eddie!" Terry snarls and slams his desk. "*This* is getting to me!" he shouts, motioning to all the grisly photos scattered around him. After a moment of silence, he leans back and rubs his forehead.

"I'm sorry," Terry says and takes a deep breath. This isn't the rise that Eddie was hoping to get out of him. Ordinarily, Terry would finish the story with an awful impression of Eddie apologizing for being late and they'd both laugh because instead of correcting Eddie's err of time and telling him to go back to sleep, Terry only responded with "Hurry up," and hung up the phone.

"I," Terry pauses and finally looks up to his partner. "Honestly, I *haven't* been sleeping right, Eddie, but it's not the darkness. It's this case… and Hannah—"

"You got to get over this shit, Ter."

"Excuse me?"

"Hannah. It's consuming you. You act like you're the only person to ever have their heart broken and it's pathetic."

"Oh, what is this—that fucking stripper?" Terry barks getting to his feet.

"Is there a reason why I hear raised voices in my precinct before seven o'clock in the goddamn morning?" Chief Eddowes asks in an austere, but not exactly loud voice as he steps into the office.

"No, sir," the two of them answer, turning to him at full attention.

"I would think the two of you have more pressing matters to attend to than a pissing match. Terry—my office. Now."

"S I T D O W N," Eddowes says as Terry closes the door behind them. "What the hell was that out there? You're supposed to be *training* him, not getting in stupid fights while we're trying to hunt down a monster. If either of you had an ounce of grit, you'd go outside and handle it like men and get back to work."

"Sir—"

"Shut up. What the hell's been going on with you, Terry? You've been coming in later everyday, your face is hanging off—when's the last time you shaved?"

Terry considers answering but believes he'll just be told to shut up again.

"Explain this to me," Eddowes says, placing his palm on top of the Card House police report.

"You didn't even read it—" Terry manages to get out before Eddowes pounds his fist on the stack of papers.

"Do not sit there in front of me and try to act like there's something this report that can justify for what happened yesterday!"

"Chief," Terry tries, but trails off. The image of Chief Eddowes as a little boy secretly reading war novels by the glow of a flashlight under his bedcovers fills Terry's mind.

"*Terry*," Eddowes' voice commands him back.

"That house…"

"If you trail off on me one more time, I'm going to drag you outside, lock you to the fence with your own handcuffs and beat the piss out of you myself."

"I didn't sleep at all last night," Terry confesses and quickly tacks a "sir" onto the end. "I was up all night going over everything again—replaying it all in my head… These fucking kids—"

"We have *two* young girls sadistically *cut-in-half*. An innocent girl shot in the *head*, and what else now? A third victim—or an entirely new homicide?"

"I guess we'll find out today."

"You should've stayed in the house with your protégé and let Hasson and Peery pursue the blood. It was *your* duty to contain the situation and now *I'm* the one that has to clean up your mess. *I'm* the one that has to hold a press conference and mandate a curfew while I try to plead with the public that it's not the police that the people in this town need to be afraid of."

Here it comes.

"What is it, Terry?" Eddowes asks solemnly. "You were never in it for the glory, and I certainly didn't peg you for a career climber when I took you in. Do you really think that catching this guy is going to get Hannah to come running back?"

"Sir—"

"If you were thinking about anyone but yourself yesterday, this wouldn't have happened. You're lucky I don't put you on leave. If you and Hasson ever try to pull something like this again, I'll have both of your damn badges on my desk, and you'll be directing landslide traffic until your arms are too tired to jack your pricks off. Is that clear?"

"Yes," Terry says with a nod. "Anything else?"
"Would it kill you to wear a fucking tie?"

"L A B R E S U L T S came back from the letter," Liam says as he leans against Terry's desk. "Nothing surprising there, unfortunately. No prints or DNA on it whatsoever—besides the blood drop, that is." Terry clears his throat to say something, but Liam continues eagerly. "However, this next part, you're not going to believe."

"What is it?"

"The fibers from the paper hit a match from a previous case," Bressi says over Terry's shoulder. "One from Bloodrun. One of yours, actually. Do you remember a 'Stephen James Albot'?" The name triggers a vivid flash in Terry's mind: Fullsend Steve slipping from the top of the water tower and his body flipping off every rung on his way to the bottom. He remembers when he first envisioned it—high on acid—that he hoped one of the support beams would catch Albot's body like a folded piece of laundry on a clothesline and save him from splattering on the concrete below.

"Get this," Liam says, reading the recognition on Terry's face. "The paper that the killer used to write his letter on came from the same batch of paper that Albot's acid was blotted on. Now, it's possible that it's just a freak coincidence, but this is where it gets even weirder. I brought up Albot's file to find his whereabouts, and guess who just got released from the Anvil yesterday?"

Terry hunches over in his chair with his elbows on his knees and taps his fingertips together.

"He never snitched on whoever supplied him the acid?" Bressi asks.

"No," Terry says and inhales deeply as he sits back up. "The court was willing to cut his sentence in half if he'd cough up the name of the dealer. Albot claimed that he wanted to help, but he couldn't put a face to him, let alone a name."

"Like Tashira Roddy?" Liam asks.

"His story was that on the night before Bill Sullivan's murder, he met some guy at a dive who 'just gave it to him.' Vague blacked out memories were all he could provide—mostly about pushing it off on college kids down in Anchorage for some extra beer money—even bought a clunker. He was *burning* the money to stay warm when we found him. It was nothing more than *luck* that allowed us to find the kid who killed Bill from it all. The whole thing was more absurd than the murder itself."

"Ter," Liam says. "If it's at all possible that he can remember who gave him those blotters—"

"I know—we gotta find him," Terry says looking up to the agents.

"Where would he be?" Bressi asks.

"We can start by checking every dive bar in town—namely the Buckaroo," Terry says. "He has a cousin living in Penland park. Last I heard they weren't on good terms, but we oughta send a car over there too. Beyond that—"

"Wait a minute," Eddie says and bites down firmly on his toothpick. "Penland Trailer Park, yeah. I have a report—there was a car stolen from there last night," he says as he searches through the clutter of murder porn for the papers that Joycie relayed to him earlier. "Here it is: *Jack* Albot," he reads.

"That's his cousin," Terry says.

"You think he's on the run?" Liam asks.

"Hopefully not without having a drink first."

"J U N I O R!" Terry calls across the parking lot to Eddie and then whistles loudly. "Listen," he says awkwardly as Eddie comes nearer. "Your report from the other day, it was good—well put together."

"Thanks," Eddie says, already over the fight that they were about to have.

"Better than Wertman's, at least."

"Alright, don't ruin it. Apology accepted—"

"Eddie, can I ask you something serious?"

"What?"

"What made you want to be a cop?"

"Jeez… Well," Eddie says and adjusts himself. "Chicks dig the uniform, for one."

"Of course," Terry agrees flatly.

"I don't know—I got sick of working for old bald white guys. They're all sociopaths. All the worst jobs I've ever had were run by one of you bald motherfuckers. There's gotta be some kind of correlation there; old bald white guy—horrible business."

"I think you're onto something Ed—you're getting a real knack for this detective thing." Eddie grins and then thinks about the mysterious werewolf story his anaana told him as a child.

"I guess, at the end of the day, I just want to make a difference—help people—save lives—catch the ones that get away," he says. "Plus, now look: our Chief is a black man with a full head of hair—gotta be doing something right."

"Is that what were doing?" Terry asks. "Making a difference? He's still out there, Eddie. We might never catch this one."

It pains Eddie greatly to hear the man who once inspired him talk like this.

"Maybe," Eddie says, "but meanwhile, we got one, Ter—thanks to you. Those suits were gonna tie that kid up in court cases for the rest of his life before they ever connected the dots with Audrey."

"Alright, keep your pants on, kid," Terry says and turns his key in the ignition.

"I'm sorry I called Hannah a bitch, by the way."

"Wait," Terry says, going over their argument from earlier. "When did you call her a bitch?"

OFFICER WERTMAN is sent over to Penland Trailer Park to find out if Jack Albot has been in contact with his family's latest felon while Terry and Eddie begin searching the local bars.

"Steve didn't kill that old man and he sure as shit didn't kill those girls!" Jack shouts. "He was still in fucking prison when they started turning up and he's *sober* now." He feels stupid saying this last part.

"He did steal your car last night and flee though, right?" Wertman asks. Jack looks down to his rug at an old piss stain of Steve's and wonders what the hell he was thinking. "We're not saying that he killed anyone, Jack. We only want to question him about his potential involvement," Wertman continues. "Now, has your cousin ever mentioned LSD to you?"

A FTER AN UNPRODUCTIVE DISCUSSION with Jack Albot, Wertman decides to take the long way back to the station. Knowing that drunk drivers often think that they're less likely to get pulled over if they take the scenic route home through the woods, Wertman wonders if Fullsend Steve perhaps *fullsent* himself into a tree.

A mile and a half away from The Buckaroo Club, he parks his squad car on the side of the road and gets out. He crushes through the fresh snow as he walks up to the back of Jack's deserted Plymouth and scans his collection of bumper stickers:

"GOD LOVES SLUTS"
"MY OTHER RIDE IS YOUR MOM"
"ONLY GAY COPS WRITE TICKETS"
"SHOW ME YOUR PITTIES!"
"MUSIC TOO LOUD? CALL 1-800-EAT-SHI—"

"9 0 7, THIS IS UNIT 2 2, I'm on Blackrock Pike out by the pine grove. I got eyes on the missing vehicle but there's no sign of the suspect, over," Wertman says into his radio. He looks inside the car from the open driver side door and sees a bottle of Russian Standard lying in a puddle of its own contents.

"S HERI DUSTED THE INSIDE for prints—she says she found two clear sets," Hasson says. "The feds are running them through IAFIS right now, but they're most likely just Albot's and his cousin's. No real sign of foul play—just the liquor bottle and the open door."

"Looks like he got a flat," Terry says and kicks the back tire.

"So, he abandoned it?" Eddie asks. As Terry's foot bounces off the rim, he notices something protruding through the deflated rubber.

"Well, he was probably ruined for one thing," Hasson says. "Stumbles out; drops the bottle; realizes he's stuck—" but Terry cuts him off.

"Look at this," he says and yanks the object free from the tire. Terry stands up holding about three inches off the tip of an arrow.

"Jesus," Eddie says. "That's a nasty point on there—those are for bear."

"He could've just run over it—especially if he was drunk," Hasson says.

"Jack told Wertman that he got rid of all of his booze prior to Albot's release."

"Well, he obviously got some from somewhere," Hasson says motioning back to the car.

"If Fullsend Steve was drinking," Terry says, "he wouldn't leave a whole bottle behind to save his soul. Something's not right here. We need to get the dogs…"

* * *

A COP CAR SPED DOWN Brigantine Boulevard with its siren wailing. The sun was beginning to make its appearance over Bloodrun, but the red and blue roof lights of the cruiser still lit up all the small business storefronts as it passed. Tina Sullivan looked out the front window of her café and narrowed her eyes as the car headed towards Hilldrum Road.

"The Buckaroo is clear, over," a voice said into the short waves.

"Copy that," Hasson replied and turned to Terry. "Still don't think he skipped town?"

"On foot?" Terry asked without shifting his gaze from the alternating glow of red and blue snowfall. "It's coming down too heavy for even that hairy bastard to get far."

"I hope you're right. What's with the sunglasses?"

"He's still here, Rudd," Terry said and pointed where to turn.

THEY DROVE THROUGH the snow covered pines past the Lepus Estate towards Sedna's Crossing. When they arrived at the tracks, both traffic arms were up and there was no one in sight.

"Turn the sirens off," Terry said. "The lights too."

"You think he's waiting for his posse to get out of school and save him?"

"I don't think those kids give a rat shit if he's dead or alive," Terry said as Rudd Hasson slowed the car down to a halt and took a good look beyond the rails. "He's not dumb enough to come back here."

"Then why are we here—you think he's in the mine? I thought they sealed that up long ago."

"They did. Keep driving. In about another mile or two we're gonna have to get out."

"It's fucking freezing," Hasson moans.

"You've really never made a bust down here, huh?" Terry asked amusedly and Hasson shook his head.

"Chief doesn't put the big dogs on breaking up high school parties in the woods," Hasson said, driving more cautiously down the old crumbling mining road.

"Everyone in town knows about the mine; the old people who've seen the inside of it; the kids who spray paint it; the dumb tourists who hear about vampires trapped inside from the Thompsons," Terry went on listing. "But there's only a small handful who know about the ruins back here."

"Ruins?" Hasson asked, letting go of the wheel for a moment to rub his gloved hands together. "What ruins?"

"Back when Bloodrun was just a little mining town, they built a church nearby. I think, if I remember correctly, it was more of a... what do you call'em—'missionary'?" Hasson nodded—he knew, albeit in the back of his mind, that the conversion to Christianity was a common practice during Alaska's transition towards statehood.

"Hannah and I stumbled upon it once while we were hiking back here. It's completely dilapidated—the roof's collapsed in and it's overgrown with brush. There's not much left of it besides some stone walls and a couple of no trespassing signs. I wouldn't even have noticed it if it wasn't for Spart, who ran over and pissed on it. When we got back to town, Hannah wanted to check out the museum," Terry paused to make sure that Hasson knew which museum he meant, "but there were hardly any records of it—only that the original town had a 'church' and was abandoned a few years after the mine was dug."

"I'm surprised I never knew about this—I grew up here," Hasson admitted.

"Well, you probably never got invited to any parties out in the woods," Terry jabbed before continuing. "Fortunately, the tour guide was able to tell us a little more. She said that the official reason the ruins are largely unacknowledged is because of the danger they pose—falling stones or something—not to mention the difficulty of getting to it. But according to her, the real reason was because the borough doesn't want to be associated with the inhumane treatment of its native people in the past."

"Boy, if the Thompsons ever catch wind of this, they're gonna have a field day with it," Hasson muttered. "*Satanic Church Invoked Zombie Séances!*" he continued, mocking Greg Thompson's foreboding voice.

"In the town's defense, when modern Bloodrun was rebuilt in the 40s, it was filled with a whole new group of people, so there's really no point in drawing attention to the atrocities that happened back then. Park right here, we're gonna have to walk the rest of the way."

"What makes you think Albot knows about it?" Hasson asked with dismay as Terry opened the passenger side door and let in the cold air. "He's not exactly the museum-going type."

"You'd be surprised how much Albot knows," Terry said, remembering the man's impressive knowledge of Philadelphia sport stats. "I figure, a guy who spends most of his time a step above homeless—constantly getting evicted and shunned from every corner of town—must know a good spot to camp out and take refuge when he's run out of people willing to let him pass out on their couch. His own family closes their doors to him and we know he disappears for weeks. The shit he must succumb to drinking when he's out scrounging." Terry shook his head in disgust as he recalled a time when he found a half-drunk bottle of mouthwash mixed with paint thinner in Albot's coat.

As they walked into the woods, the only sounds came from the snow crunching beneath their feet and Rudd Hasson's teeth clattering.

"Are we close yet?" Hasson asked impatiently and seemed to give the evil eye to the puffs of steam he made as he spoke. Terry turned around and raised a finger to his lips.

"You smell that?" Terry whispered.

"Smoke," Hasson said gratefully, inhaling a large breath through his nose.

"It's somewhere up ahead," Terry said quietly. "Let's split up, we can cover more ground and box him in. Try to follow the smoke and look out for his tracks." Hasson nodded and they parted.

Terry pushed aside some branches and tried peering through the trees for any sign of a bonfire; flickering flames, rising smoke—an unconscious drunkard. Though he knew that Albot posed no physical threat, Terry wasn't ignorant of the fact that they were at last in the thick of it—bear country—and roaming through it silently no less; the perfect conditions to happen upon a hungry mother and her cubs. He took another breath as he drew his .38 and proceeded deeper into the woods.

TERRY COULDN'T SEE THE FIRE itself when he came across it because there was something in the way—remains of one of the dilapidated stone walls, maybe—but he could see the golden sparks floating upwards and flickering out as they burned into ash. They reminded him of the snowflakes that melted on his windshield—random fading memories burning off and on—like fireflies vanishing into the dark. As Terry got closer, he could see that the shivering mass blocking his view of the flames was none other than the man that they were searching for.

Fullsend Steve was sitting on a stolen case of Lionshead with one of his gaunt hands wrapped around a dark brown bottle. With the palm of his other hand, he raised a beer cap up to his squinting eyes—attempting to solve one of the trademark rebus puzzles that were printed underneath. Terry advanced another pace into the clearing and was right about to yell Albot's name when the sound of snapping branches startled them.

"Freeze!" Hasson yelled as he clumsily swatted his way through an Alder thicket. He reached for his gun as he broke the last web of hanging branches but slipped on the slick surface of one of the fallen stones and fell hard onto the ground. Seizing the opportunity, Albot impulsively sprang to his feet and took off around the fire.

Terry quickly holstered his pistol—knowing that he could catch the old man without even breaking a sweat—lest he slipped on the uneven terrain too and accidentally shot himself in the dick. He ran towards him, leapt over the fire and slid in yellow slush where Albot had been relieving himself. Without taking his eyes off the flailing man, Terry propped himself up on the remnants of a stone wall that once enclosed a stained-glass window and swung his legs over to the other side, hoping to cut Albot off in his tracks—equally hoping that there wasn't a mound of Albot's shit waiting for him this time.

Terry's feet broke through the crust of an untouched snowdrift and he sank up to his knees. Fearing that Albot might change directions from the noise, Terry began stomping his way free when the old man ran out in front of him. Without thinking, Terry launched himself at Albot with far more force than what was needed, and they both nearly crashed through an old wooden post with a sign nailed to it reading:

DANGER
UNREINFORCED MASONRY
KEEP AWAY!

The thunderous clap of the impact immediately broke one of Albot's ribs and set him back to his customary surrender. Terry rolled over with snow packed under his aviators and straddled the old man blindly as he cried. With Albot's face wet with tears, and Terry's with melting snow, he snapped handcuffs on him for the first time.

"I said, 'Freeze!'" Hasson yelled again as he limped around the smashed rubble of the church steeple that once rose above the altar. He caught his breath as he winced from the pain in his hip and then laughed as Terry knocked off his snow-caked shades, revealing watery dilated eyes. "Shit, Volker, we might just make a detective out of you yet..."

* * *

"THINK WE SHOULD TRY THE RUINS AGAIN?" Hasson asks. "If he ain't over his cousins or at a bar—"

"That's a far walk from here," Terry says.

"Maybe he got a ride from our acid man," Hasson suggests, and Terry thinks about the conversation he had earlier with Eddowes:

"...directing landslide traffic until your arms are too tired to—"

"You go," Terry says. "You remember how to find it?"

"I think so—it'll help if he has a fire cooking again."

"Don't let him know you're coming this time."

"You're staying here?"

"Spart's a hound; he can start picking up a scent until the K-9 gets here."

"T E R," Eddie says, following behind as Terry leads Spartacus around Jack Albot's abandoned car. "Can I ask *you* something now?"

"Sure."

"How did you guys catch the kid?"

"What kid?"

"The one that Fullsend sold the acid to—who killed Bill. I get that you and Rudd caught up with Albot in the woods, but how'd you find the kid?"

"It ended up coming down to surveillance footage," Terry says and then whistles for Spart's attention.

"I thought there weren't any cameras outside of Sullivan's back then."

"There weren't." Terry crouches down and holds the vodka bottle cap in front of Spart's nose and watches his nostrils flare. "But once we knew for certain that Albot was involved, we obtained security cam footage from the Buckaroo on the night before the murder and traced Albot's movement. There was a window of time where he disappeared outside, which we figure must've been when he got the acid. After he came back in, he started talking to some college kids and luckily, Albot isn't very discreet, so we were able to catch a clear transaction he had between one of them. Fortunately, the kid paid his tab with a credit card so we were able to get his name. His DNA matched what we had on file from the clothes in the alley and that was it; easy confession."

"Do we still have copies of those recordings?" Eddie asks as Spartacus puts his nose to the ground and blows up a couple bursts of snow.

"He's got something," Terry says, and Spart begins turning circles beside the open driver side door. "Um, we should. Joycie can probably find them—why?"

"Because," Eddie says as they follow the pudgy badger hound sniff his way towards the back of the car. "If the acid dealer from ten years ago is the same guy who wrote that fucking letter—"

"Now you're thinking without your dick for once," Terry says over his shoulder and Eddie mocks him behind his back. "Follow up on it with your girlfriend when we get back to the station and make a list of everyone who was there that night."

S P A R T A C U S L E A D S T H E T W O M E N about 20 yards away from the car and then stops. He raises his nose to the air, back to the ground and then spins around to Terry, wagging his tail for a treat.

"I guess that's it," Terry says and crouches down to give Spart some kibble.

"Maybe Rudd's right. Maybe someone pulled over and gave him a lift." Terry nods and wonders if there are tire tracks under the fresh snow when Joycie's voice comes over Eddie's radio:

"You can nix the search, Rudd," she says. "They found him at St. Dot's, over."

"Copy that, heading over now. Lemme' guess, Father Murphy let him sleep inside the vestibule and couldn't wake him up again?"

"Not exactly," Joycie says and waits a moment. "He's dead."

CHAPTER XIII:
|T|O|O| |C|O|L|D| |T|O| |C|H|A|N|G|E| |S|I|G|N|. |M|E|S|S|A|G|E| |I|N|S|I|D|E|!

IN THE BASEMENT of St. Dorothy's Parish, which also serves as the cafeteria for the catholic elementary school, four rows of lunch tables have been pushed aside to make space for a circle of folding chairs. In the center, Stephen James Albot lies facedown in two pieces. On the linoleum floor above his head is a blood-colored cocktail with half-melted ice cubes floating in it.

Sheri photographs the scene quietly this time; there's no need to recite it all out loud anymore—they've heard it enough. Until Terry and Eddie descend the steps to the church basement, the only sound comes from the shutter of her camera.

Click-click.
Click-click...

"FATHER MURPHY SAID he found him like this about half an hour ago," Hasson says. "He came down to set up for the morning AA meeting, but when he turned the lights on—well, looks like we got number four."

"Three," Eddie says and looks to Terry for confirmation, but his mentor is captivated by the red drink in the tumbler glass.

No, Terry says to himself.
You son of a bitch.
"You *fucking* son of a bitch," he whispers.
"What is that?" Eddie asks.

You were there, weren't you?

You saw us. Terry shuts his eyes and tries his best to reconstruct the night when he was drugged at the Buckaroo. He can hear the guitar roaring, smell Albot's breath, taste the—

"Crimson," Terry mutters with disdain.

"A what?"

—but he can't make out any of the faces. The memory is too faded—too distorted by the acid.

"One of Albot's go-to's," Terry says opening his eyes. "Rye whiskey over Dr. Pepper and cranberry or some shit."

"Why is it here?" Eddie asks.

"...I don't know."

WHILE SHERI CONTINUES SWEEPING the room, Eddie wanders over to the church bulletin board and scans the multicolored flyers pinned to the cork. In addition to the monthly AA schedules, he sees group therapy sessions for battered women, suicide survivors and adults who were sexually abused children. As he reads, he notices Terry walk back upstairs behind him and go outside.

Click-click.
Click-click.
Click...

CHAPTER XIV:
Detective Koyukuk

"IT'LL TAKE ME A MINUTE," Joycie tells Eddie as she plugs a thumb drive into her computer, "but I can find it. What do you need that for?"

"Where's Terry?" Chief Eddowes demands as he enters the lobby—his voice catching them both off guard.

"I-I don't know," Eddie flinches as he spins around from Joycie's desk. "I thought he was at Albot's autopsy?"

"Helduser just called me," Eddowes says, trying to compose himself. "Terry was supposed to be there at 2:30, but he never showed up."

"Did you try calling him?"

"Yes, Eddie," Eddowes says clenching his eyes shut, unable to contain his frustration. "That's why I'm asking *you*—he's your partner isn't he?"

"Well, y'know, not officially—"

"Find him," Eddowes snaps. Eddie turns back to Joycie and tries not to examine her figure as he looks down to the floor where Spartacus is lying in his bed.

"The dog's still here."

"I could see that," Eddowes calls down the hallway as he walks away. "You're a *real* detective, Koyukuk!"

"BECAUSE, LITTLE *NIVIAQSAAQ*," Eddie says as he turns back around and sits on Joycie's desk. "They think whoever

265

supplied our townie with the acid is the same freak who wrote that letter. So—" Eddie spouts proudly.

"Anyone who was at the bar that night is now a suspect," Joycie says. "Wow—did Terry come up with that?"

"Just get me the footage, alright?"

EDDIE PULLS UP A CHAIR at an open computer, double-clicks the .mp4 file from Joycie's flash drive and begins surveying the clientele on the Buckaroo security cam footage from the night before Bill's murder: Kazimir Panas—or as Eddie refers to him, "the guy with the wrench," who he saw fixing a hydrant once; Mark Donahue—"the candy man"; and of course, "Fullsend Steve". As Eddie fast-forwards the clip, each of the barflies are replaced by others; "the cowboy", "the lady with the tits" and various other faces that Eddie recognizes but doesn't know the names of. Finally, Albot walks back inside from where he is assumed to have obtained the LSD in the parking lot and Eddie presses PAUSE.

...*the man with the lisp*, he writes in his notepad.
...*the tall blonde*...
...*Geoff Selover*—Eddie only remembers that name because Geoff once caught him having sex with his younger sister in the bed of Geoff's truck and broke Eddie's nose.

"SO," Chief Eddowes says, "Steve Albot mysteriously acquires some acid from a stranger in a bar one night which he then sells to a kid who kills Bill Sullivan. Ten years later, the son of a bitch returns with a letter, kills two innocent girls three days before Albot is released from prison—taking a day off for Talon Warth to coincidentally kill Émile Lepus the same way—and then decides to do Albot in too, for good measure. Is that about the gist of where we're at?" The room falls silent as Eddowes glares around for an answer.

"Maybe it's *not* a coincidence," Eddie speaks up. "I mean, at this point, it can't be, can it? The guy must've put that line of Émile's about death in the letter for a reason—it led us right to him."

"Yes, Eddie," Liam says, "that was the whole point. He wanted us off his trail."

"Right, but he must've known that Talon was going to kill him—why else would the killer have held off that day?"

"Well, his next victim—who may've been able to identify him—wasn't out of prison yet," Liam says.

"He would've killed that drunk 10 years ago if he was worried that he'd rat on him—plus, why would Fullsend wait until now to finally give him up?" Eddie asks.

"Alright," Bressi says, "and how would the killer have possibly known that Talon was going to kill Lepus?"

"I don't know," Eddie says meekly. "Maybe he manipulated Talon into doing it or—"

"Talon killed Lepus because of whatever the old bastard did to the Audrey girl," Bressi says. "That cut on her cheek—"

"Let him finish," Eddowes says, surprising everyone. "Go on, Eddie."

"The girl was definitely the motive, but," Eddie stops and looks around the room wishing that Terry was there. "I went back and checked the security footage from the Buckaroo on the night before Old Sully's husband was killed. Steve walks out and comes back in with the acid, just like it says in the report, but maybe the dealer came in too. Maybe—" Eddie stops and looks around nervously.

"Eddie, are you trying to say you think this person may have *manipulated* Bill's killer too?" Eddowes asks.

"Remember the clothes in the alley? There weren't any shoes, and—" Eddie stammers as he looks at all the piercing skeptical eyes. "It made me think of the shooting at the Rod & Reel," he says, his cheeks blushing now. "*That* kid had no shoes either. Maybe it's all the same guy. We *know* whoever gave Albot the acid likely wrote the letter. Maybe he's drugging these kids up and getting them to kill people in addition to the ones he's doing himself—"

"Jesus Christ," Eddowes shouts and rubs his temples. "The shooting at the Rod & Reel was what—15 years ago?" The

267

room falls silent again and everyone looks dubiously at Eddie, but none of them can refute the eeriness of his theory.

"How long does LSD stay in your system for?" Hasson asks, turning to the agents.

"About three or four days—depending," Liam says.

"Maybe we should have Talon tested," Hasson suggests and tries to give Eddie an encouraging look.

"When the hell did Koyukuk become a detective?" Eddowes asks.

"I made a list of everyone who was at the Buckaroo that night," Eddie says, handing the Chief of the Bloodrun Borough Police Department a scribbled page torn from his notepad.

...the guy with the wrench, Eddowes reads and looks up furiously.

"'The waitress from Yuki Hana'?"

"...Joycie can help me get all of their names."

"Eddie," Eddowes says gravely. "Go. Find. Terry."

CHAPTER XV:
Sublimation

I can sleep like a dog or an old dead log
I can sleep in a pool as if I'm in school

TERRY SWINGS OPEN a motel room door and farmer walks two 50lb bags of ice into the bathroom. He gets down on one knee, slips his pocketknife through the top of one of them and dumps the ice into the tub—repeating the motions as swiftly with the second bag. Cold water rushes from the faucet and fills up every empty space as he strips and steps in.

Within a moment of standing there, his feet begin to feel like they're being broken by an impossible pressure. His toes don't begin to go numb until after the water gnashes the arches of his feet into raw knots of fascia, but still, he forces himself to sit. The ice rises and stings—chews his flesh maddeningly all over as he submerges up to his neck and feels the intolerable pressure throbbing on his shoulders now, caving on his ribs. Every instinct in his body screams at him to get out, but this will all pass.

He tries to force himself to breathe in long even draws, but in less than a minute, he loses control of his diaphragm and pants rapidly. From past experience, Terry has learned that the intercostal muscles of the chest can produce vitalizing amounts of heat if they're kept from hyperventilating, but this is too much for him. All he wants is the cold—the numbing pain that always stills his soul—but his body revolts and shivers wildly, desperate for

warmth. After another two minutes, Terry's skin is scorched a cold dark pink, but his thoughts remain racing—
Crimson.

A S HE LIES IN THE TUB trembling uncontrollably—the ritual no longer working—the rush of pain no longer silencing his rabid mind—Terry is powerless to forestall it any longer and finally thinks back to the last time that he saw Fullsend Steve alive. Albot was a broken shell of a man then—hunched over a fire which he kept alive with wet money and rotting wood.
Rotting wood.
Split a piece of rotting wood—
"No!" Terry yells.
"No dream is fit to end until the making of a fire."
CRACK!
Terry feels the killer's letter between his soggy fingers and the paper begins to slither in his palms like insect larvae—like Albot's strips of undulating blotter acid.
I am the home of the worm—
"Ellis could see where the batter was going to swing," the old drunkard believed, *"before he even wound up."*
Terry thrashes in the tub and a wave of ice water spills over the edge onto the floor.
"666," Liam's voice now.
"For tomorrow—we die," Albot's again.
"Get off of me!"
"Get off—"
Terry sucks in a huge breath of air and lowers his head below the surface. He doesn't want to close his eyes, in fear of what he may see, but the freezing water is excruciating—his eyeballs feel like they're going to burst. It isn't until the ice cubes floating above him go blurry that he squeezes his eyelids shut.
"The shower's leaking," Hannah whispers and he can feel the dripping on his toes so strongly that he forgets he isn't home.
spells cannot be —
—undone—

Undone.
Something's left undone.

The ice cubes shift and rattle around Terry's head as tremors run down his back. The sound of the freezing water sloshing in his ears reminds him of the whirring static heard over the speakers of the Buckaroo—when an open mic-er missed the input jack of her red guitar. Something that feels like an electric current accompanies the noise and vibrates in his head—as if she dropped the guitar in the tub with him while it was still plugged in.

I have felt the Earth rumble.
Drip-drip.
I've heard the mountains reply.
Drip-drip.
I was once one of the countless gods.
Drip—
I stayed while they have all—
"*Die alone,*" the water voices as it drips on his toes.
I can't do this.
"*Why?*" Hannah asks, "*What's your damage?*"

"N-n-no," Terry garbles below the ice water and tries not to choke as bubbles rise to the surface amidst another convulsion.

"*Don't let anything(one)—*"
"*Die alone,*" the water continues saying as it drips.

This is just the drug, Terry tries to tell himself again, but it's no use this time. He's stone-sober, freezing in a motel bathroom miles from The Buckaroo Club.

"Paper—paper... paper..." Terry says inaudibly below the water and more bubbles escape between the ice.

HANNAH VS. TERRANCE
B-dee b-dee b-dee, that's all—

TERRY FINALLY BREAKS THROUGH the surface of the water and ice cubes splash all over the tile as he gasps for air. His teeth clatter together and his curled numb hands shake fervently as he grips the side of the tub.

"*I can fix this—*"

"Cooooooooooooooooooooome," the same throat singing hum that he heard from the mountains so long ago calls to him again.

CHAPTER XVI:
98.6°F

Dry again.

Terry's Bronco rolls along through the ice fog in the early morning darkness and stops at the opposite end of where Jack Albot's car was found on Blackrock Pike. The engine shuts off and all is silent. The air is cold, dry, and still.

There's a good ten-minute walk ahead of him through the pines to the water's edge and the frozen snow crushes underneath his boots. He holds an ax in one of his hands—choking the handle loosely up towards the curve of its beard. When he gets to the riverbank, he presumes to walk out onto the ice without hesitation, as if the earth continued endlessly before him. When he gets out far enough to where the water flows deeply below, Terry removes his jacket and begins chopping.

Whoosh—crack—
Whoosh—crack—
Whoosh—

Bits of ice fly up in every direction from the crashing steel and he feels the spray of the finer shavings melt on his cheeks. When sweat begins to form on his brow, he takes a brief break and stares out across the Bloodrun to the horizon. He hasn't bothered to turn around and see how far out he is, but he knows he's alone and that's all that matters. Once he catches his breath, the ax rises up and falls again.

Whoosh—crack—

Whoosh—

After another five minutes of heavy chopping, the ax breaks through to the other side and black water rushes up in the moonlight. He enlarges the hole with the butt of the handle and then dunks his blistered hands in to clear out the floating chunks of ice—the water at first soothing, then burning. Without taking another breath, Terry finishes disrobing and then slips into the river as if it were a hot spring—feet first—and doesn't reemerge.

All remains cold, dry, and still.

CHAPTER XVII:
The Abyss

"S PART, WHERE'RE YOU GOING, boy?" Terry asks jovially. The dog disregards him and continues eagerly on a scent. "What is it?" he calls again, but Spartacus is too far away now. All Terry sees is black.

"Spartacus!" he shouts, but the only response is the familiar sound of the dog's scratching paws. Terry walks forward slowly, reaching out blindly in the dark, trying to follow the persistent clatter until a faint wedge of light appears ahead of him.

"What're you doing, Spart?" Terry's voice echoes down the dim corridor as he makes out a bizarre blur of the dog's wagging tail—just like the trails that hung in the air at the Buckaroo.

"Spart, come," Terry says, but Spartacus keeps his nose to the floor and continues pawing at the closed door at the end of the hallway—the nursery which was to be for Terry and Hannah's stillborn child.

"*Spart*," Terry says angrily now, but the hound defies him and jabs at the door with his snout—*thump—thump—thump*.

"Spartacus!" Terry yells and begins running towards him, but before he can scoop him up, the little dog breaks a hole through the door and crawls inside.

"Spart, no!" Terry yells again.

A S H E G R A B S hold of the ice-cold doorknob, Terry feels his nose hairs freezing stiff as they prickle the insides of his nostrils. He lets go and backs away, but the door opens by itself.

In place of the four pastel blue walls that Terry painted and the walnut bassinet that Hannah picked out, a wild labyrinth of Card House architecture revolves all around him. Staircases bend upside down in impossible angles and break apart and reattach themselves like Tetris. Walls lower into the floor and reveal hidden rooms while other passages simultaneously rise— brick by brick—and form new chambers.

"Spartacus!" Terry yells, taking a step through the doorway and scans the churning madness. Tree branches shatter glass windows and root themselves into the floorboards. A magpie flies in through the broken glass and perches itself on top one of Émile's sculptures—an ebony clock—and mimics the sound of ice cracking across a thick frozen lake. Above it, the ceiling begins to split apart and a pillar of light beams down as snowflakes fall into the nightmarish landscape.

"Spart!" Terry calls again, but instead of a reply of barks or howls for him to chase, Terry hears a child's voice crying from the infinite depths below.

"I'm coming!" he yells and tries to follow it—hopping over chasms that are opening in the floor, climbing and trampling over the shifting floorboards as they change beneath his feet. He tries to descend a flight of stairs, but before he can reach the end, the whole thing breaks apart and bends higher than before. He runs through a passage where he hears the crying again, but somehow comes back out where he started. He yells out to the tiny bellowing voice over and over, but it fades away.

"It's over, Terry," he hears Hannah's voice behind him— a cold breath in his ears. All of Émile's twisted architecture suddenly collapses before him and falls down into the abyss as he turns to her. It's their baby's room again. It's the night she left.

"No—we can have another," Terry hears his voice outside of himself. He stands in the doorway watching the memory—watching himself go to her pleading.

"We can try again—"

"I'm done trying with you, Terry."

"I can fix this," he said and tried to hold her hands, but she pulled away.

"Not this time, babe," she said and her face scrunched up with tears.

"Please," he wanted to say, "don't leave."

But he let her go.

She walked out of the room.

CHAPTER XVIII:
Red and Raw

AS TERRY SLOWLY SINKS in the hole, a white van pulls up and parks along the frozen Bloodrun. A man, devoid of all features due to his black garments, gets out and walks to the rear. He opens the double doors and reaches inside to lift something heavy—the top half of a human body; a pale naked torso. He places it gently on the snow and then goes back to retrieve its legs.

While the shadow is positioning his composition of limbs, a distant sound enters Terry's ears which apparently goes unnoticed by the newcomer. Terry tries to listen more carefully as he walks down the hallway and sees water rising up the stairs. As it spills over the top step, he hears the noise again—louder this time—a dog's bark. He looks around for Spartacus, but there's no sign of him anywhere. Black freezing water rushes down the hall now—submerging his ankles—and he remembers what he's done.

TERRY CHOKES AND COUGHS up ice water as he tries to open his sticking eyelids—unable to see because his corneas have frosted over—but after a few frantic blinks, the rime drips away. Two hazy yellow orbs glow in front of him. He hears the distant bark again and his eyes finally focus on a van's headlights shining in the dark.

A silhouette moves leisurely in the two yellow beams—crouching and adjusting—and the glow of the moon helps Terry see what the figure is doing.

"S-s-s-sick... s-s-son of a... b-b-b—" Terry stutters quietly from the ice pit and he raises one of his frozen claws out of the black water—wincing as his flesh scrapes over the jagged hole. He's numb to the pain, but he registers the tugging and skidding as his skin sticks—freezing and ripping with the increasing weight he puts on it. The heat of his blood nearly burns his bitter flesh as it seeps into the river.

Once his shoulder is above the six-inch-thick ice, his bleeding fingers dig—searching without sensation for something to anchor onto as his other arm emerges from the water.

"Hh—hh—" Terry tries to call out between gasps—wrong phoneme. "Ey!" Terry shouts and his voice echoes across the frozen river. The graceless sound causes his throat to clasp with a sharp pinch and the dark figure turns to the river curiously.

"Hey!" Terry moans savagely as he pulls his other shoulder out of the water, drawing more blood from his ribs as he rakes his raw red body over the ice.

The faceless man watches Terry struggle for a moment and then traces his steps back to the rear of his van. He reaches inside for something heavy again—his chainsaw this time—and turns back to the river and walks out onto the ice. The motor burps as he pulls the start cord, but it doesn't fully engage. When the rope recoils, he lets the engine fall through the air and yanks it back up with the cord and the blades begin their awful buzz.

"S-s-stop," Terry tries to yell as a black plume of exhaust emanates from the saw. The whirling growl grows louder as the man approaches but Terry struggles to keep his eyes open, lying half-conscious on the ice.

The shadow walks determinedly with his saw out in front of him as clouds blot out the moon. When he makes it halfway between his van and Terry, a new set of high beams shine in the distance as a truck turns onto Blackrock Pike. The man pauses for a moment as the lights get closer and then kills the engine...

* * *

CHAPTER XIX:
The Unipqaaq of the Quiet People

"LISTEN ONLY TO ME and you will have great power
    And *true* everlasting life," the great white gull spoke again
    without speaking
    "These words that Sedna has learned from the wolves
    Create nothing but desire and fury; stubborn dreams for control
    The more words; the more anger and yearning—
    The more you will be lost in dreams
    There is only one word."

"Only death and death alone!" the people around the fire chanted as the Angatuik told their story. The faceless man sat with them and spoke their sacred words, but he didn't believe them. In fact, he believed there was no death at all, at least for him. But he wasn't there to prove this.

He was there to separate sides.

FOR A LONG TIME, all was well with the quiet people again
    Their silence and their knowledge of death
    Made them greater than the animals
    As the great white gull foretold

    But when Kiviuq returned from the sea and learned of Sedna's
    murder
    He was enraged

"Gull is deceiving you all," Kiviuq shouted
"I too have learned the many words
I can speak with the magpies
And howl like the wolves
Nothing cursed has come upon me
I am even more powerful still!
Who amongst you will challenge me?
See—where is Gull now?"

"Makchit," the faceless man whispered to a young boy in his own native tongue as the Angatuik continued. "Go and fetch me the water," he instructed, switching back to the people's language once he had the child's attention. The children were always excited to gain permission from the elders to approach the river because it was otherwise forbidden, but even more so, because they marveled at its strange properties. But the faceless man was not truly an elder; he wasn't truly one of them at all.

He's spent years watching them—learning how they talked, how they dressed—to mimic them perfectly.

The boy dipped an ivory ladle into the crystal-clear water, poured it onto the stony bank and watched in amazement as it froze in a tall column. He laughed and then followed his orders and refilled the ladle—being careful not to spill a drop as he returned.

THE GREAT WHITE GULL remained silent
    And so, the quiet people were drawn to their old desires
    They encouraged the wolves by their fires with fish
    And the people began using the many words to argue and complain
    They told lies and spoke of horrible things
    And we're confused by pain instead of empowered by it

    At the height of their madness
    The wolves began breaking their sled reins
    And eating the quiet people one at a time

When the boy returned, the faceless man was holding a stone bowl in which he mashed an ergot mixture. He signaled for the boy to dump the liquid into the bowl and he stirred the powder into a paste—then a froth—and then something that resembled a tea. As the boy watched intently, the faceless man wondered if he could be made into a pupil. Perhaps, someday even a brother.

He raised a finger to his lips and then peered into the flames as they continued listening to the unipqaaq. His favorite part was coming and unlike the rest of them, he remembered it firsthand.

S O, THE PEOPLE BEGGED for forgiveness from Gull
    And the countless other gods
    They howled out like the wolves that were devouring them
    But the gods were not sentimental
    They looked upon the people like straw-dogs

    When only a handful of the quiet people remained
    Igaluk finally said, "Enough."
    And Gull gathered up the wolves and butchered them—
    Splitting them apart—
    And dumped their bowels into the river until it was red as blood

    In his wrath,
    Gull flew into a deep roll
    And plunged into the river with a great splash
    When he reemerged,
    He was no longer an unsullied white seagull
    But a black raven
    "Do you see me now?" Raven roared from his clasped beak
    "You defied me and learned to speak like the gods
    And made friends with wolves
    So come and join me in hell and you will know no death
    And be alone forever—
    Quaqtiluk!
    I have warned you that words become flesh
    And now the flesh will reap upon you
    Those who stay will not be saved—

A curse is your lot."
And Raven disappeared into the sky…

* * *

CHAPTER XX:
The Water

A BLACK GLOVED HAND holding a Municipal Department of Public Works card reaches through the driver side window of a white van. The scanner beeps as it reads the barcode and the traffic arm rises to Bloodrun Borough's water treatment plant. The driver is the only person scheduled to work on Sundays and his only tasks are a few routine checks. Today, however, he's taking it upon himself to do a couple extra things.

He drives past the screening building, where water is pumped from the influent waste pipes, as well as the Bloodrun River itself, and parks by the sedimentation bay with its large round water clarifier. He's already begun making an impressive collection of blue barrels beside it and supplements them with even more from the back of his van.

He swipes his badge through another scanner and enters the filtration control room. As instructed, he checks the biochemical oxygen levels of the tower's current supply and records it with the suspended solids report. The turbidity he assesses by eye in a sample drawn from the test faucet. After pouring the beaker into the sink, he casually flips a switch which turns off the scum collector. There's hardly any fog to be stripped from the tank today, but this isn't part of his usual assignments for the weekend—nor within his authority. It's also not his duty to turn off the flow of sodium hypochlorite, but he does this too. Naturally, there's no need to leave the electrolyzers on then either.

Now, he just needs to find a forklift.

AFTER DUMPING all of his blue barrels into the clarifier, he goes back into the control room and turns the flow of water back on via the two large pumps. He drops his head back as he listens to the massive pipe running above him. He can hear the water rushing through it as half of the supply channels its way to the P-trap within the stumpy graffiti-covered beach tower at Point Woronzof where it drains back into the river. The other half will serve the town's 5,000-some residents as it pumps its way up into the tallest structure in the borough—the water tower.

As he stands there with his head titled backwards and his eyes closed, he remembers the countless times that he walked around bonfires passing his stone bowl. They'd all sip from it—one by one—and continue with the ritual.

Even the children.

IT WAS HARD TO LIVE without the gods
    The people could no longer hear the eagles
    Or feel the wind
    They tried to stop using the many words
    But they were ingrained in their minds
    And shaped their thoughts
    And their thoughts shaped their flesh

    The river stained the snowbanks with its blood
    And it drowned all the fish
    And even Kiviuq's kayak could not float on it
    But still, a few quiet people stayed—determined to fix it
    To save their god from his Quaqtiluk

    Seeing their efforts,
    Igaluk took pity on them
    And came down from the night sky
    He instructed them on how they could cleanse the water
    And that one day Raven would return

"Your words cannot be unspoken," Igaluk said
"Your songs cannot be unsung,
But I will make a new covenant with you."
And he spread two of his glowing fingers,
Dipped them into the river,
And marked the people's arms with the sign of his order

CHAPTER XXI:
83.5°F

"T E R R Y?" Eddie whispers and places his hand on Terry's bandaged forearm as his eyelids struggle to open. "Nurse!" Eddie yells and spins around to the door and shouts down the hallway. "He's waking up!"

"M R. V O L K E R," a woman in teal scrubs says a few minutes later with a bit of annoyance. She has other patients to tend to that are suffering from ailments that didn't result from their own doing. "You're lucky to be alive. You've suffered extreme frostbite on your hands and feet." Terry looks down to the IV, not fully grasping what she's saying. "As well as severe hypothermia. Your wounds are going to require multiple skin graft—"

"Miss," Eddie says. "Now that he's awake, do you mind if I speak to him alone? We were working on the Butcher case before—"

"You have a long road of recovery ahead of you, detective. A few more minutes out there like that and you would've frozen to death. The hemodialysis machine you're hooked up to right now is working on rewarming your blood until your body can thermoregulate your core temperature again. It's not going to be comfortable, but hopefully it'll save us from having to perform a surgical peritoneal—"

"*Please*," Eddie begs. "I don't think he's ready to hear any of this."

"W H A T... H A P P E N E D?" Terry asks weakly after the nurse turns back down the hallway. His voice comes out slow and hoarse.

"*What happened?*" Eddie repeats. "What do you mean, 'What happened'? You tell me—why the fuck were you trying to kill yourself?"

"I wasn't trying t—ugh," Terry groans as his voice fails him and he remembers the sound of his ax. "I just... needed to cool off."

"Is that a fucking joke?" Eddie asks angrily. "In the fucking *Bloodrun*?"

"Eddie," he stops and winces. "Did we... catch him?" Terry manages and Eddie looks away shaking his head.

"You saw him?" Eddie asks and Terry closes his eyes. He can only make out a silhouette approaching him in yellow headlights—black smoke raging from a chainsaw.

"Not his face," Terry says. "White van."

"Any decal?"

"No. He pulled up just as I got in. I saw him dumping a body—he didn't know I was there," Terry stops, his face contorting with pain. He can feel the hot blood recirculating back into his arm. "Fuck—I think he had a mask on... He came towards me but—"

"Jesus, Ter," Eddie starts again, "What the fuck were you doing out there?"

"Eddie..." Terry tries futilely to find his old voice. "I had to clear my head."

"Yeah, well you're fucking lucky this freak didn't bash it in or cut it off when he spotted you. We can't afford to lose you right now. Don't quit on us."

"I *wasn't* quitting," Terry groans, becoming more and more aware of the pain all over his body.

"Thank god the candy man—er, Donahue, right?—goes in early to start the saltwater taffies. He saw the body on the side of the road in his high beams and just happened to find you out there freezing to death. How the hell were you planning on getting out, huh? And why'd you park so goddamn far away?"

"I don't need this right now," Terry moans and shifts his body below the blankets. He can feel his skin splitting beneath the bandages.

"I need you, Ter… You scared the shit out of me."

"I'm sorry," Terry whispers as he slips back into unconsciousness, fearing he'll return to the Escher-esque nightmare. "…I'm… sorry…"

"He's awake," Eddie says into his phone as he steps outside of the hospital. "Well, he was. The nurse says he'll probably keep drifting in and out for a while. You're okay with holding onto the dog for awhile?"

"Of course," Joycie says and pats Spart's head. "Are you going to stay with Terry?"

"No, Chief wants me back at the station for something so Wertman's gonna hang here. Where are you?"

"I'm heading to the museum—like you said—'undercover', remember?" Joycie asks playfully.

"Alone?"

"Yeah, *alone*. What are they going to do—stuff me and put me on display too?"

"Okay," Eddie says, resisting the urge to make a joke about how he'd like to be the one to *stuff* her. "Just… be careful. I'd go with you but—"

"I can do more than answer phones and dispatch cars, Officer Eddie."

"Alright—" but before he can say, "Good luck," she hangs up on him.

289

CHAPTER XXII:
Syrpynt

"Herod is sleeping, child," Clara Thompson says with a vampiric smile as Joycie enters The Red River Museum to the recurring sound of the droning igil huur. "Don't be afraid."

Joycie looks up from the bear skin rug and then walks around it to the counter.

"How much for one admission?" she asks.

"Only one?" Clara asks with mock pity.

"Yes."

"Where's your boyfriend?"

Hopefully finding something to put your ass away with— Joycie stops herself with an artificial smile.

"I'm meeting up with him tomorrow in Fairbanks. We're going to see the Northern Lights!" she says as touristy as possible.

"Ah, isn't that sweet," Clara says. "Would you like a guide then?"

"That won't be necessary. I'll take the headphones though."

"Certainly."

Joycie had enough of Greg Thompson's phony voice after the first exhibit, but she's determined to listen until the end. By the time she gets halfway through the museum, she stops jumping from the cheap jerking animatronics and random screams that Clara most certainly recorded herself. She looks to her watch and sees that she's already wasted half an hour and $55.00 without finding a single thing of value.

"…and that was the last that anyone had seen of the serpent—until today," Greg whispers in her ears and then laughs maniacally. Hanging from wires before Jocycie is a giant taxidermy of a black alligator gar that Greg had shipped up from Hurst, Texas and was obviously sewn together with a dozen porcupine pelts and other miscellaneous claws and fins—the Thompson's version of the Loch Ness Monster. The placard by its tail reads, "The Syrpynt of Bloodrun."

"Ugh," Joycie groans, but continues following the red footprints painted on the floor through a black curtain.

"Next, we come to the Order of the Moon," Greg says. "The Bloodrun River and the land surrounding it, which is now simply known as 'Bloodrun', did not always go by this name. Long before all the *wasi'chus* moved up here, the Ahtna referred to this area as '*Qimaksis Imalutit*'—but these words do not mean 'blood' or even 'river' to them. In fact, they have no literal translation in any of the known Athabaskan languages. This name is but a remnant of a much older language—mostly lost and obscure—but many still believe that an evil *Ahkiyyini* spirit will haunt you for even uttering it—"

"Qimaksis Imalutit," Joycie repeats, rolling her eyes and then looks to a suit of laminar armor made from walrus bones.

"Archaeologists believe that unlike most of the early nomadic Inuit tribes that migrated across Alaska, there was a clan whom they refer to as 'The Order of the Moon', who settled in Qimaksis Imalutit—possibly right where you're standing." Joycie takes the bait and looks down to see that the red footprints have changed shape into those of a wolf's. "This order was an ancient blood cult that made human sacrifices to appease the tides. They gathered when the moon was full and cursed our cherished river, causing it to run red with blood…"

* * *

When the unipqaaq was finished, the Angatuik stood and raised the ergot stone bowl up to the waning moon.

"Igaluk!" he yelled. "We've refrained from *the many words*—just as our ancestors had—taught without talking. We've emptied our hearts of desire and filled our bellies with raw meat and souls. We've cast out the wolves and guarded your sacred waters. We have done all of this, but still, the Raven has not returned. Why have you forsaken us?"

But the moon only shone back quietly.

"There is no death but death!" someone yelled and the rest of them chanted:

"Only death and death alone!"

The Angatuik lowered his head at Igaluk's silence and turned to face his people.

"It's true," he said to them, "he has broken the covenant—"

"No, I haven't!" a man with a rope around his neck shouted as he was pulled inside the circle of torches. "There's a wolf amongst us!"

"Silence," the Angatuik commanded. "The wolves are all dead."

"It's him!" the man with the noose yelled and pointed at the faceless man. "Look at him! He's not aged a day in years! He's bathed in the water—he's living the curse!" But the faceless man and the rest of the order ignored him and began to put on their masks.

"*Qamyllugu! Uvaguk piirluqu ivvillu uqak!*" the Angatuik shouted, motioning to his tongue as if cutting it with a knife. The men who restrained the prisoner then dragged him to the river's edge and stripped him of his clothing. "His *mugluks* too," the Angatuik said, and they removed his sealskin boots, exposing his feet.

"I'm not the one," the man pleaded and crossed his arms over his shivering chest.

"Now, remove the tie," the Angatuik commanded, and the hunters pulled the rope from around the man's neck. "*Quaqtiluk*," the Angatuik instructed—their word for death by suicide. Death by the river.

"Please, you're making a mistake," he tried, but the men drew their bows on him—compelling him to submit—and he took an unwilling step backwards into the freezing water. The river was so cold that it felt as though his ankle bones were being crushed into shards. He screamed as he waded out up to his knees before stopping—feeling like the flesh was being flayed from his shins with daggers made of ice.

The faceless man had no concern that this outlier would gain the same powers of immorality that he had from when he soaked in the river. None of his pupils had yet—he alone was free of death and rebirth. And should the gods bestow the gift to another, he knew of ways that would still assure death—bodily dismemberment, for instance. Exsanguination. Poison. For he knew that even he himself still bled. He still scarred.

But the river was not what it used to be—the people had seen to that with their prayers and ascetic devotions. The blood was gone, and the fish were back. His only real fear was that if they continued to purify the water with their antics, that he might be forced to renounce his clandestine magic completely. As it was, he no longer felt hunger or ever grew old, but that could change. Everything always did. And soon, they'd all be dead and covered in earth.

And then the Earth itself would change—

"Quaqtiluk!" the Angatuik yelled again, and when the prisoner would go no further, the Angatuik motioned to the faceless man.

"Y-y-you," the man struggled as his adversary entered the river after him. "Y-y-you're the d-devil," he said, "a wolf under whoev-ever's face that is." He turned over his forearm, bearing the inverted Y shaped tattoo, which they all were given in commemoration of their ancestors—when Igaluk marked them with his two glowing fingers. "W-we will h-hunt you d-down... F-f-f-forever," he stammered as the faceless man waded towards him with a stone knapped blade.

"There is no death but death!" the Angatuik praised, and they all rejoined from the shore:

"Only death and death alone!"

"The Order of the M-moon will n-never f-f-forget—" the prisoner whispered before the masked executioner plunged the long, jagged knife into his gut and tore it out in a vicious swipe. Blood splashed into the river as one of the naked man's sides was completely separated and he collapsed below the waves.

"Makchit," the faceless man called to the boy before he could have his sip from the bowl. His boots, which were made to protect him from the river's curse, dripped onto the stony shore as he removed his mask.

"Come," he told him as he patted the boy's back and dropped his breastplate into the snow, leaving the circle of torches behind them.

There were too many of them now, but the vision mixture would soon drive the ones that sipped it mad. The rest would inevitably become suspicious of his never-aging face soon if they hadn't already. He had to kill them all and start over again. He'd done it before. He had the time. He might even claim to be one of the countless gods in the next unipqaaq. In the meantime, he'd have to hide until the poison took its effect on the ones who drank it. Any remaining of the order would continue pursuing him, just as the dead man warned, but he'd lead them up into the Tuqujuq again before they could catch up with him—the mountain of bones—and leave some more behind…

* * *

JOYCIE PASSES THE BONE ARMOR DISPLAY and stops before a display case full of various stone tools as she continues listening to Greg Thompson's voice:

"No one knows what exactly caused the sudden disappearance for the Order of the Moon, but after large traces of ergot fungus were discovered in many of these carved vessels, it's assumed that a mass suicide was likely to blame—never drink the Kool-Aid, kids," Greg chuckles. "Small doses of this fungus contain *ergotamine tartrate*; a powerful precursor to LSD, which has also recently been discovered in the pottery of many other ancient civilizations including the early Greeks and Egyptians. The high concentrations found in these hallowed bowls, however, would've certainly resulted in *ergotism*—or, as you may've heard this poisoning referred to in honor of the patron saint of grave diggers, 'St. Anthony's Fire.'"

CHAPTER XXIII:
Scars

"How is he?" Chief Eddowes asks over his shoulder as he washes his hands.

"Not good," Eddie says. "They've amputated some of his fingers and toes—"

"Christ," Eddowes blurts, drying his palms on his shirt.

"They've stabilized the hypothermia, but he's still slipping in and out," Eddie continues as the Chief steps back into his office and sits down. He props his elbows up on his desk and then clenches his knuckles.

"Is he the Butcher?" he asks.

"What? No!" Eddie shouts. "I know it doesn't look good, but it was just a coincidence that Terry was there. How could you think that?"

"I have to ask, Eddie. Finding him like that—" Eddowes rubs his forehead as he tries to think. "What the hell was he doing?"

"The candy ma—Mark Donahue," Eddie corrects himself, "said that he saw taillights speed off once he got close—he must've scared the real Butcher away."

"That still doesn't explain why Terry was there."

"I don't fully understand that either, but it wasn't to dump a body," Eddie pauses. "Wait, is *that* why you have Wertman watching over him instead of me?"

"Look, Eddie, more feds are going to be coming soon. If this wasn't a goddamn mess already it's going to be a real shitshow now. We don't have the manpower to patrol the whole town and pull over every plumber or electrician we see driving a white van. They think that's the only way we're going to catch him."

"I guess that makes sense," Eddie says nodding.

"Your theory—about it all being connected with the kids; the Rod & Reel, Bill Sullivan—Talon—I want you to get back on it."

"Without Terry?" Eddie asks. "I wouldn't even know where to start, Chief."

"Start at the beginning," Eddowes says, and takes a sip of his coffee.

EDDIE GENTLY RAPS on the door of Paige Glore's apartment and her mother greets him and leads him inside.

"Can I make you some tea?" she asks.

"No thanks Eileen—I just want to take one last look around before you box everything up."

"Please, Eddie, whatever you need," she says and guides him into her daughter's bedroom. As Eddie looks away from the stuffed animals on the dead girl's bed, he notices a pill bottle on her nightstand.

"Zoloft?" Eddie asks, holding up the orange prescription bottle.

"Yes," Eileen says sniffling. "I thought I lost her once before. She tried to overdose on one of her previous medications—I forget which one, Sertraline maybe—we tried a few. Her doctor said that they might have mixed results so, we kept at it until we found the right one and—things were going so great—" she chokes, "I'm sorry." She drops some of Paige's books into a plastic bin and leaves the room to grab a tissue.

Eddie walks out of the apartment building with the pill bottle in a plastic evidence bag and throws it on the passenger seat of his cruiser. He stares at it for a moment and then shifts his eyes to the tin of toothpicks in his cupholder...

* * *

THE PINK AND BLACK snake tattoo on Mellisa Nestor's left butt cheek perfectly matched her lingerie and Eddie was mesmerized by it as she got dressed. After hooking her bra back on, she made her way past the DJ booth and came straight to Eddie.

"Hi," he said bashfully.

She stared down at him for a moment and then straddled his waist with her knees and placed her hands on his shoulders. Smiling as she looked into his dark brown eyes, she pushed his toothpick through her teeth with the tip of her tongue. Eddie opened his mouth as she motioned forward—as if about to kiss him—and slid the toothpick back between his lips without sticking him.

"Hi," she replied—suddenly shy—and moved a strand of hair behind her ear.

"What's your name?"

"They call me, 'Ms. Meliss.'"

"What's your real name?" Eddie asked again. A smile formed on her face as she considered telling him.

"Nestor," she said finally, and then more gently, "Mel Nestor."

"I'm Eddie."

"I can read. *Edward Koyukuk*," she said and poked him hard on his nameplate. "The other cops change out of their uniforms before coming in. I think they're afraid someone might recognize them and tell their wives." Eddie raised up his left hand to show her that there was no wedding band around his ring finger.

"Shall we go to the champagne room then, Officer Eddie?"

"I don't like champagne," he said. Mel rolled her eyes as she leaned forward and whispered into his ear:

"Well, what do you like?" Eddie raised an eyebrow, and she nodded to the hallway where the private rooms for lap dances were. Inside each room was a cushioned bench and a jukebox for the patron to choose a song. Eddie had his selected even before he proudly stood up with an erection: "The End" by The Doors—runtime; 11 minutes and 35 seconds. It was the longest song that he could think of.

Mel pulled him to his feet, guided him into one of the empty rooms and shoved him onto the bench. Upon finding the song on the jukebox, she turned around and giggled.

"This song's almost 12 minutes long, bud," she said. "You have a screw loose if you think I'm going to dance to that."

"One screw loose is better than them all too tight," Eddie said, not knowing where he pulled that from.

"How about we do something else with the time?" Mel asked and tapped the PLAY button. As she got back into Eddie's lap, she brought her hands up to the sides of his face. It was then that he saw the raised scars beneath both of her palms.

"Oh no—sweetheart," Eddie let out sadly and pressed her wrists to his lips…

* * *

"L E P U S T O O," Eddie says to himself as his eyes begin darting. "Terry said that Émile Lepus tried to hang himself… And Fullsend Steve's been trying to drink himself to death for the past—"

You try to cut your own threads.
But it's me who has to—

"Fuck—Terry!"

Eddie stomps on the gas pedal and swerves all over the slushy road as he takes off back towards the hospital.

"10-66, this is Officer Eddie Koyukuk, I repeat: 10-66! All available units head to Fitz-Mercy Hospital, ASAP!" he shouts as he flips on his siren and the flashing lights.

"Eddie, what's going on?" Joycie asks, snatching her walkie from under her coat and swatting the audio tour headphones to the floor.

"He's going after Terry!" Eddie shouts back as he struggles to keep the car straight.

"Wertman, come in," Joycie calls with no response. "Wertman, give me a copy!"

P OLICE LIGHTS FLASH outside of Fitz-Mercy ER and a confused ambulance drives around the parking lot in circles.

"Play it," Eddie says, leaning over the hospital security desk to watch the grainy black and white surveillance footage from the hallway where Terry is supposed to be recovering. Joycie shuts the door behind her and the security guard restarts the footage from the beginning but then turns away from the screen; seeing it once was enough.

The footage begins with Officer Eric Wertman sitting casually in a chair outside of Terry's room staring at his cell phone. He cracks his neck, looks down the hall towards the nurse's station and then gets back to tapping and swiping.

After a few minutes pass, one of the doors at the other end of the hallway opens and a man in black steps through and waits until the door closes behind him. Eddie leans in closer to try and make out his face, but the figure is standing too far away from the camera to see any details. Once the door fully closes, the man pulls a black mask down over his face that donned the top of his head like a long-knit ski cap. He stands there motionless for another moment and then begins walking towards Wertman.

He doesn't even hear him, Eddie thinks and wonders if Wertman had his damn volume blaring while he tapped away, or if the figure was just that quiet. He wants to ask the security guard if there's any audio or if they can go back and enlarge the frame with the figure's face in it, but he knows that neither will be of any use to them.

When Wertman sees black boots stop in front of him, he looks up. A beat of stillness passes between the two men as they stare at one another and then Wertman scrambles to his feet.

Before his heels can properly grip any leverage on the waxed floor, one of the black figure's gloved hands snaps around Wertman's throat and smashes the back of his head into the wall. He slams him again, and again, and then slides the dazed cop up the wall with the same hand still clasped beneath his jaw. Wertman kicks reflexively in defense, but his feet tangle with the overturned chair and then hang limply.

He instinctually reaches for his pistol with all of his remaining strength, but the instant that he has it free from his hip, the figure effortlessly strikes it to the floor with a black pipe—breaking Wertman's right-hand like a twig. Wertman's face contorts as he makes a last-ditch effort to beat on the iron-like arm strangling him with his non-dominant hand, but the figure crushes down further on all the soft exposed tissue beneath Wertman's chin. As both of his arms fall lifelessly to his sides, the black figure winds his pipe back again and spikes Wertman's head into the floor like a deflated volleyball.

The figure then disappears into Terry's room while Wertman lies motionless on the floor in the hallway. Eddie watches a dark puddle form around Wertman's head as the black figure reappears in the doorway pushing a wheelchair with a man wearing a hospital gown in it.

CHAPTER XXIV:
75.6°F

T E R R Y ' S E Y E S F L U T T E R as a cold chill crawls over his body. A series of lights pass above his head that he first mistakes for more headlights, but these are different—fluorescent bulbs—like in a long hallway. His head bobs and dips around his shoulders as he tries to see—too heavy to hold in one place—and he realizes that it's not the lights that are moving, but him. Someone is pushing him in a wheelchair.

Terry tilts his head back and looks up, expecting to see the same aggravated nurse from earlier, but it's a man. A man's jaw and neck, at least—that's all Terry can see from this vantage point. There's something oddly familiar about the shape of him though, like he's seen him somewhere before—or even knows who he is—and it frustrates him that he can't remember how.

"Where are we going?" Terry asks him, or at least tries to—he's not sure at all what the noises were he just made, if any came out at all.

When the man looks down to respond, all of the skin and muscles of his face split apart in a violent flash and the only thing remaining in their place is a red rotting skull—sheening with slick dark blood. Its lipless jaw falls open and a wave of slithering insects spurts out all over like a blanket of death.

T E R R Y G A S P S with an irrepressible shiver and his frost-encrusted eyelashes snap apart painfully. He looks down with watery eyes, but sees well enough to know that he isn't covered in blood and bugs—in fact, nothing is covering him at all; he's naked again. His gut feeling is that he must still be freezing to death in the Bloodrun—that it was all just a dream—but as his eyesight slowly sharpens, he sees that this is not the case at all.

From wherever he's seated, he can see the entire borough. He can see where the river bends, where the train passes at Sedna's Crossing, and with the help of a few other landmarks, he can even roughly make out where the water tower stands.

The adjacent mountaintops to his left and right assure him that he's been stranded atop one of the forgotten peaks of Mount Tuqujuq. As he sits there with his skin stiffening, his heartbeat slowing steadily—the relentless shaking beginning to ease—he finally feels the tugging. He traces it down to his lap and sees that his wrists and ankles are bound together—just like the Tuquji Iceman. A tear freezes to Terry's cheek as his eyes shift to the tattoo that he shared with Hannah and he fades back into the cold dark abyss.

I can sleep... he thinks.
I can... sleep...

>I can sleep with rats inside a cave with bats
>I can sleep on stones or a pile of bones

CHAPTER XXV:
ASAP

"How the hell did this happen?" Chief Eddowes yells into his phone.

"I don't know," Eddie says. "The cameras in the hospital parking lot show someone loading Terry into an unmarked van and then take off—fuck!" Eddie shouts and smacks his steering wheel anxiously as he drives. "It's suicides, Chief," he says, trying to explain whatever it is that he discovered. "He's killing people who've attempted suicide—Paige and Mel, Émile, Fullsend—now, Terry. They've all tried to commit suicide before. Somehow, he knows," Eddie trails off, remembering something that he saw pinned on the church bulletin board the other day.

"Eddie?" Eddowes asks, "—Are you there?"

"Yeah—we're heading back to Dot's."

"What? Who's *'we'?—*" but Eddie hangs up before answering and drops his phone into his lap so that he can steer with both hands through the falling snow.

"What's back at St. Dot's?" Joycie asks curiously from the passenger seat as she places her coffee into one of the cruiser's cup holders.

As they pull into the church parking lot, Eddie notices that Father Murphy has already changed the letter board marquee out front from the cute message about the cold to:

|D|O| |N|O|T| |F|E|A|R| |T|H|O|S|E| |W|H|O| |K|I|L|L| |T|H|E| |B|O|D|Y|, |F|O|R| |T|H|E|Y| |C|A|N|N|O|T| |K|I|L|L| |T|H|E| |S|O|U|L|.

They waste no time trying to find the priest for a key and instead go right to the backdoor of the church basement. Eddie slides his pocketknife down the seal of the police notice and after two kicks, the door bursts open. Cold air falls in behind them and makes steam rise from the freshly mopped floor. Eddie treads over the slick surface towards the wall of flyers with great trepidation—not wanting to slip and fall onto the spot where Fullsend Steve was found dead—and scans hastily.

"SUICIDE SURVIVOR MEETING
Bloodrun Borough High School Gymnasium
Sunday, January 16th @ 4:00pm"

"3:47," Eddie says looking down at his watch. "The hospital tape showed Terry getting abducted about three hours ago—I think there's still time. Come on, we need to head over to the high school, I think this guy might—"

As Eddie turns around, he sees Joycie mesmerized by the swirling clouds of fog rising from the wet floor.

"What the hell are you doing?" he asks, and she looks up startled.

"I DON'T KNOW—I feel weird," Joycie says a moment later as they get back in the car. "Like, my breathing," she stops talking and inhales deeply through her nose. "It's like—I could just keep breathing, y'know?"

"No, I don't know—what the fuck are you talking about?" Eddie asks, turning from the road to look at her eyes. "You're tripping!" he shouts, seeing her dilated pupils and then lifts up her coffee cup. "Where did you get this?" he asks and looks in the visor mirror to check his own eyes.

WHEN THEY PULL INTO the high school parking lot, a deserted yellow school bus is parked halfway up on the curb with its flashing stop sign extended. It should've been en route making drop-offs over an hour ago. Random students are scattered all around the premises acting exceedingly strange; some shout gibberish and dance erratically while others sit and stare at handfuls of snow. Textbooks and crumpled homework assignments are littered everywhere and Eddie notices various abandoned jackets and gloves and boots with no foreseeable owners.

"Chief, it's me again—give me a call back as soon as you get this, we got a real problem here," Eddie says looking over to Joycie, who is rubbing her hands all over the dashboard. "And don't drink anything in the meantime—stop it!" he yells, swatting Joycie's hands away from the phone.

"Let me talk," she begs. "I wanna taaaalk."

"Something's going on," Eddie says as he pushes Joycie's face away. "I need to talk to you ASAP, Chief—"

"ASAP, Chief," Joycie imitates Eddie's voice. "ASAP—ASAP, ASAP-P-P!" she shouts giggling and Eddie hangs up before she can continue ranting.

"Would you shut up?" he shouts back and her smile flips into a childish pout.

E DDIE GETS OUT OF THE CAR and ducks below a few snowballs thrown at him from random kids as he rushes to the passenger side door. "I'm not sure if it's safe for you to stay here—can you walk?" he asks, opening Joycie's door.

"Am I pretty, Eddie?" she asks, looking up to him admiringly. Eddie bites his lower lip with annoyance and looks back down into her large round pupils.

"Yes, Joycie, you're very pretty. Now look, don't open the door for anyone until I get back, okay?" She bats her black eyes at him and plays with her hair as Eddie slams the door shut.

CHAPTER XXVI:
Only Death and Death Alone

THE HIGH SCHOOL GYMNASIUM is quiet except for a low murmur. Eddie closes the door gently behind him and then draws his pistol as he tries to make out the voice.

"'Listen only to me and you will have great power

And *true* everlasting life,' Gull said to them,"

He pokes his head around the bleachers and looks to center court where a group of barefooted teenagers sit in a circle around a man dressed in black. They nod their heads as he speaks and drink from paper cups which one of them pours from an orange cooler. On the floor by the man's feet lies a chainsaw flecked with dry blood.

"But I too have learned the many words

I can speak like the ravens

And howl like the wol—" but before the masked man can finish, the double doors behind Eddie burst open and Joycie runs in swinging the tranquilizer gun from the cruiser's trunk.

"Freeze, motherfuckers!" her voice echoes all around them and she laughs hysterically.

"Joycie—Joycie! Put the gun down," Eddie says and then snaps back around to the group of kids. "Everyone, stay down!" He points his gun up at the faceless man and steps towards the foul line. "You, take that fucking mask off and put your hands behind your head."

"No!" Joycie cries, suddenly panicking, and the dart gun wavers in her hands.

"Damnit—Joycie, get back in the car!"

"Is that him?" she blubbers over Eddie's shoulder.

"Yes," Eddie says calmly as she stumbles up beside him. "It's okay; it's over now."

"It's far from over, *Officer Eddie*," the faceless man calls as he takes a step towards his weapon—his black mask remaining motionless as he speaks. "And there's no going back. But you and your girlfriend don't have to die here. The others... they *wanted* it—"

"Is that what you tell yourself? Get on the ground!"

"It makes no difference—everyone is going to die soon. In the end, you're all just blood flowing back—"

"Only death and death alone!" the intoxicated students chant.

"Shut up!" Eddie yells.

"They were going to *waste* it," the man says furiously, taking another step closer to his sleeping saw. "The blood must be given to the river. The gods *must* return," he says almost mockingly. "I've heard the Raven speak and—

"I said, shut the fuck up!"

"There is no death but death!" the circle resounds, drowning out Eddie's voice.

"I am the *word*. I *am* the blood!"

"Take that fucking mask off now and get on the ground!"

"No!" Joycie cries out again. "I can't—I can't, Eddie, please!" In her drug distorted eyes, the man's mask is not clinging tightly to his nose and cheeks, but to the hollow bones of his skull. "I can't see it! I can't—"

"Stop it—stop!" Eddie yells as Joycie tugs on his arm—both of their guns swinging before the terrified circle of kids.

"Don't make him take it off!"

"Joycie—let go of me!" Eddie growls, trying to push her away without hurting her.

As the two of them struggle, the faceless man advances the remaining distance that he needs and crouches down. When he comes back up, the roaring buzz of his blood-stained chainsaw shrieks out across the gymnasium—abruptly rooting Joycie and Eddie to their positions as they turn their heads—but he's already upon them. The spinning blades plunge downward in a swift arc and catch Eddie on the shoulder as he shoves Joycie away with all of his might. The tranquilizer slips from her hands as she hits the floor and it skids towards the circle of entranced teenagers as Eddie's Beretta clatters onto the court with trickles of blood.

E D D I E S P I N S A R O U N D, half-numb to the gushing laceration, but the faceless man shoulders him hard in the nose—snapping the bridge to one side—and Eddie spills onto his back. The stars clear after a moment, but his vision remains doubled as he looks up helplessly—hardly aware of the whirling saw that hovers inches above his face.

"STOP!" Joycie screams—her voice just loud enough to be heard over the mowing buzz of the engine. The faceless man pauses and turns to her curiously for a moment before he straightens his stance and dismisses her altogether.

"Stop it!" she cries again, but he resumes lowering the saw closer to Eddie, who is now coughing up the blood that's leaking down his throat from the broken nose. The man goes to tighten his grip on the saw before moving further in, but his arms seem to defy him and begin to go slack. His back curls as he heaves the saw back up to his hip, but one of his hands comes loose and the chainsaw swings through the air—a ravenous pendulum.

Eddie raises his hand up to shield himself, but the spinning chain snags him in the webbing of his middle finger and rips through his last two digits. He screams and rolls out of the way as the saw topples to the floor and dances in a menacing circle—spitting a fine mist of Eddie's blood all over as it twirls.

"No!" the faceless man snarls and grabs the side of his neck. Eddie can make out the yellow tuft of a flechette sticking out between the man's gloved fingers as he stumbles towards Joycie.

"Get back!" she shouts and pulls the trigger again with a soft *pop*, but the second dart whizzes by him and into the bleachers. He sways side to side—trying to fight the ketamine bear sedative—and reaches out with both hands as he falls to his knees.

"Joy-gu... ri-kuh... lluh... you—vud—sss," the man mumbles insensibly and collapses forward.

"Eddie!" Joycie shouts as she drops the gun to the floor and runs over to him. "Are you okay?"

"Motherfucker," Eddie moans as he lets go of his mutilated hand to assess the damage.

"Oh my god," Joycie cries as she watches streams of blood flow down Eddie's elbow.

"It's alright," he musters as he closes his hand back over the wound. "Listen to me, okay? Take my handcuffs—"

"No, no, no, Eddie, please—"

"Joycie, look at me," he says and glances back to the motionless body. "You have to handcuff him before he wakes up. Okay?"

"I can't!"

"He's going to be out for awhile; those darts are rated for 300lb bear. I promise, he can't hurt you—but you have to do it now; I need to wrap this. He got my shoulder good too," Eddie says, and Joycie watches the acquiescing red puddle spread out underneath him.

"Okay," she finally agrees and unzips her jacket and drops it to the ground beside him.

"W-what're you doing?" Eddie asks, trying not to stare at her as she pulls off her shirt.

"For your hand," she says, dropping it into his lap.

"Oh, right," he says, almost disappointed, "thanks."

BY THE TIME Joycie returns to him, the circle of kids has disbanded and Eddie has her shirt tied tightly around his reduced hand.

"Can we go now?" she asks, slipping her jacket back on over her bra. Eddie nods and she helps him to his feet. They stare down hesitantly at their prisoner as his bloody chainsaw skips around in a ring of blood.

CHAPTER XXVII:
Rot

JOYCIE DRIVES REMARKABLY WELL, considering that she can't rely on any of her senses. She keeps the car straight and slow—too slow at times, and Eddie nudges her and groans from the pain radiating in his scapula.

"I'm sorry," she says and speeds up as they pass an old burning Colony Park station wagon. "Did you see that?" she keeps asking—checking in with him every time they see something bizarre.

"Yes," Eddie moans, "just focus on the road." He tries to look in the backseat without hurting himself and sees that the handcuffed man is still unconscious.

CARS ARE PARKED all over town in random places—some abandoned, some with people in them blaring music or screaming. Joycie steers around one car with a naked man dancing on its hood by the side of the road. An overturned ambulance sits in an intersection with three paramedics urinating on it as if trying to put out a fire. She honks as they pass them and then honks again at two people fighting like children on the sidewalk across the street.

"Enough with the horn," Eddie says as Joycie goes to beep at a woman climbing a telephone pole in her bathrobe.

Within a few blocks of the police station, they drive by a man hollering and kicking his lawnmower as it fails to clear a path in the snow where someone else is lying down making a snow angel. Far in the distance, a cloud of smoke rises and a pack of dogs run down the street barking wildly.

WHEN THEY FINALLY GET BACK and pull into the lot, Joycie discovers—after smashing into three stationary cop cars—that parking is a lot more difficult than rolling leisurely between other slow-moving, drug-possessed pedestrians. Hoping that Eddie hasn't noticed, she decides to simply stop the car in the middle of the blacktop and exclaim:

"Alright, we're here!"

Eddie takes another look in the backseat to make sure that the masked man hasn't moved and then winces as he sits up.

"Are you sure you're okay, Eddie?" Joycie asks, but immediately gets distracted by a group of children rolling an enormous ball of snow down the sidewalk and claps giddily.

"I'm fine," he says, "come on."

EDDIE WAS HOPING that the hard part was over, but lifting the heavy man up again proves to be even more difficult the second time around. Joycie keeps stopping every few paces to either hysterically laugh or cry and Eddie himself requires a break whenever he feels dizzy—or the pain in his shoulder becomes too intolerable. Upon entering the lobby, Joycie hears the phone ringing from behind her desk and she drops the man's legs to run over to it.

"Hey," she greets warmly. "This is... *the cops*," she giggles and then raises her eyebrows at the screaming voice on the other end.

"Stay here," Eddie grunts and begins dragging the unconscious man around the corner.

"Eddie!" Joycie calls as he disappears down the hallway, which seems to her to be alive—shrinking and expanding with her breath. "Koyukuk-uk-uk-uk-uk—" she chants insanely, but quickly gets sidetracked by more calls of the madness going on outside.

"Oh my," she says, scribbling illegibly onto her desk, "—I'll send a car over right away!"

The phone slips from Joycie's hand as she tries to cradle it and she stares out the window at another plume of smoke rising beyond the water tower. As the phone swings by its cord, a terrified voice raves about leaking faucets and toilets overflowing with blood.

E D D I E   S T A R E S down at the unconscious man lying in the middle of the holding cell as he catches his breath. He can hear cars honking and people screaming from outside, but he ignores them. He can hear a siren going off from the firehouse and a bullhorn speaking gibberish, but he ignores them too. For five whole days, Eddie has been waiting for this moment—but now he's too afraid to act.

Terry should've been the one to catch you, he thinks.

He sees dried blood all over the man's clothes as he bends down closer, reaching for the black mask with his good hand. He's certain that the man will wake up the second that he tugs on it, grab his wrist and crack him like a whip against the steel bars. Eddie hesitates for another moment to collect himself, and then yanks the mask off all at once and throws it like it's a venomous snake.

The guy with the wrench, Eddie thinks as he recognizes his face—the man he waved to once while he was fixing a busted water main one exceptionally cold winter.

"Kaz—"

"Eddie!" Joycie cries. "We have to go!"

Eddie looks up and sees Joycie coming around the corner with her hands stretched out in front of her as if she were blind—feeling for what's real and what isn't. With the monster's immense strength still fresh in his mind from the hospital videotape, Eddie drops his eyes back down and jolts with a sudden panic as he sees the man's eyelids fluttering.

"Get back," Eddie yells to Joycie and he rushes over to the steel bars—pulling them closed with a loud *clank* as it locks. They both watch as Kazimir Panas begins to stir from his stupor and burble incomprehensible words—neither of them feeling particularly safe, despite the bolted barrier.

"Where's Terry?" Eddie asks, crouching down to him once the dazed man is finally able to keep his eyes open. Kaz shows no sign of hearing him and his head bobs around like an infant as he looks about the holding cell confused—and then angry.

"You... bitch!" the lipless skull shouts at Joycie.

"Hey!" Eddie yells but stops himself from getting closer. "Where's Terry?"

"Quaqtiluk," Kaz says and smiles as he sits up clumsily.

"What the fuck does that mean?" Eddie asks, unfamiliar with this branch of Inuit—if that's even what it is. It isn't the Alutiiq that he learned from his mother, that's for sure.

"Let me out of here," Kaz whispers as he wobbles up on one knee.

"Fuck you," Eddie says, drawing his pistol.

"No, Eddie!" Joycie screams.

"LET ME OUT OF HERE!" the man's voice floods the entire cell as he grabs the steel bars with his cuffed hands and pulls himself to his feet. "You won't shoot me, little Koyukuk," the man says in his strange accent, "and you can't keep me here either."

"I'll keep you here as long as I wan—"

A car crash booms from outside, followed by the sound of broken glass and the steady horn of a lifeless head weighing down on a steering wheel.

"Eddie, please—we need to go *now*," Joycie cries and places her hand inside of his elbow. "Come on."

"What did you do to him?" Eddie asks, ignoring Joycie—keeping the Beretta aimed right at Kazimir's forehead.

"I gave him what he wanted," Kaz says with a grin and turns around, averting his face from them. "—what they *all* wanted. There was nothing in him to save."

Eddie blinks and a tear rolls down his cheek as he thumbs the hammer back.

"Eddie, stop!" Joycie shouts and tugs on his arm. His grip tightens around the handle, but he lets her pull him a step away towards the hall. "It's what he wants," she says, tugging him again and he starts to lower the gun. "Come on."

"Eddie?" Mel Nestor's worried voice suddenly emanates from inside of the cell. *"Don't leave me here with him! Please, let me out!"*

"It's not real," Joycie says.

"Eddie, please, I want your cock!"

"You mother fucker!" Eddie yells, as he shrugs Joycie off of him and cringes from the pain in his hand.

"How about I put her face on for you, Officer Eddie, and you can fuck her one last time—"

Blood sprays all over the floor in front of Kaz as Eddie blows a 9mm hole through one of his kneecaps. As the man falls forward with a scream of pain, Eddie raises his gun and points it at the back of his head.

"Eddie, no!" Joycie shouts.

"Oh, *pui*," Kaz hisses tauntingly. "What would your hero Terry do, huh?" he asks, still facing the stone wall. "Stick your other hand through the bars and let me even you out first, then you'll really match him. Then you can shoot me in the back too, just like he did to that boy—"

"Shut the fuck up!" Eddie yells and cocks the hammer back again.

"Eddie!" Joycie cries, *"please."*

"—he was out of bullets," Terry's voice suddenly plays in Eddie's ears.

"Let him fucking rot—"

"A thousand years just like an hour, right?" Eddie asks, dropping the gun to his side. "How fast do you think it'll go by in here with no one coming for you?" Eddie stops as he watches Kasimir's shoulder rise. "What? Doesn't your patience break time? You've got nothing left," he says and wipes tears away from his face with his mangled hand. "No *saw*. No *mask*. No more *kids* to brainwash. You wanted them to worship you, didn't you, you sick fuck?" Eddie asks and Kaz tilts up his chin. "I bet

315

killing them made you feel like a god, didn't it? Well, I got you, motherfucker, don't you see? You're nothing but a caged animal—all alone. And you're gonna die alone. No more *pupils*. No *brother*—"

Kaz spins around in a fury and Joycie's eyes widen with horror as the decaying bloody skull hangs its jaw open in a deafening howl.

"Go!" Eddie yells as a nest of worms and roaches boil out of it onto the floor. He pushes Joycie around the corner as she cries hysterically and the skull's voice echoes down the hallway:

"I can wait, Eddie!" it yells and laughs madly. "I can wait *forever*!"

E P I LO G U E:

A S E R G O T I N F U S E D B L O O D pumps through the black pipes of Card House like the tubes of a giant heart—ready to burst—Spartacus laps up the last of the water from his little bowl. He trots into the living room, hops up onto Terry's computer chair, and clumsily skips onto the desk. He walks around an open laptop—which has a picture of Terry, Hannah, and him for its wallpaper—and then curls into a ball beside the window. He whimpers for a few moments and then closes his eyes.

    The sound of a small explosion down the street makes him jump and his ears rise at the thunderous rumble and cries of people screaming. Sirens shriek as a police car speeds down the street and Spart sits up and looks out the window hoping to see Terry's Bronco. His tail wags for a moment but then stops as he realizes no one is coming. In the distance, smoke rises in various places from the center of town and he tries to sniff it through the glass. He whines again and paces around in a circle—no longer able to sleep and wait for his master to return. As the chaotic noises outside begin to soften, Spartacus lies back down and sighs deeply.

T H E D A C H S H U N D is about to close his eyes when he hears the familiar jingling of Terry's keys outside the front door. His tail wags uncontrollably as he leaps off the desk onto the swivel chair and then down onto the carpet. He runs over to the door excitedly—his rear-end wiggling with unbridled joy—and he howls eagerly as he hears the lock turn.

"Oh, Spart—baby!" Joycie shouts as she picks him up and rubs his belly. He licks her cheeks as she squeezes him against her.

"I got him!" she calls to Eddie as she turns around and staggers. "I told you; I dropped him off here so he'd be safe while I was stomping mud holes over at the Thompson's."

"Alright," Eddie says, "I'm just saying, you haven't exactly been in the right state of mind for the past couple of hours."

"Let's go," she says and mashes Spart's face into her breasts.

"Okay," Eddie says and gives Joycie a smile as she walks past him towards the cruiser. He stands there for a few moments and looks all around the inside of Terry's living room. On the floor, he sees an open book discarded carelessly beside a shelf and picks it up.

> "O child, even though your
> body has been cut into pieces,
> you will not know death. You
> may try to enter your old corpse,
> but the winter will freeze it and
> the summer will make it rot.
> And so, you will enter a new
> body, like water poured into
> the sea.
>
> Open your eyes, from first
> being a man, you have now
> become a dog and you will
> suffer in a dog-kennel. With
> one secret you may be
> recovered—without words
> you will be freed."

"Come on!" Joycie yells and honks on the horn. "Koyukuk-uk-uk-uk-uk!" She raises Spartacus over her head and he barks insanely with her. Eddie wants to say something before stepping away, but nothing comes to him and he begins to feel stupid. He drops the book back onto the floor and leaves Terry's door open as he walks down the pavement to join Joycie and Spart and any other survivors fleeing the carnage.

"You're gonna have to reset my nose before it heals like this," he tells her as he gets in.

As they pull away, the pipes creak in Terry's bathroom and his showerhead drips blood into the tub.

Acknowledgements

Thank you to Joe Shacklock and Katie Stamper for helping me edit this. Thank you to Mike Curry and Ryan Crepack for assisting with the cover design. Thank you to Nick Kurth and War & Peace Party for letting me reference their music. Thank you to Chili for keeping me reasonably sane. And lastly, thank you to all of my friends and family, especially my mother, for their support while I was a hermit.

Made in United States
Orlando, FL
23 December 2024